Saida & Autumn

Saida & Autumn

A MENSURA COLLEGE NOVEL

ARILIN THORFERRA

Print ISBN: 978-1-61450-567-9

Published by FurPlanet Productions, Dallas, Texas

Cover artwork © 2022 by Ransom Dracalis

First Edition, July 2022

Contents

Preface

So, this started as roleplaying. Sort of. But not really.

Let me back up.

Many years ago, when dinosaurs roamed the earth and internet forums were still popular, a forum called BigFurs started a shared world setting: "BigFurs Community College." Contributors brought their ideas and characters to a loosely defined scenario of a mixed-size college, and wrote a shared ongoing story in that setting. My character Arilin Thorferra became a professor there, despite her first story appearance, "Cheating at Solitaire," casting her as a sociopathic villain. I folded in what she'd done on FurryMUCK as canonical for BFCC, as she'd become decidedly less villainous over time. (She also obviously became a pen name—and, yes, to a degree her author's fursona. Is Arilin-the-character supposed to be the author of the stories under her name, including this one? I don't think so, but never say never.)

BFCC was nominally contemporary, but had magic and mad science and aliens and God knows what else. It was glorious fun—and conceptually, a steaming hot mess, with no regard for worldbuilding consistency and power balance. While it faded into furry history, I took inspiration from it as part of Arilin's background as she moved away from being a villain. The ever more byzantine backstory drew from it as well as ideas—and even other characters—from the nebulously defined "world" of FurryMUCK.

Eventually, I decided I wanted to make Arilin's life story make *some* kind of sense as a story. Her journey remains dubiously fantastical—as you may glean from *Saida & Autumn,* Arilin is the unwilling heroine of a redemption-arc portal fantasy that's never been written—but her new setting has its own identity and own world with its own rules.

The story "Teacher's Pet" introduced the new Mensura College and provided glimpses of the college's uneasy relationship with the (normal-sized) town it's adjacent to, as well as hints of the larger world's history. When I started my Patreon, I decided I'd do a larger Mensura College story. Originally, I planned on a longer sequel to "Teacher's Pet," but a tossed-off joke ended up leading me somewhere else entirely. The joke? That Saida, Arilin's cousin, should have a goth bunny girlfriend. And, well, here we are.

At the time I finished, this was the longest macrophile story I'd written. It's also the first story, macro or otherwise, I've written that's a romance front and center. It was written in 2018 and 2019, and re-edited in 2021. Publishing this in 2022 gets it out later than I'd planned, but [gestures wildly at 2020].

I won't lie: Mensura College is *still* a bit of a hodgepodge, and there's something awkward about creating "canon" versions of role-playing characters—especially the one I share a pen name with. On the other hand, it's fun to actually *have* canon, story-appropriate versions, and to bring out bits and bobs in my head that haven't been shared before. Writing this, I fell in love not just with Autumn but with Saida, too, who may surprise folks who know her only from non-canon jokes/vignettes. I hope you love them as much as I do.

– Arilin

CHAPTER 1

The Beanstalk

TWO MONTHS PAST HER TWENTY-NINTH BIRTHDAY, SAIDA Talirend could still usually pass for a college student, but she'd begun to feel self-conscious about it, as if her monthly stays at Mensura College perpetuated a kind of fraud. As a relative of a tenured professor here, though, she had the right to rent a little studio in the staff housing area—and there weren't any places *off* the campus a cat woman whose ears broke the eighty-foot mark could fit.

Mensura's Student Union building was a marvel of crazy engineering. Set into the side of a hill, giants entered at the ground level and littles entered from the hillside at about her waist level. They had more effective space available, getting in several floors where the giants had only one. She'd overheard giant students grumble about that, but it never bothered her. Giants weren't normal-sized here, after all—they were, well, giant. That had become the appeal for her, what drew her back regularly: being in a world where nearly everyone and everything felt toy-sized was magical.

Areas where the sizes mixed freely, though, were even *more* magical.

She'd been coming to the college two years, after improbably reconnecting with her cousin Arilin—now even more improbably a professor here—and it still seemed like a storybook every visit. The college's clever design subtly kept students of different sizes apart as much as possible, but some spaces deliberately mixed things up. Her favorite of those places, by far: the Beanstalk.

Most of the cafés at the Union tacitly segregated patrons by size. The Beanstalk, though, had floor-to-ceiling posts made to look like huge, thick vines, with "leaves" holding groups of tables at various levels—very often right over tables sized for giants. Littles could also sit "on" the bar at a separate raised bar. Catwalks criss-crossed the space everywhere, artfully arranged to be out of any giant walking paths. On her second visit, Saida realized at least two servers handled each table, one little and one giant. Food orders would always be brought out by someone at the scale of the diner, but they might well be taken by someone on the opposite end of the spectrum.

Originally Saida doubted the genius of the design outweighed the sheer madness of mixing giants and littles with alcohol and food. But her cousin assured her no one had ever been accidentally, let alone intentionally, killed, and the serving staff maintained a legendarily zero-tolerance policy for bullying. That didn't stop them from displaying a deadpan sign behind the giant bar reading 0 PATRONS EATEN TODAY.

The pizza pub was maybe half full as she stepped inside, lively but not so crowded that she had trouble finding a seat at the counter. As usual, she caught people turning to stare across or up at her, depending on their size. She suspected at least half were doing a double-take to confirm that, no, Professor Thorferra *hadn't* just walked into the Beanstalk in denim shorts and a fashionable T-shirt. They didn't look that similar—Saida had creamy fur rather than snow white, strawberry blonde hair, green eyes rather than blue— but she got mistaken for Arilin regularly.

It only took about ten seconds before the little tabby cat bartender, rather than the dog her size, looked up toward her and waved. "Hey!" He smiled, not in the least fazed by a customer who could swallow him whole. "What can we get you?"

"The black lager and a slice of pepperoni and mushroom."

He nodded, punching a few buttons on his touch screen. "It'll be right out."

"Thanks."

She spun around on her stool slowly, looking around the room again. Maybe it wasn't as busy as she'd first thought; there were just a few groups—two ones her size and an especially rowdy, all-fox-guy one at the little bar—and a handful of loners like herself, noses in textbooks and half-forgotten glasses of beer or soda to the side.

No: *nearly* all the loners were like that. The exception sat alone at a dark table in a corner, a rabbit with fur so white it looked almost unnatural. She'd accented that with black eyeliner, brow highlights, and even lipstick, then kept her wardrobe just as black, too. Jeans with so many lateral rips across the legs it was a wonder they still held together held fur-tight to her, and an oversized, plain black tee-shirt slipped off of one shoulder. Her hair offered the only break from the stark monochrome style. Most of the long strands falling down past her chest maintained a deep black, but streaks of red, orange, and green ran throughout. It wasn't a look Saida usually found attractive, but she felt her heart speed up just a beat or two.

Suddenly the bunny girl looked straight at Saida. Her eyes narrowed. Probably thinking *Shit, that's not Professor Thorferra, is it?*

But it could also be because Saida had been looking at her so intently. The cat flashed her a small, hopefully disarming smile. After a moment the rabbit's posture relaxed into a slouch and she gave a small smile back, picking up her drink.

The giant bartender set her beer down, along with shakers of red pepper and grated cheese.

She leaned toward him. "Who's that?" she said softly.

"Who?"

She nodded toward the corner.

The dog, a handsome retriever type, tilted his head, one ear flopping over. "Don't know her name, sorry. I've seen her around campus, and here occasionally. Think she's a MAP student."

"Huh." Saida nodded. "Thanks."

"MAP" was the Magical Arts Program. So Goth Bunny was a sorceress in training? That gave her some pause. Her past experience with magic was mostly as a target.

She glanced toward the rabbit again. Now she'd leaned forward, elbows propped up on her table, arms crossed, giving Saida a one-raised-brow look. The cat flashed another smile, slightly sheepish. This time, the rabbit didn't smile back; she nodded at an angle, eyes flicking down and up again. Toward the seat opposite her? Was she inviting Saida to come over?

The laughter from the group of littles on the bar grew more raucous, coincidental to her smile. Or maybe not. Her ear swiveled to focus on their conversation.

"—lesbo giants—"

"—really be a dyke if you're not really a—"

She glanced down with a sharp frown. A couple fell quiet, ears lowering, but one of the ones who'd been speaking yelled up, "No offense, big girl. We're just saying."

"You're 'just saying' what?" Saida kept her voice low and deliberately foreboding. The dog behind the counter flashed the littles a disapproving glance, too.

"Bunny's...you know...was..." He trailed off, as if finally realizing he'd headed onto dangerous ground.

"Never mind," another one muttered, voice low enough she had to strain to hear it.

Out of the corner of her eye, Saida caught the rabbit girl's expression freezing. She turned to look back down, keeping her tone deadly flat. "Leave before I use you as pizza toppings."

It wasn't just that group that went stone silent. The pub's background babble dropped to near nothing.

Just Saying Guy was the first to find his voice. "Y-you can't make jokes like that here." He looked up at the dog giant behind the bar beseechingly. "If students get caught—"

"Shame I'm not a student." Saida flicked her gaze to the frowning dog, giving him a wink. Hopefully he'd cut her some slack.

After a moment he turned away from the scene, studiously wiping down an already-clean prep area. "Let me know if I gotta change the number," he said, jerking a thumb at the PATRONS EATEN sign.

The foxes all turned to look at up Saida, each set of ears back. Keeping a steely gaze fixed on them, she slowly raised the cheese shaker.

They bolted, knocking over chairs as they scrambled to the elevator.

The rabbit was looking off to the side, away from the bar. Saida chewed on her lip, watching. Had she lost the moment? Damn little pocket frat bros—

But, no, maybe not. After a second she glanced back at Saida expectantly, long ears up.

"Here's your pizza." The dog set down a plate behind her on the counter.

"What? Oh. Thanks." She turned around. "Wait, I didn't order two slices."

"You didn't? Sorry." The dog continued to look studiously disinterested. "Maybe you can find someone to share it with."

"I...thanks." Picking up her beer and the plate of pizza, Saida headed across the room to the table, setting both down and taking the opposite seat. Across from the younger woman, the cat finally realized how much taller the rabbit was: at least a hundred feet high, not counting the ears. It was *extremely* uncommon for her people to be that big. In this world, at least this part of it, there seemed to be little limit on potential sizes—and, for that matter, powers. She liked to think she'd made her peace with it, but she might never be completely used to it.

"You're not related to Professor Thorferra, are you?" The bunny's voice had a lovely smokiness to it. Deep violet eyes locked onto Saida's.

"I'm her cousin Saida."

"Really. So you're another Rha." She folded her hands in front of her on the table, the dim light catching glittering black claw polish. "Are you a student?"

"No."

"Staff?"

She shook her head. "I live back in Stravell. But I take long weekends here at least once a month."

The rabbit lifted one brow and smiled curiously. "I hear second- and third-hand stories about Thorferra having got here through some kind of mad science accident."

"That's not wrong. Teleportation is less mad science than niche business back home now, though."

"How can you sound blasé about traveling between worlds?"

"I don't mean it that way." She shrugged self-consciously. "We can only teleport between beacon stations, so the one here is probably the only one that ever *will* be on another world. It's a strange fluke, a silver lining to what happened to my cousin. Otherwise, where I'm from is...no magic, no crazy tech. No giants, since everything is my scale. It's nice, but boring."

"So's most of this world if you get about a hundred miles from Mensura." She shook her head. "So is that why you come here? Because it's not boring?"

"That's a fair way to put it. I like being a real giantess, having the world literally at my paws. When I first got here I used to take long walks around places where people might never have seen giants." She laughed. "Although I appreciate the campus and the area around it more now, since it's nice to be a real giantess without worrying someone's going to send an army after you."

That earned her a laugh. The rabbit held out her hand across the table. "I'm Autumn."

Saida closed her hand around the rabbit's for a moment, smiling back. Autumn's palm felt fuzzy against her own velvet pads. "So you're a student here?"

Autumn nodded. "Magical Arts." She spread her hands. "I look the part, right?"

"No, then you'd have a robe and a pointed hat. But I guess you fit with the dark and mysterious stereotype."

The rabbit lifted a brow and crossed her arms. "Do I, now."

"You do. You didn't explicitly invite me over as much as signal I had permission to approach."

That brought more of a teasing smile. "And I don't give it to just anyone."

She smiled, taking a sip of beer. "I also know...let me see. By Rha standards you're extremely tall. At home, I'm five foot seven, so you'd be...how tall are you?"

Autumn picked up her own drink. It looked like a soda, most of the ice melted by now. "A hundred and one feet."

"That'd be..." She closed her eyes, working out the math. "Six foot nine."

"You can do that math in your head?"

"I'm good with numbers."

"I see that." She grinned, showing off her sharp front teeth. "I like the idea of being six foot nine. I like the idea of being a hundred feet tall better, but if I'm standing next to someone on my scale, I want to be the taller one."

Saida laughed, although she felt her tail twitch. She thought she'd seen something glint farther back in the rabbit's mouth, and couldn't help but be curious. She sighed inwardly. Had she always had an oral fixation, or could she write that off as more quirks from her curse? Shoving it to the back of her mind, she picked up a pizza slice. "It looks good on you."

Autumn's ears went up, then lowered into a more relaxed position. Even so, self-consciousness shadowed her eyes as she looked down at the table. "Thanks." She took a deep breath. "I'm glad those ankle-high jerks didn't put you off. It seemed—I mean, it looked like we had..."

The Rha smiled. "So it wasn't just me."

"No." Autumn relaxed again. "It definitely wasn't."

Saida took another bite of the pizza. "Want any? Although it's not vegetarian."

"The pepperoni gave that away. Just because I'm a rabbit doesn't mean I'm an obligate herbivore, though." She picked up the other slice. "You didn't put any of the jerks on here, did you?" Without waiting for an answer, she opened her mouth wide and took an exaggeratedly big bite.

"No, sorry."

Autumn chewed and swallowed, then smirked. "Just as well. They'd probably be bitter."

Saida laughed, then lowered her voice. "I hope I'm not going to be banned from here for making the joke. It's kind of frowned on around campus, right?"

"Did the server say anything?"

"No, he heard it all and played along with me."

The rabbit glanced toward the counter with an expression of relieved surprise. "Cool. I think you're safe, then."

They ate their pizza in silence for a few moments. Companionable silence? Maybe. Saida felt...not at ease, not even comfortable, but happy. She'd had lust-at-first-sight crushes before, some of which hadn't at all been good for her—some of which she couldn't help blame on that damn curse. But this, whatever it was, it didn't feel like that.

She realized Autumn had paused chewing, head tilted to the side, expression quizzical.

The Rha flushed. "What?"

"You were looking at me with, with...like..." The rabbit trailed off, looking to the side with another sheepish smile, then back down at the cat.

"Sorry. I got kind of lost in thought in a moment."

"Ah." The rabbit looked just a little disappointed.

Saida bit the inside of her lip. She needed to get the conversation going. "What kind of magic are you studying?"

"Hmm? Oh." She took another bite of pizza. "I started with transformation magic. That's what I came to the school to do. The instant I learned about the school, getting here and learning that became my life's mission."

"That's a very specific focus."

Autumn fixed her gaze on the cat. "I had big things to change."

Saida nodded slowly. The word choice wasn't accidental, was it? "You weren't a giant when you came to the school."

Autumn took a deep breath. "Like I said." She spread out her hands, pressing them against the table. "There's what I realized I always had been, and what I realized I should be. I knew I needed to change to be both. So it's what I did." Her expression grew more intent, and she bit her lip.

The cat reached across the table, putting her hand over one of the rabbit's. After a long moment, Autumn flipped her own hand over, entwining her fingers with Saida's and beaming. The Rha felt herself melt into a happy puddle.

"You need to tell me a secret now," Autumn said after a few moments, smile growing impish once more.

"I do?" Saida gave her a lopsided smile in return.

She leaned forward, lowering her voice. "Maybe my transitions aren't *secret*, but I don't share them casually with strangers. So we shouldn't be strangers, little cat."

"Little?" Saida drew herself up with a smirk.

"Little," Autumn repeated. "Want me to stand close enough to you to touch and compare heights?"

Saida felt her ears blush. "That's not as effective a threat as you might think coming from you."

"Oh, now I'm even more intrigued."

Saida sighed. The blush wasn't going away. Well, she had an obvious choice or two, but *obvious* wasn't necessarily *wise*. "It's just hard for me to come up with something. My choices are either boring or overly personal."

"Go with personal."

Right. Given what Autumn had shared, that was a lousy attempt at deflection. "They're...I mean...kind of...intimate for a first..." She caught herself and cleared her throat.

Too late, though. Autumn leaned forward, thin brows lifting. "Date?"

"Are we on one?"

Autumn tilted her head to one side again, then the other, then straightened up, looking intently into Saida's eyes again. "That depends on whether you let me lead you out of here holding your hand. If you do, then I'm going to take you to a great coffee place, buy you coffee, and we're going to call this our first date."

Saida laughed. "All right."

"All right." Autumn stood up slowly, still holding Saida's hand.

The Rha stood up too, not letting go.

Autumn walked around the table, eyes on Saida's, then slowly walked past her, fingers still entwined with the Rha's. Saida tightened her grip on the rabbit's hand and followed.

CHAPTER 2

Higher Grounds

When Autumn had led her out of the Beanstalk, Saida hadn't expected the rabbit to head right for the main campus road. More precisely, for the sidewalk that ran along it, set a good two meters lower than the road's surface to make it harder for small cars and big paws to accidentally meet. "You ever been to Higher Grounds in Parkcrest?"

"No. I'm guessing the name's a size pun? I didn't think the town had anything built for us once you got off campus." Saida looked up at the college entrance archway as they walked underneath it. To her, it felt like a small garden gate on an old money estate, but had to be staggeringly imposing to someone used to the rest of the world's scale.

"It's a pun on coffee." She pointed ahead into the city. "It's just few blocks that way."

As the ground shifted from poured concrete to broken asphalt, the sound their sandals made shifted from hard slaps to softer crunches. The neighborhood right past the college gate had become unofficially known as the DMZ. It had been run down for years, in the way light industrial areas often were; the college's construction brought added fear of what might happen with giants and magic just past the huge walls. The DMZ had been left as a mix of increasingly squalid slums and outright abandoned buildings. The desolation all but invited giants to come out and "play monster"; what was the harm in kicking over an already-condemned building? Arilin had told her this had been one of several ongoing tensions with the city. "Wait, it's little?"

"That doesn't mean it's not built for us, does it? Everything's built for us." She laughed. "Sorry, that sounds like it should be followed by deep maniacal laughter. I just mean we live here, too, and we can go where we want as long as we're careful about it."

The next block was in better shape; the block after that, not too many giantess-steps ahead, looked like Tiny Hipsterville. Tiny LGBT Hipsterville, to boot: rainbow flag banners hung from storefronts and lamp posts. If she were the same scale as the town, she'd love to explore it. But now, at normal size, her sandals took up more than half the width of a road lane. In the DMZ almost nobody had parked on the side of the road, so she could walk normally without fear of causing damage. Tiny Hipsterville had wide medians full of grass and flowers and even trees and benches, and parked cars lined the roadside.

Autumn seemed to notice her hesitation and grinned. "Hey, I have way bigger feet than you and I walk here all the time. We're specifically allowed to be on these roads."

"'They can't stop us' isn't the same as 'allowed.'"

"If we weren't allowed, we wouldn't have the traffic signals, would we? For someone who says she loves being giant, you're awfully nervous about...being giant."

Saida furrowed her brow. "What do you mean, traffic signals?"

"You haven't seen them? Stop at the intersection here for a moment."

Saida stopped and glanced behind her. The closest car was more than a block back, going *very* slow to avoid being too close to the four giant paws ahead. She bit her lip and looked down at the fragile buildings and cars and pedestrians. She'd expected the two of them to be attracting more stares, but everyone just kept going about their little business below.

Abruptly, the tops of the lamp posts lining the avenue ahead lit up red.

"Wait for green." The rabbit had pulled a phone out of her pocket and was tapping on it with both thumbs.

"Those are for us?"

"Mmm-hmm."

"Are you...turning them on with your phone?"

Autumn glanced down at her with a laugh. "No, goof, I'm texting our coffee order ahead. What do you want?"

"I..." Arilin had never mentioned giant-safe roads, but Saida had foolishly preferred walking around—and through—town many miles away, where giants were less common and she *had* been putting both the littles and herself at risk. She'd caused more than one traffic accident, sent more than one crowd of pedestrians screaming away in panic, and angrily kicked one set of traffic lights into a strip mall when she nearly tripped over it. She might not have been a monster, but she'd been callous. If she'd learned earlier to be a *good* giant like Autumn, she might not have been cursed—

Autumn tapped her on the shoulder. "Green."

"Oh." Saida steeled herself, then took a big step forward, over the entire cross-street. Her sandal came down hard enough to set off two car alarms. Oh, *there* were the scrambling panicked pedestrians. Her ears flattened.

Autumn laughed. "Walk normally. Just watch where you're placing your feet and keep them in the lane."

"There are cars!" she protested. "Moving! In the same direction!"

"Yes. Don't step on them." Autumn walked ahead.

Saida gritted her teeth, but did her best to follow the rabbit's lead. How did the *drivers* know where she was putting her feet?

But—somehow—it worked. As she moved forward, the traffic moved forward, too. The car behind her got uncomfortably close, but it didn't try to go under her. She could see the red "landing lights" on the block ahead changing to green, then the next block; the cars on cross-streets got red lights. So giants had right of way. Lights set at ground level also flashed, perhaps alerting drivers they now shared the road with giants.

By the second block she'd gotten comfortable enough to increase her speed—and the car behind her had gotten comfortable enough to pass. It startled her, but she barely had to change her stride. She just had to be aware of where the car was. And where the pedestrians and the parked cars and the trees and the little yappy dogs were. But it wasn't hard. And all the littles around her paws stayed aware of where she was.

"You've never walked through a city?" Autumn kept her eyes on the road and her own paws, even as she made intermingling with the auto traffic look barely more difficult than breathing.

"I have. But it wasn't like this. They didn't plan for giants. Here they're trusting me not to be a monster."

"And?"

Saida laughed as she realized the answer. "The trust is way more of a rush."

Autumn grinned back over her shoulder, then looked forward again. "Okay." She pointed. "The shop's right there."

The Rha looked down. From her angle, she couldn't see the storefront; it was just another little dollhouse. "What do we do?"

"Lower your hand to signal people behind you that you're stopping, like this, but right over the street." The rabbit raised her hand, palm up. "Then move as close to the sidewalk as you can without blocking it."

Saida followed suit as well as she could. One parking space nearby was empty, so that made it—ah, there was another one, around the corner. It wasn't too awkward a stance. She hoped.

Crouching, Autumn leaned over the building's roof. People on the sidewalk backed away warily, but she smiled and pointed at one with a black claw. "Go inside and let them know Autumn Caligo is here to pick up her white mochas?" The rabbit's tone and manner made it sound like a polite question, but her phrasing—and size— made it more of a command. The fox nodded and ducked in hurriedly.

"Hey, *your* paw is blocking the sidewalk."

Autumn glanced down. "Not completely. Besides, if somebody touches my foot, it's good luck."

She laughed in spite of herself. "A white mocha, huh? You didn't wait for my order."

"You were slow. But you'll like it."

Shortly a goat walked out, paper cup in each hand. From above, the most noticeable thing was her shocking blue mohawk. If Autumn had a perky-goth vibe, this woman looked like she'd just leapt off the stage at a punk club. "Hey, Autumn," she called up. "Who's your friend with her paw in the loading zone?" She set both cups down on the sidewalk, about six feet apart, then leaned against Autumn's lucky foot to look up.

"This is Saida. Saida, this is Kim."

Saida crouched. Her balance felt steady, but if she fell she'd take out at least one store even if she put her hand out to catch herself. Great. "Hi."

Kim's eyes swept up and down Saida. "Hey. Nice to meet you." She looked back toward Autumn's face and gave her a thumbs up, with an expression that clearly read *good catch!*

Autumn grinned down, then looked to Saida. "So, you're probably wondering how we drink those."

"That's a leading line, isn't it?"

"It is. Everyone clear?"

Kim stepped back. "Clear."

Autumn lifted a hand and traced a symbol in the air, murmuring under her breath. Her claw-tip flared and sparked like a just-struck match. Then she carefully tapped it to each tiny paper cup. The cups sparked, too, then abruptly expanded in size, each one now standing taller than the goat woman.

Saida's eyes widened.

Scattered clapping came from watchers on the sidewalk, including a couple big claps from Kim. "That's always so cool."

Autumn picked up both cups, then straightened and handed one to Saida. She took a sip from her own. "Great as always, Kim."

The goat gave her a thumbs-up, grinning, and headed inside again.

The rabbit motioned with her free hand. "There's a park a couple blocks away with enough space for us to sit down in."

"All right." Saida smiled. "Let's go."

This time the walk seemed almost normal, even with a couple

drivers tapping their horns. (Autumn explained they were just letting her know they were underneath her.) A forest Saida had seen in the distance turned out to be in a huge municipal park, three blocks wide and eight blocks long. The trick was finding enough *empty* space for them.

"There?" Saida pointed at an open meadow between one of the gardens and a soccer field.

"Sure."

As they walked through the grass, over paths and benches and by thankfully-sparse crowds of littles, Saida found herself grinning. Autumn didn't comment on it until they'd both sat down, the Rha with her legs stretched out, the bunny cross-legged in a lotus position. "What?"

"I went out for pizza, and suddenly I'm on a sunset date with a younger woman who's showing me how to be out on a little town without accidentally trampling it." She laughed, shaking her head.

"What's the unexpected part? The not trampling, that I'm younger, or that I'm a woman?"

"Yes." She grinned. "Although I've always known I was bi."

Autumn nodded. "I am, too, although my experience with boys hasn't been great. But have you been out in little towns and accidentally trampled them? Or not-so-accidentally done it?"

"Yes and no." She sipped her mocha. "This *is* really good."

"They're always good there, but Kim makes the best. So tell me about the yes and the no."

"When I first started visiting here, Arilin drilled into me that the campus is the only safe place for giants, and that we're all trying to make a good impression on the town here. But I started going for... long walks. Through other towns, farther away."

"To be a monster?" Autumn's beautiful violet eyes focused on her with uncomfortable intensity.

"I don't think so," she said slowly. "But I guess I just didn't want to worry much about whether people thought I was. I don't think I did much damage, but I got into enough trouble that I stopped." She knew leaving things hanging there made it sound like she'd had people try to kill her, but she wasn't up for explaining she actually *had* been killed—and set up by a twisted curse to have it happen again.

"I hope it wasn't too much trouble. What did you do? Dance across a city kicking over buildings? Swallow annoying policemen whole?"

Saida's eyes widened, and she looked up, fluffy tail lashing once.

The rabbit tilted her head, the sunset glinting off her earrings. "I just want to know who I'm on a first date with."

"I've done a little damage here and there, mostly by accident, not always. I've...what-ifed about eating people, if I'm honest."

"Really. Huh." Autumn sipped from her own mocha, looking out over the city with an unreadable expression.

As the silence stretched on, Saida fidgeted. Maybe honesty wasn't always the best policy.

Autumn looked down at her. "I don't want to hang out with someone who's enthusiastic about being a monster, but that doesn't mean I expect everyone to be giant nuns or something."

"Do I pass, then?"

The rabbit nodded. "I'm pretty good at reading people." She lowered her voice again. "Besides, I won't pretend I *haven't* thought about being a monster once in a while."

"I thought it might be different for someone who..." How had Autumn put it? "Didn't grow up the size she should have been."

The rabbit's smile grew warmer. "Maybe." She took a sip of her own mocha, looking thoughtful again. "I love knowing I have the power I do, but just taking it because I can is..." She shook her head. "I can do anything I want with someone who fits under my paw. But if they *want* to be there, if I get them to say, 'Oh, Autumn, *please* do anything you want with me...'" She smiled, letting that hang in the air as she took another sip of her drink.

Saida glanced down at Autumn's shapely sandaled paws and found herself gripping her own drink tightly enough that the cup started to crease. "I hadn't thought of it that way before."

"Like you said, the trust is a hell of a rush." She focused that intense gaze back on the cat. "Now I'm trying to think how I'd react

17

if some cute little thing I was holding in my hand gasped out, 'Please, Autumn, swallow me!'"

"And how would you?"

"I'd probably be freaked out." Autumn looked down at the Rha again. "But if they had resurrection magic, and I'd be able to see them again and ask how it was..." She grinned slightly. "Yeah, they'd be going down my throat." She tilted her cup and her head all the way back, exposing her long neck and visibly swallowing as she finished the drink.

"Oh." Saida felt a blush rise to her ears. Before she could think of anything to say, her phone started buzzing. Frowning—but a little relieved at the distraction—she pulled it out of her purse. A text message, relayed from the office through the off-world beacon. She sighed. "Hang on."

It was Jonry, of course: her patronizing problem child, following up on a sales contract he'd been having trouble working out yesterday. Reading between the lines, he'd made the problem worse, and was sending her new document revisions and by the way it would be *so helpful* if she could get on a phone call and smooth things over in person. It was a miracle that the hack she and her brother had put together for cross-dimensional data worked at all; she'd have to go back to Stravell to actually make the call. She tapped out a few curt lines of advice and a promise to follow up in the morning. "Goddess Arvya, what an idiot," she muttered as she put her phone away.

"Problem?"

"Work. I'm going to have to get back to my suite and review some documents before I get to bed."

"Did—did you just get a text from another world?" Autumn looked incredulous.

"Yeah." She grunted, sipping from her own drink. Unlike Autumn, she still had a third left. "Just being on another world doesn't get me off of being on call."

"What do you do?"

"I mentioned how teleportation beacons are a niche business now. I'm the sales director for the company that makes them."

"You're—" Autumn looked taken aback. "Wow. You don't seem much older than I am, and you're a corporate executive?"

Saida sighed; this wasn't the time to go into this. "I wouldn't have the job if I wasn't family, and I'm sure it's only because I'm family that I get enough slack to keep a home here and take long weekends. Not that anyone but my brother knows where I go."

"Keep a home here," Autumn echoed.

Saida started to feel more self-conscious. "I mean, it's a studio here I rent with Arilin's staff discount, and I have a flat back home. Still renting there, too."

"Mmm. You being a bigwig over there makes me more surprised you'd want to come here."

"I like the place. I like feeling giant. And I like the people I meet."

"Like me?"

"Like you. When I first saw you earlier tonight you seemed so dark and mysterious. Then as we talked, you seemed gentle. But still with an edge."

"Everyone's a bundle of contradictions." The rabbit put her hand on Saida's shoulder; it looked slim and elegant, even though it was larger than the Rha's in every dimension. "I'd like to think I'm gentle *and* dark and mysterious." She grinned.

"So will you dance across the city with me?"

"Only if we place our paws very carefully. But," Autumn rose to her feet and leaned down to offer her hand to Saida, "you wouldn't do that."

"You're sure?" She took the rabbit's hand and stood up.

"Yes." They started walking back toward the street. "Like I said, I'm good at reading people."

As they approached the main street, the landing lights switched back on for them. The walk back toward the college was easy, despite higher traffic. "So other than mostly gentle, how do you read me?"

"Dark and mysterious."

Saida laughed. "I don't feel like I'm either, but I'm going to take it as a compliment."

"You should."

When they reached the college's gate, Autumn stopped, looking down at the cat. "So now what?"

"Are you asking how far I go on a first date?"

"I know you have to leave to do work." She put her hands on the Rha's shoulders, looking down into her eyes. "So I'm asking if there's going to be a second."

"If you want it, yes."

Autumn kept her eyes locked on Saida's for long seconds. "When will you be back in town?"

"A couple weeks."

"I'm going to give you my number, and I expect you to call."

"I will."

Autumn touched her lips to Saida's lightly, holding there. The Rha leaned up, tightening her hands on the rabbit's shoulders, purring.

When the kiss ended, Autumn brushed her muzzle against Saida's ear. "You still haven't told me a secret, little cat. Don't think I've forgotten."

Saida shivered, eyelids fluttering. "Next time."

CHAPTER 3

Volunteer Work

"ARE YOU HUMMING UNDER YOUR BREATH?"

Autumn frowned down at the hyena who'd asked the question, a broad-chested, thirty-something guy in tight blue jeans and an equally tight purple tee. Tom stared right back up, unfazed, grin even wider than usual.

"Yeah." She resumed her work—watching little volunteers at a dozen tables within her reach repacking bulk dry goods and produce, from rice and beans to fresh fruit, into family-sized bags for distribution. The tables sat to one side of a warehouse floor, the work area partitioned off into a "room" with no ceiling; she sat just outside that area on the main warehouse floor. The rabbit's job was to see when they'd either emptied one of the bulk boxes and move a new box over to them, or filled up one of the distribution boxes and move the finished product to the receiving area. As one of the food bank's few paid staff members, Tom's job was handling all the actual shipping and distribution coordination. And, apparently, giving the giantess shit. "So?"

His grin grew. "Are you...*happy?*"

"Look, we've been over how my fashion sense isn't a subtle statement of existential despair. I'm a happy person."

"You're not a *humming* happy person."

Rolling her eyes, she hurried to move a few more boxes into place. "Look, I just happened to be humming."

A grey fox vixen glanced up from the rice she was weighing out. "So I guess you had a good date last night?"

Autumn nearly dropped the box she was holding between thumb and forefinger, staring down at her.

The vixen's ears lowered. Autumn wasn't sure of her name, maybe Carolyn or Karen or something, but she recognized her. Always immaculately professional-looking, someone you wouldn't guess would volunteer monthly at a food bank. "I...didn't mean to assume, but..."

"Autumn went on a *date?*" Tom's grin grew even more. "Oh, come on, who's the lucky guy?"

The vixen opened her mouth, closed it, then cleared her throat and went back to her rice.

Autumn reached down and tapped a black claw on the concrete floor by the woman. "Out with it."

The vixen jumped, barking, sending a scoop of rice flying into the air, then looked back up at the rabbit giantess, tail between her legs now. "I saw you and your friend last night because you're both, well, hard to miss. I shouldn't have assumed it was a date, but..."

"It was. And sorry, I didn't mean to scare you."

Tom put his hands on his hips. "Oh, you don't date normal-sized people? I thought I had a chance! Have you been leading me on?"

Autumn sighed again, returning to her box-moving task. "Sometimes you're lucky I like your boyfriend."

"I like him, too," he replied in a sing-song voice. "All right, everyone, five more minutes."

Five minutes later on the dot, Tom led the volunteer group—everyone but Autumn—off the warehouse floor into a no-doubt charming lobby area she couldn't even see into, much less enter. Other than the vixen, she hadn't recognized anyone from past shifts. That wasn't uncommon. A lot of white-collar managers took their work groups to the food bank for a shift as a team-building exercise. There'd always be people who'd enthusiastically talk about coming back on their own, but almost no one ever did.

Her own entrance and exit was less dignified, crawling on her hands and knees—carefully—to a set of giant rolling doors barely big enough to accommodate her when she crawled through on her stomach. It took slow, careful wiggling to make her way out, and once a frantic "No! No! To your left!" yell from the staff.

By the time she made it outside and dusted off, Tom had walked out, too, setting down a can of Diet Dr. Pepper. She traced the power-drawing rune in the air—sloppily, Professor Snep would tell her, but she'd done it so often it had become automatic—and muttered a focus word under her breath, then tapped the can carefully. It shimmered, expanding to her scale. "Thanks."

Tom waved a hand dismissively. None of the other volunteers were given free snacks from the staff break room, but shifts Autumn worked on ran close to three times more productive than the average. Then the hyena grinned. "Four today."

"Four, huh? Is that a record?"

Tom frequently reported on how many volunteers—or staff—were, quote, "ogling that cute giant puff tail." She'd grimaced and rolled her eyes and half-heartedly told him to stop it, but he'd correctly guessed she was less offended than conflicted. She didn't want to be objectified, but it could still be annoyingly gratifying to hear people thought she was sexy.

"Maybe." He laughed. "I think the coyote in the blue floral print shirt was all but drooling."

"Yeah, that doesn't surprise me. He was looking up at my chest when he thought I wasn't noticing." She shook her head.

"But I shouldn't be bothering you with this anymore, should I?" He punched one of her toes. "Tell me about your date!"

"It wasn't...I mean, it was a date, yeah, but we just went out for coffee."

The hyena crossed his arms, looking up expectantly.

She sighed theatrically, rolling her eyes. "She's a cat I met at the Student Union."

"Oh. *Oh.*" The gears turning in Tom's head might as well have been clacking like a switchyard. "Another student?"

"No. She's a professor's cousin."

"How old is she?"

"I don't know." She took a long drink of the soda.

"Older than you?"

"Yeah."

He wagged his tail. "What's she do?"

"She's a sales... VP? Director? Some kind of corporate executive."

He tilted his head, looking up with raised brows.

Autumn sighed. "What?"

"I would *not* have bet money on 'high-power capitalist' being your type."

"She's not like that. I mean, she must be doing well, since she lives and works...wherever Rhas live, and rents a studio here. But she's sweet."

"Rha?"

She waved her free hand. "Giant cat. I guess. Professor Thorferra and Saida are the only cats I know who use the word, and I think they're both from another world or something."

"Another world? Like, another planet or dimension?"

She nodded.

"Come on."

"Yeah, explain to the giant sorceress-in-training you're sitting here talking to how that's completely crazy."

"Point." He shook his head, looking back at the warehouse. "Speaking of that, any luck on coming up with a spell that multiplies food instead of just making it bigger?"

The question of why the spells that enlarged food to her scale didn't let wizards breezily solve world hunger hadn't led to heated arguments when she and Tom first met, but only because he was still too terrified of a real live giantess to dare contradict her. By the time he was comfortable enough to tease and argue with her, he'd come to understand she wasn't bullshitting him when she said it didn't work. Giants could eat little food without a problem, and littles could eat "naturally made" giant food if they dared. But magically size-shifted food played by fiddlier, arcane rules. Shifting food at Tom's scale up to hers would be fine for her, but it'd render it about as nutritious as packing peanuts for Tom.

So the next obvious question: why can't you take a bag of rice and cast a spell on it that makes it ten bags of rice? "No. The only textbooks I can find on it don't go into detail about why it doesn't work, though. Half of them try to make it sound like a moral question and the other half make it sound like an impossible physics problem, which is probably closer to the truth."

"*You're* an impossible physics problem, but you're still here."

She grinned wryly, taking another sip of the soda. "I know. But enlarging objects is easier than multiplying them. It's transmutation versus creation. I've researched turning inedible material into food, too, but it's not promising. Turn a brick into a pear and you get something that looks, smells, and tastes like a pear, but still has the nutrition value of a brick."

"Great. And transmutation isn't easy, even though you're an expert at it."

"Not an expert, just...some kind of savant. There are common first-year spells I'm terrible at."

"You're selling yourself short. Ha!" Tom waved a hand. "But back to your mystery date. When do you see her again?"

"That's up to her. She's supposed to give me a call when she's back in town."

"You didn't get her number?"

"I gave her mine. I don't know if she even keeps the same number between visits."

"Oh, honey. You go out of your way to make your life difficult sometimes, don't you?" He sighed and patted her toe again. "I need to get ready for the afternoon volunteer group. You staying?"

"I can't. Too much school work to do."

"Got it." He snapped his fingers and pointed up at her. "Speaking of work. Did you ever write that letter?"

"No."

"It's been a month."

"That depends on how you measure it." Her parents had sent a birthday card two years ago; it took her nearly six months to work up the nerve to write back and correct them on her name. Next year she got two birthday cards: one from her sister, addressed correctly; the other from her parents, addressed to her dead name. She hadn't written them since. Or heard from them, until the email from her sister.

"You can't avoid it forever, dear."

"I can do whatever I want. I'm a giantess." She downed the rest of her soda, then pushed herself up to her feet. "See you next week."

Maybe Tom was right, and she *should* have gotten Saida's number. In the moment, making Saida promise to call had seemed romantic, but maybe she should have opted for practicality.

She's not like that. But Autumn had no idea what Saida was like, did she? No matter how much she deflected about her wealth and position, the cat was a rich executive. An older rich executive. Being looked at in the adoring way Saida had looked at her—seemed to have looked at her?—was thrilling, but people like that didn't get seriously involved with moody broke college students.

Did she want to just be a fling?

She made her way through the parking lot carefully, then picked up speed on the empty street. The food bank's warehouse sat close to the DMZ, just a few minutes from the campus; she'd seen other students volunteer occasionally, although never any other giants.

When she reached the gate where she and Saida had shared their first—and so far, only—kiss, she stopped, looking across the campus in the direction of the staff housing, then back out across the city.

"I should have asked for her number," she muttered.

CHAPTER 4

Buckle Down

"THEY WEREN'T GOING TO TAKE THEM AT THAT PRICE." Jonry spread his hands apart, fixing Saida with his patented, patronizing *let me 'splain to you* expression as they walked. He must have thought he looked authoritative, but he just looked constipated. "I know how much we're eatin' on the installation costs, but trust me, it'll work out."

She suppressed a sigh. As much as she liked the theory of these "walking one-on-ones," it was an unconscionably hot day, approaching 94 degrees, with what the weather claimed was 50% relative humidity but felt more like 500%. Wanting to stop and wring out her tail made this intolerable conversation somehow even less tolerable. "And how much are we 'eating' on installation?"

"Just under five million." He managed to say that not only without sounding sheepish, but with an edge of disdain, as if she should have already known the answer.

Unfortunately for the swaggering gray tabby, she *did*, in fact, already know the answer. "If that's correct, we won't break even for fourteen months."

"Right, but—"

"But that's *not* correct, because you assumed all of the client's eighteen remote offices match our standard cost structure."

"It all evens out!"

"No, it doesn't. The four cross-country ones are in metro areas with taxes and regulations that run their cost up about thirty percent. The six in other countries range from two to four times as much when you add import duties, infrastructure improvements, and security updates. And your contract doesn't pass on the costs of the extra security we'll have to hire in Lantalvo, since it's a war zone. Our breakeven point is *three years*."

Jonry's ears had steadily lowered as she spoke. "But I wouldn't have gotten the contract."

They turned a corner, heading back toward their office past the new war memorial. This city had come through the lightning-bombing of the previous decade with little more than scratches, but these austere, cheerless "memory parks" had become perversely fashionable displays of patriotism. "Jonry, you're a good salesman, but you need to stop treating teleportation beacons like HVACs. We aren't trying to undercut the competition."

His tail lashed. "Do you know how much cheaper the competition is? I do my research, little lady, and let me—"

Her voice rose into what she'd heard the staff call the "Saida Screech," but she couldn't help it. "We have no fucking competition!"

He stopped mid-stride, eyes widening.

"Every other company on the market selling teleporter beacons is just rebranding Melovi units, and they're cheap because *they're cheap*. The bigger the payload, the shorter their range. None of their units can send something heavier than a paperweight cross-country and they have to recharge for ten minutes after each transfer."

"I know—"

"Only *one* of their models is certified to send people, a max of a hundred miles. This company wants to send staff between international offices. If they don't use us, they're using airlines. We don't compete on price because we don't *have* to."

"So you would have just walked away?" He sounded genuinely affronted by the idea.

"I'd have given them a final offer that was within the discount guidelines I've already given you, and if they said no? Yes, I'd have walked away. If they needed us, they'd be back." They'd reached the warehouse-like office building, walking past the understated but expensive marble sign with the Talirend Dynamics logotype carved into it. She'd had to push Mradhi hard to replace the sheet metal one, to make *some* attempt at giving the offices an upscale look. It had improved the sales by about twelve percent within a year. She'd tried to get him to move the sales and executive offices downtown, too, but he'd balked at the cost, no matter how much data showed that sales to status-conscious millionaires would cover it in under a year. Convincing him wasn't her job now, anyway. She tried not to grit her teeth.

Jonry's tail was between his legs now, but he sounded more resentful than chastened. "Point taken. Ma'am."

"What other prospects are you working on?"

He walked through the door ahead of her, letting go just in time to make sure she had to catch it to walk through herself. Terrific. The only thing worse than false, patronizing chivalry was a macho sulk. At least the blast of blessed air conditioning lessened her irritation.

"Got a few. Harrison Media Group is looking at an interoffice system, and there's a couple movie moguls who want to set up JetNets."

She nodded. "Those sound promising." JetNet was their trademark for a personal system, what the excessively rich would set up between their offices and their various homes. They weren't much cheaper than the commercial systems, but people making that much didn't care. Technically, she had a JetNet, although it was a prototype unit that predated the company. Back from when it was just her brother trying to make their late uncle's mad science project into something real.

"Thanks. So." He shuffled back and forth on his paws, keeping his eyes on her but turning the rest of his body back toward his cubicle. "Anything else, ma'am?"

"No. Is there anything you need from me?"

He'd already started to head away. "Nah, we're good," he called, without looking back.

Saida headed back toward her own cubicle, forcing herself not to look at Raiben's office as she passed by. She had the biggest, nicest cubicle of anyone in the company, not just the newly combined sales and marketing division. It was barely a step down from an office.

But it *was* a step down from an office. Specifically, *that* office. The one she'd been in six weeks ago.

Dropping into her chair, she slumped back, staring dolefully at the computer. As futuristic as their business had sounded to Autumn, the consumer tech around Mensura was at least a decade ahead of Stravell's. Her PC wasn't as powerful as the *phone* she carried on her weekend visits to the campus. She wasn't sure Mradhi had ever completely given up on the idea of finding a way to commercialize a smuggling operation between the worlds, despite his reluctant agreement to both her and Arilin's objections.

She skimmed her email, ignoring most of it until she hit a missive from Raiben. She scanned over it, eyes narrowing.

Tail lashing, she pushed back from the desk and headed toward the CEO's office, doing her best not to make it an angry march.

Her brother was six years older than she was, but didn't look it. If he put effort into it, he'd pass for a fashion model—something he stubbornly remained disinterested in. His new wife, though, surely didn't. Since the marriage he'd been dressing more sharply, button-down shirts rather than polos, slacks rather than jeans, colors that complimented his light tan fur—although Saida was still pretty sure he bought off the rack. But his disinterest in "the good life" was also a saving grace, an inoculation against the excesses one might expect from a multi-millionaire in his early thirties. He'd spent a bit lavishly on his home theater setup, but the house he and his wife had recently moved into was, well, a house. Not a mansion estate, just a pleasant house in a nice suburb, not even that big for its neighborhood. Big for only two, but she expected they'd have a child within the next couple of years.

He saw her and held up a finger, swiveling around in his chair as he continued talking on the phone. Saida crossed her arms.

It only took him a few seconds to disengage with a typically curt, "Call back later." Then he spun around again to face her. "You're here to complain about Raiben's plan to move our sales team to commissions."

She sighed, tail lashing, then turned to close the door behind her. "I'm here to complain about him not even running it by me."

Mradhi frowned. "He said he'd clear it with you. I'll speak to him."

"So he cleared it with you."

"I'm the CEO."

"And I'm the Director of Sales."

"Again, yes, he should have run it past you. But as the VP of Sales and Marketing, he can make this call."

"Commissions? We're not selling air conditioners, Mradhi. Or cars."

"Earlier this morning you were moaning about Jonry all but giving away beacons to get the service contract. Do you think he'd have done that if he were working on a commission basis?"

"Bluntly, yes." Saida's tail lashed. "And for Arvya's sake, Raiben wants to put me back in the field."

"He just said he wants you more hands-on with the biggest contracts."

"That means in the field. Instead of getting a promotion, I'm getting a demotion."

Mradhi leaned forward. "Saida, you've grown into an excellent manager, but when we talked before I brought Raiben in, *you* said you didn't think you were ready to be a VP. Are you reconsidering that?"

Her ears lowered. "No." She sighed. "Maybe."

"I still think your self-assessment was right. As good a manager as you are, you're distracted. I don't expect you to live for your job, but I expect you to focus more on the company than on your weekends playing giantess." Mradhi turned back to his computer.

Her ears went completely flat, and she hurried out of her brother's office. She didn't stop at her desk, instead heading out of the building, back into the broiling sun.

She'd risen high and fast—higher and faster than she likely deserved. She had a knack for planning, a head for numbers, but she'd never been that good a salesman. *Was* she a good manager? Did she get the pushback she did—never from Mradhi, to his credit, but nearly everyone else—because she was a woman, or because she just wasn't as competent as she tried to convince herself she was? Her trips to Mensura helped her put all those doubts aside.

At least, they *had*. Since the curse she'd been too spooked to keep exploring off-campus, and after a mortifying encounter a few months ago—another temporary death from being swallowed alive, all the more horrifying from the way the curse made her own body betray her, reacting to the act like it was the best sex ever—her enthusiasm for the campus had cooled.

Until meeting Autumn.

She covered her face. Did it even make sense to call her again? It'd been a magical evening—literally—but talk about a long-distance relationship. And she'd all but promised to tell the rabbit about her curse. Letting more people know about it was the last thing she should do. She'd gotten the uneasy feeling there were rumors about her among the more predatorily inclined campus giants. Hell, Autumn might *be* one of those giants.

And she knew just which big contracts Raiben would want her to be "hands-on" with. She hated to admit it, but he wasn't wrong. Dammit, maybe she had to buckle down, behave like the high-power executive she was rather than the college dropout she felt like.

But maybe she should do that tomorrow. Right now, she needed a good happy hour.

CHAPTER 5

Maybe Not That Interested

BY THE THIRD TIME THE LITTLE HUSKY HAD STOPPED JUST on the balcony just behind her to stare, Autumn had had enough. She turned around abruptly enough to make him jump. "Can I help you?"

He looked around wildly, as if she might be speaking to someone else in the library standing right behind him, then gripped the railing. "Um. Y-you're in Snep's advanced alchemy class, right?" His voice shook in time with his whole body shaking.

If she was in a better mood, she'd try to sound reassuring, but this wasn't shaping up as a good mood day. Besides, if he was in that class, he had to be at least a second year student, so he should be way over the whole giants-are-so-terrifying thing by now. "Yes."

He nodded quickly. "There's, um, nobody else who looks like you. Um. You're one of his favorite students."

"That's a stretch." She sighed. "Did you just want to say hi, are you looking for homework help, or were you just hoping to keep staring at me without me noticing?"

His ears folded down, although not before she caught them turning bright red. "I...um. I dunno. I was just looking. You're... you're very pretty."

Autumn barely managed to stifle her sigh. Before her transformation, she hadn't realized being a giantess would attract littles constantly fantasizing about what creative things girls they were ankle-high to could do with them. "Thanks."

He nodded, shuffling on his paws. "I just. Uh. What...do you think about littles?"

"They're fine." She kept her voice flat.

The husky nodded again, looking down, then up, then down again. "I, uh. Maybe see you later."

"See you in class."

She waited until he'd turned around and headed out of sight before sitting down and staring at the ceiling with a groan. At least he'd picked up on the go-away-now-please vibe before asking if she'd ever thought about dating a little.

No, she'd thought about dating more often than that, ha ha. She'd been on six dates total since she transitioned, and maybe ten in her whole life. Granted, it was validating that she'd had more not only after she'd become a giantess, but after she'd consciously adopted what her sister Kelly called a "dare you, bitch" look. And, yes, that had included a few kinky things with people ankle-high to her, but she was pretty sure they'd been more fulfilling for the littles. Being giant didn't stop you from being objectified—if anything, it made it worse.

And then there was Saida.

She'd spent the first couple of weeks after their meeting almost floating. *God,* she was cute—and there was something else she couldn't put her finger on. An almost kitten-like sense of wonder, maybe. The way she got flustered when Autumn did something that reminded the cat she was the small one. The way she clearly enjoyed being flustered.

Playing it over in her head made Saida sound dismayingly like the little husky she'd just dismissed. But crap, if the Rha was just out for some kind of kick, that should have been *more* reason for her to call. But she hadn't called in two weeks. Or two more weeks. This upcoming weekend would make it two months.

How had Tom put it? High-power capitalist. Maybe Saida had realized she wasn't interested in dallying with a freaky-looking college student after all.

She pushed back from the desk, sweeping up the books and dropping them off on the nearest book cart. "Maybe I'm not that interested in dallying with her, either," she muttered aloud.

Her black mood propelled her out of the library and back toward the Union, although she didn't have a destination in mind. Another Friday afternoon with no weekend plans in sight. So, one of her typical weekends. Good thing she usually believed herself when she insisted she liked being solitary.

Once inside, she scanned the atrium. She still remembered how awe-inspiringly huge this building seemed when she'd arrived as a little—there had to be *acres* of floorspace between the multiple levels. As a giantess, her relationship to the space changed substantially. It wasn't as if it were cramped, but the options became far more limited: the open space she stood in right now with a few food kiosks, the Beanstalk, and the Union Café and Lounge, a small sit-down restaurant with a positively tiny bar. There were only three other giants in this central sitting area, but there were never that many giants, period. She doubted there were more than six or seven dozen total at the school; it was a wonder as many "non-essential" services existed for them as they did.

If she went back to the Beanstalk, she'd start thinking about Saida and be pissed at her again. But she didn't want to spend the money at the sit-down place. Finally, she just dropped onto the nearest sofa. Sometimes deciding was too damn much work.

She let herself space out for a few minutes, then realized the little husky was back. Sort of. He was walking along the edge of one of the two overlooking balcony levels. The upper one ran over a hundred feet off the floor, past her ear tips; the lower one ran a bit above her waist level. That's the one he was walking along. It didn't look like he was trying to spy on her this time, at least not until he caught sight of her. He didn't look at her, but the hitch in his step was almost a stumble.

Man, how had he made it this far staying all googly-eyed over giants? Sure, she'd had some of that, but she'd also been looking up at people Saida's size and thinking *I'm taller than you are, you just don't see it yet.* Well, maybe having a little fun would pull her out of her mope. "Hey," she called.

He stopped, looking down with a wary expression.

She stood up, walking slowly toward the balcony. "I was a little tough on you back in the library."

"That's...I mean, I think I was kind of a jackass. I'm not great at talking to girls my size, and...um..." He trailed off as she got closer, head tilting back and eyes getting wide.

One of the more unusual mandatory classes at the school, and one of the very few with segregated sizes, was a seminar on little-giant etiquette. Autumn was one of the only students who'd attended the versions for both scales. One of the lessons was that the perception of appropriate personal space didn't scale linearly, but grew with the size difference. Someone her height should stay back at least twenty feet from a little they didn't know, and let them choose to close the gap if they wanted. She slowed even more as she reached that distance, but didn't stop. "And you've got even less practice talking to giant ones."

"R...right. I say hi to giants in class sometimes, and Professor Thorferra likes to pair up mixed-size students in composition class, but..." His words ran dry again as she stopped barely a foot from the railing. He had to look almost straight up to see her face, which he did, ears visibly reddening. His tail clearly couldn't decide whether to wag or to curl between his legs.

"All right, then." She rested her hands on the railing, one to either side of him. "Practice." If this had been one of the catwalks common to campus interiors, he'd be trapped, although that would get a giant student reprimanded by staff if they saw it.

He whined. "I...I'm Charlie." His voice cracked like he'd just regressed to the edge of puberty.

"I'm Autumn." She kept her voice level, neither threatening nor welcoming, eyes remaining locked on him.

"Nice. Um, nice to meet you, I mean." The husky swallowed loudly. "So...um. How's it going up there?"

"Exactly the same as it is for you down there. Being a hundred feet tall doesn't give me my own weather system." She sighed, relenting. "Look, Charlie, if you're going to try to flirt with giant women, think about the *woman* part first. You're signaling that you think the most interesting thing about me is that I'm big enough to swallow you whole."

Charlie's mouth opened, but no noise came out.

Autumn's pocket started buzzing. She pursed her lips, then backed away a step, pulling out her phone. "Hang on." The number wasn't one she recognized, but it was local to campus. "Hello?"

"Hi. Autumn?" The voice on the other end of the connection sounded hesitant. "This is Saida."

She lifted the hand that was still on the railing off it, so when she made a fist it didn't break anything. She heard Charlie back away fast with another whimper, but didn't look down.

She didn't realize how long she'd stood there silently until Saida continued, now sounding more worried. "You...remember me, right?"

"Yes," she said curtly. What kind of stupid question was that?

"I'm sorry I haven't called before now. But this is the first time I've been able to get back to Mensura since our date."

Autumn closed her eyes. She didn't know if that made her more or less angry. "You said you came here every two or three weeks."

"I know." Saida's tone had edged into forlorn misery. "It's... work's gotten not just busy but...complicated. I just...I couldn't take a long weekend and work remotely like I had been."

Oh, your job is more important than seeing me? Yes, dumb bunny, the executive is probably gonna put her job ahead of the goth girl she shared a light kiss with. Autumn rubbed her forehead. "Fine." She didn't mean it to sound as sarcastic and bitter as it did, but fuck it. She *was* bitter.

"No, it isn't, and I'm sorry. I'd still like to meet again."

The pleading in Saida's voice was plain, but dammit, she could have popped in any other weekend, couldn't she? "I don't know."

"Just a lunch on campus, then. A quick coffee, even. Please."

She closed her eyes. "I can do dinner tonight."

"You can?" Saida sounded almost comically relieved. "That's great. Where? I'll pick up the tab."

Damn right you will. "I..." She opened her eyes again and glanced around. "The Beanstalk again, I guess, unless you want the sit-down place. The Banyan Tree, I think it's called."

"We can definitely do sit-down. Have you ever been to Chimayo? They have a few giant tables."

Her eyes widened. "Chimayo," she repeated. It was on the edge of campus, one of a handful of private businesses that leased space from the school with the condition they provide service to multiple scales. The upscale restaurant, owned by a celebrity chef she'd seen on television a few times, had only been open a few months—to rave reviews and solid bookings. "You think you can just get a table at the hottest restaurant in the city for a Friday night on a couple hours' notice."

"For giants, maybe. And I kind of have an 'in.'"

"I..." She shook her head. "Sure. All right."

"Great." Saida sounded excited now. "I'll call you back in a few minutes with the time if I can get it. Okay?"

"Okay."

She put the phone back in her pocket, and looked down at Charlie. "Sorry. I have to go."

He nodded. "Okay. Um. Thanks for...not eating me?"

Autumn paused, then crouched down. "You're cute, Charlie. You just need to relax. Get more comfortable around people *you* think are cute, regardless of their size. Remember girls are people, not objects. Then remember giants are people, too."

He nodded again, smiling uncertainly.

She straightened up. "Now, I have to go find something to wear." Shaking her head, she hurried back toward her dorm.

CHAPTER 6

Chimayo

THE "BUSINESS DISTRICT" SAT NEAR THE SOUTHEAST corner of campus, close to the staff housing—which must be where Saida's suite was. Technically, the district sat both on campus and in the off-campus DMZ, but at the edge of a low artificial cliff designed to put little street level at average giant chest height. Autumn had only been to this part of the campus maybe four times since she'd been a student. Five? There were no student services here, and she'd never had much interest in the Giants' Club, a bar that Professor Thorferra apparently co-owned. Some people said it was kind of cliquish, the name seemed silly, and the Beanstalk was closer anyway.

She slowed down as she approached the restaurant. Smooth tan stone formed the exterior walls, lines curved rather than hard, softly lit from below by lanterns—spotlights, she supposed, to littles—hidden in the foliage. Logs from either magically enlarged or unimaginably intimidating trees supported the roof. It looked like something from a high desert city, taking cues from ancient architecture but remaining modern.

No other giants stood outside, although a handful of littles milled around at street level. The sheer drop-off of dirt and rock that she remembered from a few months ago had been finished into a four-story wall of dark brown stone blocks, water trickling down in rivulets to a pool at the base. Some littles saw her and waved up cheerfully; others gawked gracelessly. All of them were dressed better than she was.

No, she admonished herself. *They're dressed more expensively. You're dressed great.* On her way out of her dorm, she'd been waylaid by Judy. The plushly curved raccoon had the eye of a fashion critic, and she'd immediately noticed the unusual lack of rips in Autumn's pair of black jeans. When the rabbit confessed she had a date, Judy briskly ushered her back to her own closet and commanded her to switch to that dark purple, design-free tee (tucked in), bring that black jacket, borrow this silver necklace. She'd bristled, but had to admit it not only all worked, but still fit her own style.

"Autumn!"

She turned to see Saida hurrying toward her. The Rha had traded her own jeans and tee look for a dark green sheath dress, a tight sleeveless wrap ending just above her knees, the V-cut neckline bordering on risqué given the cat's buxom build. She'd also added jewelry, by way of a matching bracelet and anklet, both simple gold hoops—albeit possibly real gold, or at least real gold plating. She started to feel underdressed again.

Before she could say anything, Saida stopped in front of her, looking her up and down. "You look stunning."

"Thanks. So do you."

Saida smiled self-consciously, fluffy tail flicking. "And thanks for giving me another chance." She hesitated, then motioned toward the restaurant. "Have you had...I guess they call it 'Southwestern' food? We don't have anything quite like it in Stravell."

Autumn followed. "Like tacos and burritos? Fajitas?"

"I don't think so. We don't have those in Stravell, either, although our breadpockets are close." She reached the door first, holding it open for the rabbit.

Inside, the restaurant looked like—well, like places her parents would never have taken her to. Soft, warm indirect light, walls that matched the waterfall stones, solid dark wood furnishings from each table to the host stand. Tasteful, restrained, expensive without being overtly excessive. She liked the look, but admitting that even to herself made her vaguely uncomfortable.

A tigress in a formal black suit—a tuxedo? Autumn wasn't sure, but it even had the bowtie—stood behind the host stand, smiling as they approached. "Good evening. Welcome back, Miss Talirend."

Autumn's brows lifted.

Saida smiled. "Thank you."

The tigress checked a display in front of her, then tapped the screen a few times. "Right this way." She gathered two menus and headed into the dining room.

Past the entranceway, the reality of giant and little reasserted itself. The room for them held only five tables, although it didn't feel cramped. One wall, though, had a break just a bit over halfway up: the little dining room, separated from the giants by a railing. That space had dozens of tables, and she caught a glimpse of the separate entrance and host stand. The wall for the giants continued about twenty feet over the floor for the littles.

When she took her seat, the tigress handed her one of the menus, then handed Saida the other one after the Rha sat down. Autumn opened the menu, saw a column of prices, and immediately choked.

Saida blinked across the table, looking alarmed.

"They're just higher prices than I...wait, these are just the *appetizers*?"

"They're not—I mean—look. Don't worry. Order what you want."

"You were going to say they're not that high?"

Saida's ears flicked back. "I've seen lower, and I've seen higher."

Autumn shook her head, looking down at the menu. She didn't want to pick a fight. "Sorry," she murmured. "I just feel out of place."

Saida tilted her head and flashed a wry smile. "I don't know what to say that won't sound like 'when I was your age.' But I remember being a broke college student. Then a broke college dropout."

When the waiter, a smartly dressed coyote, approached the table to take their drink orders, Autumn decided not to argue when Saida ordered a bottle of wine to split. The Rha seemed comfortable navigating a fancy wine list, but she'd seemed just as comfortable sharing pizza and coffee in a paper cup.

"So, you've eaten here before."

"Twice. I'd always wanted to go to one of Chipotle's restaurants." She waved a hand at the room. "This is the first one I could fit in."

"Chipotle...Layotl? The owner? Don't tell me you're on a first-name basis with her."

"Well, actually, yes. She's Arilin's silent partner in the Giants' Club."

Her eyes widened. Before she could say anything, the waiter came back with the wine. "Are you ready to order?"

"I...um." Autumn hurriedly scanned the menu. In fact, there were no tacos, burritos, or fajitas in sight. Everything sounded alarmingly fancy and she didn't recognize half the ingredients. "Are the stuffed chiles vegetarian?"

He nodded. "They're roasted poblano peppers stuffed with huitlacoche and sweet corn, topped with a walnut cream sauce. They're delicious."

"Okay. I'll have that." She had no idea what *huitlacoche* was, but evidently it wasn't, like, chicken entrails or something.

Saida offered her closed menu to him with a smile. "I'll have the honey-chile glazed salmon."

"Excellent choice." He took both menus, lifting Autumn's out of her hands unbidden, and disappeared.

"So." Saida took a big sip of her wine, looking across the table but not quite meeting Autumn's eyes. "I don't want to throw a lot of my office politics at you because they wouldn't mean much and I know they're not an excuse. But a few weeks before I met you, my company hired a new director of sales and marketing. Up until then, I'd reported directly to the CEO. My brother. Now I report to this new director."

So she was second from the top, now she was third. "Is that a demotion?"

"Officially, no. But whether it is or isn't, I've got much less slack now." She let out a long sigh. "It hasn't been said in so many words that I need to stop taking long weekends 'out of town' so often, but...it's been made clear."

Autumn picked up her own wine glass, mimicking Saida's swirling motions, giving it a careful sniff and an even more careful sip. It tasted like red grape skins rubbed on an oak leaf. Gah. Didn't wine have at least some sugar? "This feels like the start of a 'it's not you, it's me' speech."

"No, no. I mean..." Saida trailed off, looking into her own wine glass.

"It's okay." Autumn spread her hands. "Look, all we've had is pizza, coffee, and one kiss. First dates don't always work out. I guess I get a dinner I could never afford on my own out of it, right?"

Saida's voice tensed. "Could we maybe *start* dating before we break up?"

"Look, if it's either your job or your weekend world-hopping, it's better if we *don't* go any farther, isn't it?" She shook her head. "You're at a family business. You *must* be paid a lot. You've got a boss, but you're still management."

"Autumn." Saida leaned forward, meeting the rabbit's gaze now. "I didn't come back to tell you I had to make a hard choice between seeing you and keeping my job. I came back because I realized that choice is bullshit."

She felt her ears flush, and she looked away. "So now what?"

"Now we have a nice dinner. If anything else happens after that, it's up to you."

Autumn took another sip of the wine, this time trying to roll it around in her mouth like she'd heard you were supposed to. All right, now she could pick up other fruit flavors. Strawberry and cherry, maybe. "So were you really a broke college dropout?"

"I was. I'm not from a rich family. There weren't many rich families left after the war unless they were military contractors or something, but we weren't rich before it."

Autumn tilted her head. "War?"

"Arilin doesn't talk about it in class?" Saida let out her breath. "I guess she wouldn't. The accident that sent her here happened during the first big attack. Well, Mradhi thinks the attack's probably what caused it. The lightning weapons—"

The rabbit felt her eyes growing wider as the Rha spoke. Clearly,

Saida noticed it, catching herself and smiling a little sadly. "Just say a lot of people in Stravell lost a lot. Arilin was never interested in coming back. She'd built a whole life here, one she never had there." She waved a hand around. "She was...antisocial. I don't think she had any friends, and Mradhi and I were too young to know her before the accident happened. We're it for her family now."

"You're—her parents were killed in the war?"

Saida nodded. "We thought she was, too."

Her own crazy life started to seem blessedly mundane. "Uh—and your parents?"

"Physically, they came through the war fine. Dad never got another steady job, as far as I know, though, and they divorced... twelve years ago? I don't know where he is now. Mom's doing okay, thanks to a pension Mradhi set up for her."

"Oh." She bit her lip, looking down.

"How about your family?"

"Less dramatic than your story, but complicated. They're not thrilled at having a giant for a daughter, and I can't tell if it's the 'giant' part or the 'daughter' part that bothers them the most. And my father has some kind of cancer now, I think, but I only hear this second-hand when my sister bothers to get in touch with me." And when I let myself read her emails. "I'm going to have to deal with them again sometime, but I'm putting it off as long as I can."

Saida grimaced in sympathy.

The waiter reappeared, setting down their plates. Autumn's stuffed pepper looked like a work of modern art, split down the middle and overstuffed with a filling of not just corn and huit...whatever, but finely diced onions and what looked like some strange cross between squash and apple, drizzled with the cream sauce, sprinkled with pomegranate seeds and surrounded by multicolored wild rice. The cat's salmon looked no less carefully plated, set on a bed of what looked like spinach and polenta. "Oh, wow." She just studied her plate. "I'm pretty sure this is the fanciest food I've ever seen in real life."

Saida cleared her throat. Autumn looked up to find a cheetah woman standing by the waiter, holding out a silver tray. On the tray stood a short ringtailed woman—not a raccoon, a, what was it, cacomistle—wearing a chef's outfit. "I hope you like it." She folded her hands behind her back and smiled. "I'm Luyu, the sous chef. Since you're friends of Chef Layotl's, I wanted to introduce myself. Is this a special occasion?"

Before Autumn could shake her head, Saida said, "It's our first dinner date."

"That's lovely!" The cacomistle clasped her hands together. "We'll make a special dessert you can share. In the meantime, let Ferran know if you need anything," She indicated the coyote, who nodded.

"We will. Thank you so much."

Autumn stared at Saida after they left. The cat smiled self-consciously. "I didn't plan that, I promise."

"That's more worrying, somehow." She carefully cut off a bite with her fork, put it in her mouth, then melted into her seat. "Oh my God."

Saida grinned. "I'd say 'wait until you see the dessert,' but I don't want it to sound like innuendo."

Autumn waved her fork at the cat. "You don't get to make innuendo yet. You still owe me a secret."

Saida swallowed her own bite of salmon, looking down at her plate. Then she look back up and took a deep breath. "I'm cursed."

Autumn swallowed her own second bite, and looked into the Rha's eyes. "You're serious."

Saida nodded, ears lowered. They were both silent for a few seconds, until she straightened up and cut off another bit of the salmon. "Want a bite of fish?"

CHAPTER 7

The Curse

WHEN THE WAITER CAME BY WITH THE BILL, SAIDA already had her phone out, payment authorized, so she could tap to pay before Autumn could glance at the final number. She didn't count on the rabbit trying to use her height advantage to get a glimpse anyway.

"I said I'd cover it!" She covered the reader's display with her hand, handing it back to the coyote.

"I didn't see it." Autumn's shocked expression belied her words. "But how can you pay a bill here with money literally from another world?"

"My brother and Arilin set up some kind of currency exchange. They have my banking information from Stravell, and it's tied to an account I have here with the school's credit union." She stood up, raising her hands. "I suspect it's breaking banking laws in both places. Sometimes it's better not to ask."

Autumn stood up, too. "Every day since I've been at this school the world's become a little stranger."

"Tell me about it."

The rabbit leaned closer to her as they headed out of the restaurant. "No, you tell *me* about it. You dropped that grenade then put it off through all of dessert."

"It was a great dessert, wasn't it?"

"It was, and I don't know how someone even thinks of mixing apples, green chiles and cheese in a pie, much less makes it work. Also, you're changing the subject."

Saida glanced around, at other giants just twenty feet away— well, a hundred yards, by local standards—and at littles milling about at their street level. "Let's walk."

"Where?"

"We can go to my suite."

Autumn's ears stood up.

Saida cleared her throat. She hadn't meant that to sound like *come on back to my place*, and it seemed even more awkward given she'd bought the rabbit dinner. "No pressure. Just, you know, a quiet place for a self-conscious cat to talk."

"Okay."

It was a short walk to the staff housing block. The long, single-story rows of identical doors, bland pastel colors set against the off-white exterior, reminded her less of an apartment building than a motel. "I'm down at the end here." Unlocking the door, she held it open for Autumn.

"Huh." The rabbit had stopped in the center of the sitting room, looking around. The suite had just two rooms, without a full wall between them; the larger part featured a small kitchen separated from a living room/office by a breakfast bar, and a half-height wall separated that from the single queen-sized bed. "This is pretty nice."

Saida nodded, taking a seat on the couch. "It feels...a lot like an extended stay hotel in Stravell. Maybe a little more institutional."

"Nicer than any place my parents stayed at." Autumn took off her jacket, tossing it across an armrest, and sat down next to her. "So."

"So." The Rha clasped her hands in her lap. How could she tell this story? "We talked on our first date about resurrection magic."

Autumn furrowed her brow, then half-grinned. "Right. I teased you about how I might eat someone with it."

"Yes." Saida's ears colored and she looked away. "Which makes this a little harder to say. I, uh...have...that."

The rabbit looked blank for several seconds, then tilted her head to the side. "Resurrection magic."

She nodded.

"Are you bullshitting me? That's your 'curse?'"

Saida nodded again, ears lowering. "But—"

"Someone 'cursed' you with one of the most powerful spells of protection known to magic." Autumn made finger-quotes as she said *cursed*, looking less amused than annoyed. "If this is a weird joke, I am *not* getting—"

"It's not a joke!" Saida snarled, teeth bared.

The rabbit froze, for a fleeting moment showing the primordial reaction of prey confronted with angry predator that no amount of civilization could completely erase.

Saida dropped her gaze, rubbing her face. "Listen, all right? The curse is that I was given some kind of—death wish to go along with it. Some...I don't even know what he was, other than a stag named Kenley. But he wanted to punish me for being a predator by making me prey. And some day I'll be eaten, or killed somehow, and I won't come back. Every time it happens I'm rolling dice for my final life."

Autumn had folded her hands in her lap as she'd continued talking, and remained quiet for a few seconds. "Were you really that monstrous, or was he?"

"I told you I did some damage when I first got here. I was way too cavalier. But I don't think I was ever that bad, I truly don't. I didn't kill people. I played giant movie monster a couple times, but in places that were already abandoned. I've heard of students who were worse." She shook her head slowly.

"And the death wish? You're cursed to seek out things that are going to kill you?"

Saida looked up at the ceiling, taking a deep breath. "This is embarrassing." How could she put this? Maybe as straightforwardly as possible. But maybe she could just duck out. She only promised *one* secret, after all.

"You're turned on by things that are going to kill you?"

She swallowed, looking back at the rabbit dolefully.

Autumn had a wry, joking expression. But her eyes widened at

Saida's stare, and she lowered her voice. "Oh my God, you *are,* aren't you?"

"No. Not...exactly. I'm turned on by saliva."

Autumn furrowed her brow, remaining silent for long seconds. Then she covered her mouth, choking back a giggle.

Saida flattened her ears, turning away. God, why did she try to explain this to anyone? It was just asking for—for this.

"I'm sorry." Autumn touched her shoulder. "I just...you've described one thing that most people *wouldn't* consider a curse, even with its limits, and the other thing? I mean, you could just tell me it was a fetish and I wouldn't bat an eye."

"Put them *together,* though, and it's a recipe for getting eaten."

"As it were."

Saida gave the rabbit a death glare.

"Sorry, I couldn't help it. But come on. You're a giantess. No matter how delicious you look—and you totally do, at least metaphorically—you can't be on many menus."

"There are people who can become *really* huge."

"And people who can shrink you. But not many of either."

"But there are people in both groups right at this college."

"Sure. But you're not going around telling most people about this."

"No, but I think there might be...rumors about me." She snorted. "At least according to the last person who ate me."

Autumn's ears skewed at different angles, making her look like she was trying to send semaphore for a moment. "Oh. Three Lords. Um, how often has that actually happened? You being eaten?"

"Five times."

Autumn rubbed the back of one of her own ears with two fingers. "Well, I guess it's four times more than almost anyone else could say."

"I assure you it's five times more than I'd like."

"Yeah." The rabbit let out a long breath, whistling faintly through her front teeth. "So do you want it lifted?"

"What?"

"Do you want the curse lifted?"

Saida flicked her tail. "Of course. Can you—can you do that?"

"Me? Shit, no. I've studied curses, but I'm *totally* unqualified to mess around with death magic. But there are people on campus who could. I might be able to get Professor Snep to take a look."

Her heart leapt. "That would be amazing."

"Well, give it some thought first. I don't want to sound like I'm saying it *isn't* a curse, because I can see how upset you are by it. But it almost sounds like the curse is more the psychological effect than the physical one."

She felt her ears flatten. "What's that supposed to mean?"

Autumn took Saida's hand, looking down into her eyes. "I mean coming back from death itself is immensely valuable, even if it's not guaranteed. And the other part..." She cleared her throat. "That could kind of be sexy, with the right person."

That made her ears color. "But not putting them together."

"The first person who ate you was the one who cursed you in the first place, wasn't it?"

Saida swallowed and nodded.

"So what if his whole story about cursing you as punishment is bullshit? What if eating you was his version of acting out a rape fantasy? This just sounds too much to me like it's all about power. About making you feel helpless." The rabbit shook her head, baring her own teeth. "He's given you a power that people literally die for —*without* coming back—and made you feel miserable about having it. Maybe that's the real curse."

"You make it sound like I don't need a magician, just a therapist." Saida sighed.

Autumn slid closer to her on the couch, putting an arm around her and pulling her to her side. She kept forgetting just how much taller the rabbit was; her ears came just past Autumn's shoulder. But resting against her felt nice.

"I don't know. Maybe." Autumn tilted her head down, muzzle close to the cat's ear. "Maybe you just need to not dwell on it for right now."

"I should just relax in the company of my maybe-girlfriend who talked about how she might like to swallow someone if she knew they had resurrection magic." She smiled wryly.

"Saida." The rabbit put a hand under her chin, tilting her head up so their eyes met. "If you were really worried I was going to do that, you wouldn't have told me about all this, would you?"

"No, no. I was just..." She trailed off, feeling a sudden vertigo. "What if *this* is part of the curse, too, if I can't help myself from talking about this because I secretly *want* it now and I can't—"

Her voice had been rising in pitch and speed as she spoke, cut off when the rabbit pressed her lips to hers, then enveloped her in a hug that pressed the Rha's muzzle to her collarbone. "Shhh," Autumn murmured. "Don't let him be in your head."

She hugged back, closing her eyes and shaking.

"If you want to find a way to break this, I'll help. And I won't do anything with you that you don't give me permission for."

That sounded lovely. That sounded foreboding. Could the curse trick her into giving permission? She managed a little nod of assent, though.

Autumn held her in silence for at least another minute. Then the rabbit laughed softly. "You know, now I'm worried that if I so much as lick your ear, it'll somehow be taking advantage of you."

She tilted her head up, smiling slightly. "I trust you not to."

"Is that permission?"

Saida took a deep, long breath, nose filling with the rabbit's scent —both her light natural musk and a shampoo or perfume, shimmering notes of bitter orange and cardamom and juniper. "It might be more of a wish."

Autumn went still for a moment. Then she licked her lips, leaving them glistening with more than the black lipstick, and closed them around the Rha's left ear.

Saida sucked in her breath, then clutched at the rabbit more tightly as she ran her tongue along the edges of the trapped ear, inside it. Oh, God, all her nerves suddenly buzzed. And what was— "Do you have a tongue stud?" she got out, voice embarrassingly breathy.

"Mmm-hmm."

Saida could feel more of the tongue against her ear now, the metal nib pressed against its edge. A shiver ran down her spine from shoulders to tail-tip.

Autumn slowly pulled back, sitting up straight. Then, abruptly, she straddled the cat's lap: knees to either side of Saida's hips, chest at nose level. Saida tilted her head up, eyes wide, breath still quick.

The rabbit leaned forward, pressing Saida back against the sofa with her weight, hands sliding down the Rha's side. "I want to start taking more advantage of you now, little cat."

Saida reached up to put her arms around the rabbit's shoulders, pulling her down for a kiss. "You have permission."

CHAPTER 8
Morning After

WHEN AUTUMN WOKE UP, THE CEILING LOOKED TOO LOW. She blinked sleep away from her eyes. She hadn't changed size and forgotten, surely?

A soft purring snore to her left snapped her to wakefulness. No, the bed—Saida's bed—just sat higher than hers. And it was longer, wider, more plush. And it had a nude cat woman in it.

Autumn rolled onto her side, looking at the smaller Rha, still fast asleep. Between conversation and increasingly heated play, they hadn't made it to bed until midnight, and hadn't made it to *sleep* for another hour past that.

She let her eyes wander Saida's mostly uncovered form. The cat had a pinup magazine figure, the kind of cheerleader looks that would let her lead a bevy of hot young men around by the nose. (All right: by another body part.) The realization that she'd assumed anyone like that wouldn't ever be interested in her brought up unwelcome questions about her own prejudices and self-esteem. On advice from both a therapist and more experienced magicians, as she learned to transform herself, she'd hewn closely to what would have been possible through non-magical means. Some days—not most, not even many, but some—she wondered if that approach had been a mistake.

Some days, though, she felt absolutely beautiful the way she was. Today was one of those days.

She sat up, then grinned. If the cat woke up now, Autumn would be towering over her. She couldn't help but suspect Saida liked that. Whether she'd admit liking it or would just blame it on her "curse" was a more complicated question.

The whole curse story was—well, it was just crazy. Yeah, the Rha got seriously turned on by being licked, but that just seemed like a kink. You didn't need magic to explain it. And "cursing" someone with limited immortality? That was like cursing them with a multimillion dollar bank account. Yet she couldn't believe it was an elaborate prank, at least not on Saida's part; she was telling the truth as she knew it.

Maybe Professor Snep would have some ideas on what it truly was, and if it really was a curse, how to break it. Before they'd fallen asleep, she'd suggested going after the guy who cast it, but the idea had absolutely terrified Saida. Despite Autumn's private skepticism, she had to admit the Rha had a point. Maybe this Kenley was a charlatan, but maybe he wasn't, and she had zero interest in ending up on his menu.

Her eyes settled on Saida's face again. While it was clear the Rha hadn't wanted to end up on his menu, either, her new girlfriend definitely had some kind of submissive streak. The way her tail flicked every time Autumn called her "little cat" wasn't conclusive evidence, but it was sure suggestive. Despite what she'd said on their first date, she wasn't she had the nerve to put Saida on *her* menu, but she'd be happy to tease her about it, about shrinking her. No—she'd be happy to do more than tease about that last part. She could only imagine how a palm-sized Rha would react to being licked.

New girlfriend. She felt her ears flush.

The cat's eyes opened in a squint, and she made a sleepy *prrp*, shifting on the bed and brushing hair away from her eyes. As they opened fully, they settled on Autumn, and she smiled drowsily. "Good morning." She reached up and batted at the rabbit's nipple ring.

"Hey." Autumn laughed, covering her breast with a hand. "It *hurt* when you got your fang caught there. Let's not try for a claw."

"Claws retract. You drink coffee in the morning, right?"

"I drink coffee all the time."

"Excellent." Saida rolled to the side, away from Autumn, fast enough that she should have tumbled to the floor in a tangle of sheets. Somehow the move ended with her standing on her feet, stretching gracefully. Cats. She padded into the kitchenette. "I brought some coffee from home."

"You have coffee in...what was the name? Stravell?"

"Mmm-hmm." The Rha scooped a few measures into a grinder, then got down an hourglass-shaped carafe that looked like a beaker from a chemistry lab, unfolding a paper filter into its top half. "I can't swear it's the same plant as coffee here, but we make it the same way and it tastes very similar."

"One of the unexpected lesson from the college has been how much convergent evolution the universe apparently has. Incredibly enough, you and Professor Thorferra aren't the only people here from off-world."

"Arilin's mentioned that, too." She started an electric kettle going. "Although I guess my world's an outlier for being on a giant scale. At least in part."

Autumn lifted her brows. "In—" she started to say, but the grinder drowned her out. She walked closer, repeating it immediately after the grinder shut off. "In part?"

"The Liliren are on about what this world's normal scale is, I guess." She emptied the grounds into the filter. "Little mice."

"Cats and mice." Autumn started to laugh, but found herself grimacing instead. She'd heard some of the rumors about Professor Thorferra's wild youth. "Should I ask how you treat them?"

"We're kind of jerks." Saida's tone stayed matter-of-fact as she picked up the kettle, slowly pouring water over the coffee. "Legally we recognize they're more than animals, but we don't recognize them as people."

"Just because of their size?"

"Well." Saida looked up at the rabbit. "You didn't grow up in the city here, right? What did you learn about giants growing up?"

"Not a lot, but I get your point. There's kind of a 'monster until proven otherwise' attitude. But with the sizes flipped, like you're saying, that sounds a little more horrific." As the coffee brewed, her nose wiggled. The liquid gathering in the carafe had a mahogany tint to it, and smelled unusually sweet.

Saida set the kettle down, watching the last of the water drip through the grounds. "If you'd asked me a few years ago, I'd have probably said something like 'look, it's not like they have bad lives.' They still have their own lands we set aside for them, their own towns. A lot of Liliren live in and around our cities, though, free-loading off our infrastructure, and they're mostly protected when they do. The common wisdom is still that they're better off with us than without us."

"But that's not what you'd say now?"

She poured two mugs of the coffee. "No. I've been coming here for a couple years, learning what Arilin learned. It opens your eyes to what's around your ankles, and frankly, it's pretty dark." She sighed, picking up both mugs and holding one out to Autumn. "The Liliren lived in Stravell before we did. In the story we want to tell, we settled an uninhabited paradise. In the story where we have to admit they *are* people, then we trampled over their entire little civilization, didn't we?" Saida smiled wryly. "So we like the first story a lot better."

Autumn picked up the mug she'd been offered, taking a sip. "Hmm." It had a lot of sweet fruity flavor to it that made her think of mango, or papaya, or something else tropical. A little odd, but good. Kim at Higher Grounds would approve. "So what are you going to do about it?"

"About what?"

"The Liliren."

"What—are you asking if I'm going to become some kind of Liliren rights activist?" She laughed.

Autumn glanced down at the cat, frowning a little. "Is that so crazy? You're in a really privileged position back home, and you must meet a lot of powerful people. You can start talking to them about this."

"Autumn, the last thing I can afford to do right now is to get a reputation as someone who's going to force uncomfortable conversations on my customers. I'm not so 'privileged' that I can't lose what I have very quickly."

She couldn't stop herself from digging in her heels. Couldn't Saida see the parallels here? "Like the Liliren did."

"Either argue that I can help them because I'm 'rich'"—Saida actually made the air quotes with her fingers—"or argue that I should become homeless in solidarity. Don't argue both at the same time."

Autumn scowled. "That's not what I said."

The cat sighed, tone softening. "I'm sorry. But I don't know what I can do right now beyond supporting charities for Liliren. And letting mine out of his cage more often."

Autumn choked on her coffee.

Saida unsuccessfully covered a laugh. "Sorry, I had to."

The rabbit wiped her mouth, scowling more deeply. "That is *not* funny. For all I know, Rha *do* keep Liliren in cages."

"You're not allowed to keep them as pets, and it's not legal to keep them in cages for long. I think two days max."

Autumn stared. Saida looked back, blinking once. This time, it *didn't* look like she was joking. Saida had said they lived in and around Rha cities sometimes. That meant they'd need to be "removed" when the giants wanted to rebuild or remodel, so they might very well be picked up and shoved in cages. If developers there were anything like they were here, they might just do the Liliren in, too, if they thought they wouldn't get caught doing it. And even if keeping them as—well—pets was technically illegal, how often did it happen in practice? Would some Liliren even be okay with that, or would they at best be resigned to it?

Finally she shook her head. There was a lot she didn't know yet, and it wasn't something they could hash out in a few minutes over coffee. "So how long are you in town for this weekend?"

"Until tomorrow."

"And you won't stay away another two months, right?"

Saida smiled, with a hint of sheepishness. "Not unless something goes dreadfully wrong. I plan to be back every weekend, unless I'm stuck on a business trip."

"Maybe I should play tour guide for you again, then. Although I bet you've seen more of the campus than I have."

"Maybe, but Arilin didn't spend much time showing me around. I've mostly explored on my own. And you've seen more of the town around the campus. How close are we allowed to get to the real downtown district, anyway?"

"All the way through, but just on one road, and not during commute hours. Unless we shrink."

Saida opened her mouth, then closed it.

Autumn grinned. "You know I can do that."

"Yeah, but my impression is you...don't."

She shrugged. "I don't like being little. But I make an exception every so often." The rabbit tilted her head. "It's an angle on the city you haven't seen before, isn't it? Or on the campus."

"No, I haven't." Saida's tail flicked, like she was imagining being small. But her eyes were on Autumn. Hmm. Just what was the Rha imagining?

"Of course, if you were small and I wasn't," Autumn leaned forward, "you'd have a giant friend to show you around."

The Rha's tail flicked faster.

CHAPTER 9

Perspective

"THE DORM'S NICE."

Saida stood in the center of the rabbit's small-in-scale room. Autumn had just pulled on an oversized black T-shirt, completing her transformation back to her normal wardrobe. It probably wasn't the same tee she'd been wearing when they'd first met, but the Rha couldn't swear to that. A glimpse into the taller giantess's closet suggested *all* her shirts—and pants, and jackets—were black. Maybe she'd had to borrow that purple shirt she'd worn last night.

"Really?" Autumn glanced around the room with a surprised expression. "It's okay for something they could build for giants, but it's pretty cramped and spartan. Also, now I'm sure they built it with magic, so I'm less willing to cut them slack."

"The semester I spent in a dorm, it was about this size but had two students."

"Holy hell." They headed out of the room, down the hall toward the common area. "Why just a semester? Did you join a sorority?"

"Goddess, no. A friend and I got an apartment as roommates. Looking back, it was a terrible one, but it seemed great then."

Autumn laughed. "That was before you dropped out?"

"Yeah. At the end of my second year, my grades dropped just enough that they cut my grant for the third year. So I went to work over the summer, just to save up money, and I never ended up going back." She shrugged. "Mom tried to cover my rent, but that was a stretch for her. Dad had left by then, and...he was good for holiday money. Nothing more."

"Oh." Autumn looked genuinely surprised.

Saida laughed, shaking her head. "I need to get you over the idea that I grew up sipping champagne out of a gold-plated baby bottle."

"Ha ha." Autumn led them outside, down the front steps, stopping just as they stepped onto the sidewalk. "I don't know what I'd do without the scholarship here. I get a big zero from my parents. I wouldn't have any spending money if it wasn't for the work-study program."

"Where do you work?"

"The magic archives. Not nearly as exciting as it sounds." The rabbit clapped her hands. "Okay, so do you really want to do this? I don't want to pressure you."

Saida smirked. "Yeah, you kinda do."

Autumn folded her arms. "I said I'd only mess with you with explicit consent, and I meant it."

"All right. You don't want to pressure me, but you *do* want to mess with me."

"Shit, yes."

Saida laughed. "Okay, that's honest." She took a deep breath. "Let's do it."

"You're sure."

"Don't make me think about it so much I say no."

Autumn flashed a small smile, taking a deep breath herself. "Okay." She traced a symbol in the air with her left hand, touching her right index finger to Saida's nose.

The world blurred.

The cat's body had suddenly become a plastic bag with the air being sucked out. It hurt, but it wasn't an understandable pain, not an ache or puncture, neither fire nor ice. This was something nerves weren't supposed to experience, something they didn't know how to communicate.

Even when the pressure faded and the stars left her vision, her fur still stood on end. She didn't *feel* different, but the sidewalk she'd been standing on looked like a road, and she didn't remember that platform with—a giant—

Oh. That was Autumn's sandal. And her right foot.

She swallowed, staring. A simple change in perspective made something as cute as a bunny paw suddenly terrifying. The closest toe claw, painted a black so glossy she could make out her distorted reflection in it, had to be bigger than her head. And while she'd known the whole paw was bigger than a minivan, that meant something very different when *her* paw was car-sized, too, than it did when she could be that minivan's driver.

"You okay?"

She snapped her head up. As high above as the voice had come from, the rabbit had leaned over, hands sliding down her jeans to rest under her knees.

"Yes. I just. Uh. Wow."

"Good wow?"

She swallowed, nodding. "Good wow. What's the plan?"

"First, I pick you up." Autumn moved into a crouch, setting her hand down palm up on the ground. "Then I show you around campus and maybe more of the town, and we see how long I can resist popping you in my mouth. Or, given the way you were looking at my paw a moment ago, putting you in my sandal."

"I don't think I have a paw fetish and *please* don't try and give me one because you might pull it off." Saida crawled onto the offered hand, sitting down awkwardly. She'd known rabbits didn't have pads —after last night, she knew that quite well—but this was still an unusual experience. The fur across Autumn's palm felt coarse at this scale but not bristly, short but still deep enough for her to sink her hand into.

The big fingers curled up a little, and the rabbit stood, lifting the Rha up into the air until she was about chest level. Autumn grinned down. "We'll put a pin in that and come back sometime. Are you comfortable riding on my shoulder, if you can hang onto my choker?" She touched the foot-wide black leather collar around her neck. The finely-wrought thin chain hanging off the front in decorative loops now looked surprisingly heavy and imposing.

"Probably." The Rha climbed on, sinking into the rabbit's thicker fur. The scent of the rabbit's shampoo, bitter orange and cardamom, grew intense. "I've got good balance, so I don't know if I need to hang on to anything."

Autumn lifted a hand to her waterfall of thick black hair. "If I turn my head without thinking about it, you're going to be knocked off, and that's not a way I want to test your resurrection magic."

There are ways you do *want to test it?* "Good point." Saida leaned forward—fortunate she didn't get vertigo—and grabbed the chain, wrapping it a few times around her arm. "Does this mean I'm holding your leash?"

"I think it means you're my jewelry, little cat, but you can tell yourself whatever you want." Autumn grinned. "Ready?"

Jewelry? Uh—dammit, there went her tail twitch. "Ready."

The giantess strolled forward.

As different as the view was, it was hard to describe *how* it was different. She usually saw the campus from this height, after all, but she felt like an average-sized woman moving through a world that was mostly toy-sized. Now, she felt like she was surveying a normal-sized world from a fire tower, with impossibly-sized buildings dominating the horizon. And impossibly-sized people.

Like her girlfriend.

Autumn stretched out the arm in front of Saida, gesturing ahead. "I don't know if it's worth showing you things you've already seen."

"I don't feel like I've seen anything at all now. What impressed you when you were this size?"

"Giants." She laughed. "So let's take a walk through the Union." She turned down a different path.

Saida looked down, at the "little" road running alongside the giant sidewalk. Only a few cars went by, moving faster than Autumn's stroll. A couple students on the road's sidewalk waved up at the rabbit—or maybe up at *her*. She waved back.

She couldn't say the Student Union Building "came into view" as they approached: it had been in view for miles. Instead, it came to *be* the view. How had she gotten the impression of it as simply a large building? At merely half this size it would be beyond gigantic. Even with magic, it didn't seem like it could possibly exist.

Autumn stepped inside, and the shift in air pressure rocked Saida's perch. She gripped the chain more tightly. Other giants sat in the couches and chairs scattered around the stadium-sized floor, reading alone or chatting with one another. Or looking at Autumn, standing up and walking over.

The raccoon woman approaching was shorter than Saida's normal height, with a thick, plush build and a dress that made her look like she'd stepped out of a fashion mag. One piece, low cut front and calf-length skirt slit up to the thigh, pale yellow on the right half and sky blue on the left, the vertical line where the colors met curving from her cleavage to meet the top of the skirt cut. She'd topped that off with a riot of multi-colored necklaces. "Autumn! How did your date go?"

"Great." The rabbit indicated Saida with a claw-tip, which made the Rha's ears fold back in her hair. "This is my date, Saida. Saida, this is my friend Judy."

Judy leaned forward, muzzle tilting up a bit toward the cat.

"Hi," Saida managed.

"Nice to meet you, dear." Judy tilted her head. "I admit I'd thought you'd be taller."

"I am. I mean, usually. I'm taller than you."

"Usually," Judy echoed, teeth showing in an amused grin. Saida tried unsuccessfully to still her tail.

"I'm showing her what life is like small." Autumn sounded far too amused.

"Why, how fun." The raccoon's grin grew. "Of course, I suppose some people like to be small, if they're around the *right* giants, hmm?"

Saida opened her mouth and then closed it. "I have no idea what to say to that."

Judy laughed, then looked up at Autumn, putting her hand on the rabbit's opposite shoulder. "Oh, tell me you'll leave her like this for a while. She's so cute that way."

Autumn laughed. "You're just hoping I'll leave her on an end table by your chair, aren't you?"

"Why, I'd never dream of stealing your adorable, easily pocketable girlfriend." The raccoon put a hand to her cleavage, making the necklaces jangle. "Goodness, what's that over there?" She pointed behind Autumn with her other hand, then reached for Saida, slowly enough to make the joke obvious. Even so, Saida couldn't help scrambling back against Autumn's neck, wrapping her other arm into the chain, too.

"Nice try," Autumn said, putting her hand on top of Judy's.

The raccoon burst out laughing, then smiled more warmly. "It was lovely to meet you, Saida."

Saida swallowed and forced herself to relax and smile. "Maybe we'll meet again when I'm at a safer size."

Judy laughed. "That would be lovely, too, even if a little disappointing." She winked.

Once Autumn had started walking again and Judy had moved on, Saida let out a breath. "She's not actually dangerous to littles, right?"

"Depends on how you define 'dangerous.' Everyone who goes on a date with her recovers eventually."

Saida's tail twitched. "She's that hard on littles?"

"I didn't say 'littles,' I said 'everyone.' Also, I didn't say anyone was complaining."

"Goddess."

"So, I think we can go into the Beanstalk, just look around—or I can order a slice of pizza and make you nervous while you watch me eat—and then head into town."

"That's not going to make me nervous."

Autumn turned her head to the side and ran her tongue over her lips, right over Saida's head.

"Ah..."

"Mmm-hmm." The rabbit brought her hand up, lifting Saida up toward her muzzle. "Maybe I don't need the pizza."

"Hey—"

Autumn licked over Saida's front. And face.

All of the Rha's nerves lit up. "N-not in public!" she hissed.

"Mmm-hmm," Autumn repeated, sounding smug this time. "What if I just—"

"Autumn?"

Both rabbit and cat looked down at the unexpected, unfamiliar voice. Well, at least unfamiliar to Saida. Autumn made a strangled noise when she saw the rabbit woman standing on the waist-level balcony. "Kelly?"

The smaller rabbit leaned against the railing, looking cross. "What are you doing?"

"I'm—what are you doing here?"

"I was in town and just thought I'd drop by." She put her hands on her hips. She had a heavier build than Autumn, tan fur rather than white, but her eyes were strikingly similar. "Don't be an economy-sized moron. What the fuck do you think I'm doing here?"

"Daring me to go fee-fi-fo-fum on your ass?"

Saida cleared her throat. "If I could, I'd say something neutral and sneak off to let you two work whatever this is out, but I'm kind of stuck right now."

Autumn grunted. "Maybe I should—"

"Come on, introduce me to your girlfriend, or your lunch, whichever she is, because I have no idea how the fuck you roll now that you're a giant." Kelly crossed her arms.

Autumn sighed heavily. "Kelly, this is Saida, my girlfriend. Saida, this is Kelly, my sister."

CHAPTER 10

Big Sister

SAIDA LOOKED BETWEEN THE TWO ANGRY RABBITS, quickly gathering a new appreciation for just how angry rabbits could manage to look. If they were both on the same scale, Kelly might be more intimidating than her sister, but right now Autumn won the scary contest on a technicality. "Hi, Kelly." She smiled awkwardly from her shoulder perch.

"Okay, we can add 'lesbian' to the list of things I didn't know about my sibling growing up, although in my defense that'd have been pretty hard to predict."

Autumn snorted, crossing her arms. Her shifting shoulders made Saida slip down toward the rabbit's collarbone, hanging on more tightly to the chain.

"Dammit to hell, Autumn, did you think if you ignored my emails, I'd just give up and go away? You want to just cut me out of your life like everybody else you've known more than three years?"

"If all you're going to do is try to drag me back to a home I literally don't fit in? Yeah, maybe I do. Why didn't you call before showing up here out of the blue?"

Saida tried to pull herself back up onto the shoulder, scrabbling.

"Why didn't you answer your phone when I called? Three times? And left three messages, the last one of which was 'I've booked a flight and I'm going to be there Saturday'?" Kelly slammed her hands against the railing. "If you want me to leave and never talk to you again, just tell me. Maybe give me what you want to say at Dad's funeral first, even if it's 'fuck you,' because you know I'll say it. Also, maybe help your girlfriend back up before she falls between your tits."

"What—" Autumn slapped a hand over Saida, which made the Rha squeal reflexively, ending in a wheeze as the wind was knocked out of her. The slap was quickly adjusted to cupping the cat in her hand. "Crap. Are you okay?"

"Yyyhrf," Saida managed, hand to her chest.

"Sorry. Crap. Sorry." The hand holding Saida moved to the railing, close to Kelly, who stepped back warily. Autumn tipped the hand gently, forcing the cat to hop off. "What do you mean, 'funeral?' I *know* he's not dead." The worry in her eyes betrayed the certainty in her voice.

"You do? How do you know that?" Kelly crossed her arms, cocking her head to the side as she looked up at her sister. "You're not listening to mom's messages, and now you've stopped listening to mine."

Autumn looked away. "I wasn't listening to yours because you were starting to sound like her."

"Don't you even." Kelly rubbed her forehead. "No. He's not dead yet." She closed her eyes. "But he started on home hospice care, Autumn."

The giantess ran a hand through her hair, silent for a ten-second stretch that felt like ten minutes. "I've gotta go for a walk." She spun on a heel and strode out of the Union.

"Of course you do," Kelly muttered, watching her sister go. Then she glanced over at Saida. "Aren't you a little short to date a giantess?"

Saida straightened up, collecting herself. Inch for inch, Kelly was definitely more intimidating than her sister. She stood a touch higher than the cat, light brown hair chopped punkishly short, a build beyond merely athletic. She looked like she could benchpress Saida. Possibly benchpress two Saidas. "I'm normally a giantess myself. Not as big as Autumn, but over eighty feet."

"So you're just playing tiny for some kind of sex thing? That was a hell of a lick I walked in on."

Her ears went flat. "No. This is not a conversation I'm having with someone I just met, all right?"

Kelly shrugged. "Whatever. Is there a place on this level we can get a beer?"

"I don't know. I've never been able to fit on this level before."

"Right." The rabbit sighed. "I'm gonna go look. Join me if you want, don't if you don't want. She did this at home a lot and trust me, she's gonna be gone a while." She turned around and strolled deeper into the Union.

Saida looked back after where Autumn had gone. Well, it wasn't like she could run after her like this. She didn't want to insert herself into what looked like *heavy* family drama, but if she was serious about making a go of this with Autumn, they'd have to let each other into one another's extended lives sooner or later. And Autumn did leave her here with her sister. Maybe she expected them to talk.

On the other hand, maybe she'd been too angry to think about that at all and she'd be mortified at Saida prying.

Grumbling, she headed after Kelly, jogging to catch up. "There's the Beanstalk," she said. "It's got good pizza and beer."

"I thought you didn't fit here." The rabbit gave her a skeptical look.

"I don't fit *here*, but the Beanstalk's for all sizes. The entrance for littles has got to be on this floor."

"'Littles.' That isn't something I get called real often." She snorted. "Okay, lead the way."

Saida scanned the area quickly. They'd entered a food court; she felt a mild pang of jealousy at seeing how many options were available to students who lived at this scale: a sandwich deli, a salad bar, a taqueria, a stir-fry counter, a sit-down bar and grill. Much more like living in Stravell. Of course. Well, the Beanstalk entrance had to be somewhere to the left. She headed that way as if she knew where she was going. "They say 'little' and 'giant' here so neither size gets called 'normal.'"

"I guess that makes sense, although 'little' still sounds kinda patronizing."

"It's hard to find any size words that don't." Also, *little cat* sounded hot when Autumn said it, but she didn't need to share that.

"Yeah." As they rounded a corner in the hallway, a railing appeared on the right side again, now overlooking the Beanstalk. Kelly looked down at the floor, up at the ceiling, then back at Saida as she walked. "That it?"

"That's it."

"That's...definitely a thing. Wow."

It took another minute's walk to get to the closest entrance. Up until now, Saida hadn't realized the Beanstalk was a *completely* different place when you were little. You entered through one of three different doorways on two different levels, and followed tunnels designed to look like they'd been bored through huge trees. The catwalks around and between tables curved like branches and vines, changing both elevation and direction; some thicker vertical "trunks" held glass elevators that looked like giant jeweled ladybugs. It felt like being in a huge, primeval forest that somehow gave way to the pizza pub of the demigods.

Taking the lead, Saida walked straight ahead, right out onto the bar. Finally looking nervous, Kelly followed close behind.

Saida stopped at a four-top not too far from the center of the bar. Almost as soon as she and Kelly sat down, the giant bartender—the same dog who'd been there the night she'd met Autumn—came over and looked down. "What can I get you?"

Saida smiled up. "I'd like a Naughty Hops IPA."

Kelly looked up with an alarmed expression, then checked the beer list. "Ah. Uh. Uh. How about the, um, Chance of Rain Hazy IPA?"

"Sure." The dog squinted at Saida a moment, then shrugged and headed off.

"God, this would be a crazy place to be a student at." Kelly shook her head, then leaned forward, resting her arms on the table. "So you're my sister's girlfriend. How long have you been dating?"

"That's...complicated. We've only been on two dates, two months apart. I don't live in the area."

A server on their scale walked out onto the table, setting their beers down. "Thanks." Kelly raised the glass to him as he walked away, then looked back to Saida. "You live back in giant-land, huh?"

Saida sipped her own beer. "Also complicated, but you could say that, I guess. Being here is like being in a dollhouse world. Usually."

"Except when you're one of us dolls. So what do you born-that-way giants really think about littles?"

Saida furrowed her brow, not sure how to answer that. She took another sip of beer to stall.

Kelly raised a hand. "Don't tell me. It's complicated."

She laughed. "Kind of."

"Fair enough. Growing up we didn't think about giants at all except as storybook monsters. Big dumb ugly brutes who kidnapped princesses and shit, and nothing that anyone had had to worry about for like a thousand years before this college opened up." She waved her free hand around and took another swig of beer. "But they're not. They're smart enough to get into college. They're built like us, not like weirdo monsters." She leaned across the table, lowering her voice. "And some of them I might think about playing kidnappable princess for."

Saida gave Kelly an awkward smile. "So can I ask about your family a little? You can just say 'it's complicated' if you want."

The rabbit snorted and laughed, leaning back. "Let's see. My younger sister was my younger brother growing up, and she's gone from scrawny to skyscraper. She doesn't wanna deal with our parents because Mom's still being an asshole over her transition, and Dad's..." She trailed off, then chuffed. "Maybe it *is* complicated, yeah. I mean, he was an asshole about the gender transition *and* the size shift, but I think he's coming around on both. But first he was too proud to say anything, now he's too sick to. So Autumn doesn't even know. And she won't listen."

Saida grimaced. "What's he sick with?"

"Brain cancer. They say he's got four or five months, maybe, but once you start hospice, I mean, sometimes it's just weeks."

"I'm sorry." She paused, gathering her thoughts, then shook her head. "Forgive my bluntness, but it sounds like you want to drag Autumn back home to say goodbye. I understand why you'd want to. But isn't there a good chance this is just going to make everyone more miserable?"

"Drag her back home. Right. I'll lasso an ankle and tug hard." Kelly sighed, looking down at the table and running a hand through her hair. "I just—I know it's a hard thing to ask. I guess I don't really know *how* hard it is to ask. It's not like I've had to deal with coming out to my parents. I know there's probably not gonna be some story-book ending here, and I don't know if she and Dad can make up, let alone mom. But if it's not now, it's not gonna be ever."

Saida sighed, too, picking up her beer. Kelly shifted in her seat, straightening up and then slouching moodily.

They drank in silence, until they ordered the next round. When the next pints appeared, Saida's phone buzzed. A text message from Autumn: *where are you?*

Beanstalk, she texted back.

"Less than an hour," she said to Kelly.

"Huh." The rabbit shrugged, picking up her beer.

When Autumn walked up to them, she just set her hands down to either side of their table. "I'm not shrinking down for the trip back."

A range of expressions flitted across Kelly's face. Then she looked up. "It's five hundred miles and giants don't lumber along at highway speed. You got a few weeks free each way and a map to fields you can sleep in that won't get your huge puff tail shot off?"

She rubbed her face. "Dammit, Kelly."

CHAPTER 11

Going Home

EVERYTHING OUTSIDE LOOKED WRONG.

Autumn stared through the train window, past the ghost reflection of her expressionless face. She'd taken this route three times before, first a lifetime ago on her way to college, then for her one and only visit home. The way it had gone, she'd assumed it'd be her last.

The train had left Mensura behind, and the larger city after that, and the smaller city after that. Now they were in an over two-hour stretch with no stops, streaking past endless farm country at the train's full speed of a hundred-eighty miles an hour. Kelly had been right, of course; the walking speed of a giant didn't scale up linearly. She might be sixteen times faster than a six-foot tall man, but she walked closer to a mere four times faster.

But now she was as little as the traffic, as little as the trees and the train and the seats and her loudly snoring sister. Everything that should be down was up, everything that should be small was large. After she'd cast the spell on herself, the vertigo nearly made her puke. She'd tried to explain to Kelly, but predictably, it hadn't earned her any sympathy. *You were this size for nineteen fucking years. It can't be that alien. Get over yourself.*

It wasn't alien. It was just wrong.

She glanced over at Kelly. She'd been so *very* tempted to transform to the six-foot-nine height Saida said the rabbit would be in

Stravell, but knew she wouldn't hear the end of it. Now, though, she was back to being Kelly's frail kid sister, heading back to a town and family that only knew her as the frail kid brother.

Sighing, she crossed her arms and leaned back. Not that frail anymore, she reminded herself. She'd started exercising since she'd been at college—not a lot, probably not as much as she should, but enough to have muscle tone. Kelly could still whip her ass, but that wasn't a fair comparison. She'd seen her sister deck a biker wolf with one punch.

Kelly's snoring ended in a snort, cough, and blink. She looked around. "We there yet?"

"No."

She sighed. "I told you we should have stuck with the plane."

"And I told you I couldn't pay for it. Our two tickets together on this cost less than your return flight would have. Besides, it's only a few hours more. Nicer seats, better food—"

Kelly grunted. "Okay, okay, don't do the travel agent thing again." She pulled out her phone and looked at the screen.

"She texted you back?"

"Yeah." She started to put the phone away.

Autumn put her hand on her sister's wrist, pulling it up enough that she could start to read the reply. *Let Andrew know we will set a place for*

Kelly pulled her hand back, shoving the phone in her pocket with a mutter.

"So it's going to be like that." Autumn threw herself against the window, staring up at the train car's ceiling and the overhead luggage rack.

"You know how passive-aggressive Mom can get."

"That's not passive-aggressive. Passive-aggressive was giving me the most masculine toys she could find for years after she caught me playing with your Barbie Vixen. This is just plain aggressive."

Kelly pursed her lips, blowing out a resigned exhale. "I'm sorry this is gonna be a shitty evening."

"Yeah. So am I."

They both fell silent for about a minute, until Kelly grunted again. "I don't know what even happened to that Barbie Vixen doll."

"I kind of stole her from you." She shrugged half-apologetically. "I just learned to hide it better."

Kelly lifted her brows. "Huh." She punched Autumn's shoulder. "Good on you. I always hated that bubbly little bitch."

Autumn rubbed her shoulder, but laughed. Kelly started laughing, too, and in short order they were holding each other, both fighting back giggles.

The train kept up its breakneck speed for another hour, slowing down as the railway curved into the outskirts of Port Claria, rising to an elevated track to keep it above grade. After its stop at the Transit Terminal, it wouldn't break even ninety miles an hour again, making three more stops along the coast before it reached Westville.

This time it was Kelly's turn to wake up the dozing Autumn. "Come on, sleepyhead."

"I didn't fall asleep," Autumn mumbled through a yawn, stretching.

"You did." Kelly stood up, grabbing both their overnight bags from the overhead rack. "Your whiskers always twitch when you're dreaming." She started walking toward the train's exit.

Autumn slid out of the seat and hurried after her. "Okay, I was dreaming about stomping the high school to dust."

"Fifty dollars if you let me watch, a hundred if you take out Mrs. Kinnison."

"Deal."

When she stepped out onto the platform by her sister, the heat and humidity hit her like wet sand. She got about ten feet before she felt her whole body sagging. "Ugh. How did I stand this?"

"Stand what?"

"Ninety degree heat with ninety percent humidity."

Kelly rolled her eyes. "It's like eighty degrees tops. I remember you complaining about the cold your first winter up at college."

"I've learned my lesson." She checked her phone. Eighty-three degrees, sixty-six percent humidity. Still fucking miserable. "You wanna call a ride, or should I?"

"I'll get it."

The weasel who picked them up a few minutes later wasn't that chatty. Good. The oppressive heat had nothing on the weight of seeing more and more familiar buildings go by.

It wasn't until the driver let them out in front of an old brick apartment complex, a single building three stories high that Autumn realized she'd never seen her sister's new place in person. When she'd left for college, Kelly had still been living at home, saving up to move out. This was across town, an older neighborhood that looked like it might just be starting to gentrify. "Second floor, in the back." Kelly pointed, then led them up a staircase.

The apartment's inside wasn't much cooler than the outside. The air smelled mostly of her sister, with a touch of must. She recognized a couple of the pieces of furniture from her parents' place, but mostly it looked new. At least, new to her.

"Okay. So." Kelly walked across the room, flipping on an in-window air conditioner that came to life with a grinding whirr. "The couch is about as comfortable to sleep on as my bed is, so you should be good. I'll get some sheets and a couple pillows."

Autumn nodded, dropping onto the sofa and closing her eyes. It *was* comfortable. The adrenaline that had been building up on the ride here leaked out of her all at once. God, how was she going to get through a family dinner tonight? Was this what she signed up for? Couldn't she meet her cranky-ass father at some neutral territory like a coffee shop or a dive bar? Why hadn't she just made it a goddamn phone call, find out if they even had anything to say to one another.

"Hey." Kelly pulled up a bare wooden chair, sitting on it backwards to face her. "You up for this?"

"You flew up to Mensura, browbeat me into coming back with you, and you're just asking me that now?"

"I mean this whole dinner thing. Maybe there's a way we could talk with Dad without...you know."

"Without Mom."

"I'm just saying, it's not too late to skip out and go get smashed on shitty daiquiris at Gimpy's."

"Yeah, I think it probably is too late for that. Also, Three Lords,

'Gimpy's.' How didn't we see what an ableist trash name for a restaurant that was growing up? How is it still called that?"

"We can look for a bar with a more sensitive, wholesome name."

"You're making fun of me."

Kelly nodded, straight-faced. "Yes."

Autumn smiled, then shrugged, sighing heavily. "If I'm here, I'm here. Let's do it."

"Okay." She got to her feet. "It's about a fifteen-minute drive. I mean the house, not Gimpy's."

Autumn thumped her foot. "Probably only about twice that walking."

"Are you kidding? It's like nearly eight—" She narrowed her eyes. "Don't you even think about that."

She raised her hands. "Just saying. Giant rabbits might not be as fast as cars, but they're economical *and* beautiful landscape features."

"Yeah, they're only economical until someone sends the bill for damages." Kelly made a point of jangling her car keys as she grabbed them.

"I don't damage anything!"

"You live in a town built for fifteen foot long bunny paws." She pointed accusingly with one hand, opening the door with her other. "And I've been through that bombed-out slum-fest of a neighborhood outside your school gates. Maybe *you're* a well-behaved giant monster, but those buildings definitely got some help falling down."

"They were already abandoned, you know." She got into her sister's car, a two-decade-old subcompact about a year overdue for a wash both inside and out. A myriad of other scents competed with her sister's, too many from discarded fast food bags and wrappers in the back seat. At her normal size, the whole car would fit easily in her hand. She imagined picking it up, shaking out all the trash, then running it under a faucet for a couple minutes.

"That's not real comforting to anyone at paw level, you know," Kelly retorted. The car sputtered to life on the second try, and she pulled out of the driveway, stomping on the gas until the car hauled itself up to thirty-five miles per hour—about ten over the speed limit. Her car might be an econobox, but Kelly clearly wanted a sports car.

"I guess not." Autumn couldn't help grin.

The drive back to their parents' house didn't hit any freeways; half the drive was on the fifty-mph Summerland Expressway, the rest on in-town roads that didn't have speed limits higher than forty. Again, Kelly was maddeningly right. No place for a giant to walk on or around Summerland, and the rest of the roads had small sidewalks. When they had sidewalks at all. And she hadn't realized how much of Mensura must have underground power and communication cables—not to mention stoplights that weren't strung all the way across roads—until she caught herself counting just how many intersections here would have been trip hazards.

At this point, all the streets were familiar, unchanged from a few years ago. She knew each turn, and knew when they were just a minute away.

When they pulled into the driveway of the old ranch-style house, past the maple tree she'd fallen out of multiple times, parking in front of the attached garage that carried the house's weird red brick and pale green color scheme, she let out a long breath she hadn't realized she'd been holding.

Kelly shut off the engine. "You ready?"

She nodded. "Yes."

"Not too late for Gimpy's."

Autumn grinned weakly, getting out of the car.

CHAPTER 12
Family Dinner

THE FRONT DOOR SWUNG OPEN AT KELLY'S KNOCK. Autumn found herself hanging back, partially shielded by her larger sister.

"Hello, Kelly." The older rabbit smiled up, the perfect image of a matronly suburban retiree. Maybe one from a generation ago. She even had an apron, for lord's sake. Her smile faltered, then stiffened as she looked past her older daughter at her younger. When they'd last seen one another, Autumn had been wearing blouses and denim skirts—more feminine, but decidedly less punk. "And hello." Her mother stepped back, tone as stiff as her smile. "It's good of you to come." She held the door open.

Inside, everything was just as she'd last seen it: eggshell colored walls, walnut and cherrywood furniture, knitted multicolor throw pillows arranged on the couch. She didn't know why she'd expected any difference; the only time she remembered any big change was when they'd used Dad's holiday bonus to replace the sofas and coffee table. Beyond that, furniture, even down to the television set and stereo, only got replaced when worn out or broken. They'd been talking about repainting the walls all through high school, and finally did just after Autumn left for college—with the same color. The dining room furniture, inherited from Mom's mother, was as sacrosanct as the silverware inherited from *her* mother. She only brought that silverware out for holidays and Sunday dinners. Sure enough, the table had already been set with it. If Autumn had shown up tomorrow, on a Monday, would Mom have bothered?

Dad sat on the sofa, the same corner he always sat in. At first glance, he looked the same as always, too, save for being in sweat shorts and an undershirt—clothes he'd have only worn before for yard work. At second glance, though, he looked...well, fat. He'd put on a lot of weight, and didn't carry it well. But that wasn't what made him look wrong. He looked *droopy*. Droopy. Two medical canes rested against the couch's armrest.

His eyes, though, became alert as they settled on Autumn, and he pushed himself up out of his slouch with a grunt. "You look like a singer with some heavy metal band."

Kelly nudged her forward with a shove on her shoulder. "This is Autumn. Your other daughter."

Autumn caught a soft *huff* from her mother as the other rabbit hurried into the kitchen. "I'll have dinner on the table in about ten minutes."

"My brain might have holes in it, but it's not mush yet. I know who that is. Come over here." He motioned at Autumn, then at the seat by him.

She headed over to the couch and sat down, resting her hands in her lap and fidgeting. "Hi, Dad."

He leaned back again and folded his arms, looking down at her. He'd always been a tall rabbit. "So Kelly dragged you to see your asshole old man before he kicked off, huh?"

"I wouldn't put it that way."

"Not to my face." He laughed, ending in a sharp cough and a grunt. "You always hear about chemo making people thin, you know? But it makes some people fat. Turns out rabbits, we're more likely to get fat. Figures, doesn't it. Been fit all my life and I'm gonna need an extra-wide coffin anyway." He shook his head. "So how's school?"

She shifted uncomfortably. She hadn't been prepared to ricochet between brutal honesty and small talk, but maybe she should have. Jasper Caligo, always blunt to a fault.

"It's been good. I've liked the history classes." History had been his major, even though he'd never done a damn thing related to the degree.

"But you're still majoring in magic."

She nodded.

"Ain't that a crazy wonder. Still usually a hundred feet tall, too."

She studied his face, but couldn't read his expression. Well, if he was going to go there right off the bat, so be it. "Yeah."

"You know that's gonna make your life hell once you graduate."

"There were giants before the school opened, Dad."

"Only across the Great Canyon in Monsterland."

"Great Chasm."

"Whatever." He grunted. "Seriously, what job are you planning to get?"

"I don't know."

"You don't know." He shook his head. "That's why I didn't want you to go there."

"Jobs didn't come up. You threatened to cut me off if I want there because you thought I'd get eaten."

"If you got eaten I wouldn't have had to cut you off, would I?" He snorted. "Admit I didn't expect 'oh, no, I'm actually a giantess,' though."

"You and mom seriously never suspected?"

"The giant part, or the 'ess' part?"

"The 'ess' part."

"We thought you might be gay." He shrugged. "You never said anything one way or the other, did you."

"Like what, Dad?" She didn't try and keep the hostile skepticism out of her voice.

"Fair question." He let out a long breath through pursed lips, just like Kelly did. Autumn hadn't realized that was where her sister had gotten that from. "Seeing anyone?"

"What?"

He looked down at her again. "You didn't date a lot in high school. How about now?"

She nodded after a moment. "Yeah."

"Is he a rabbit?"

Oh boy. "Uh, no, they're a cat."

"Cute?"

"Very pretty." She caught herself, correcting, "Good-looking." Yeah, very pretty good-looking. Great job there.

He glanced at the kitchen, then lowered his voice, leaning closer. "Girl, huh?"

Autumn's eyes widened.

He drew back, looking amused. He kept his voice low. "You may have been a wallflower, but you had an eye for the girls. I'm not surprised that wasn't just 'cause you were trying to see yourself."

"Girlfriend. Yeah." Where was this going? "That doesn't mean I'm not really a girl."

"Didn't say it did." He took a deep breath, looking away from her. "I know I haven't been…good about all this. I didn't know how to deal with my son telling me he's—she's—my daughter. Still don't." He shrugged, smiling wryly. "But I don't have the time left to keep pretending it's your problem instead of mine."

She closed her eyes, taking a shallow breath, and put her hand on his. "She's a giantess."

"One thing to wrap my head around at a time, kid. It's pretty brittle these days."

She choked back a laugh, not sure how appropriate it was.

"Dinner's ready," her mom called from the kitchen, starting to bring out plates.

"How…I mean…how are you doing?"

He grabbed both his canes, shuffling them between his hands and gripping the handles. "I have good days and bad days, and I'm starting to have more bad days than good." He hauled himself to his feet. "Lucky you, you're here on a good one." As he walked toward the table, he moved faster than she'd expected, despite leaning heavily.

Mom had gone all out on dinner: roast acorn squash stuffed with wild rice, mushrooms and apples, green bean casserole, twice-baked potatoes, rolls. Autumn recognized—well, everything, down to brand names. The squash and apples would be fresh; the mushrooms and green beans would be whatever cans had been on sale; the potatoes would be from a frozen box of Chef Larry's Gourmet Heat-n-Serve. She gravitated automatically to her old seat at the table.

"Who wants to say grace?" Mom phrased the question as if it were for the entire table, but looked directly at Autumn.

She felt her ears flush. She'd stopped going to church in high school except when dragged to "important" holiday services.

"I'll do it," Kelly said. Before her mother could react, she recited a prayer quickly and mechanically. "Bid the Three Lords be our guests at this table, blessing us with this bounty and their fellowship."

"Three Lords bless us," everyone finished, with varying degrees of enthusiasm. Autumn mumbled hers resentfully, which earned a piercing look from her mother and a resigned *just go along* glance from Kelly.

After a moment, her mother cleared her throat, starting to pass the food around the table. "So how has college been? I haven't heard news in some time, except what Kelly shares."

"Fine." She tried to sound casual rather than curt. "I was telling Dad that I've been enjoying the history classes."

"It's not a good major. Your father can tell you all about that, can't you, Jasper?"

Autumn passed along the squash and took a too-big scoop of the green beans. "It's not my major, remember? Magic is."

"Yes." She looked pointedly up and down Autumn's body. "I certainly can't forget."

Autumn clenched her teeth.

"So," Kelly interjected loudly. "Dad, how's your latest woodworking project going?"

"Oh, slower than this sort of thing used to go for me, but that's what you'd expect." He shrugged, chewing a bite of the squash before continuing. "Should be able to get the desk all refinished, though, before I forget what desks are."

Her mother made a little choking noise. "Don't joke like that."

"Who's joking?" Despite the words, he sounded distinctly amused now. "Audrey, pass the potatoes?"

It took Autumn a moment to realize he was looking at her. "Autumn," she corrected.

He looked at her blankly for a half-second, then grunted, tapping the side of his head. "Sorry. Kinda half power up here."

She passed the plate of potatoes to her father wordlessly.

"Audrey does sound more like Andrew," her mother muttered.

Autumn slammed her hands on the table, looking across at her mother levelly. "Neither one is my name."

Her mother sat bolt upright, whiskers twitching, eyes going wide. "You can call yourself whatever you want." Her voice trembled. "But Andrew will always be the name I gave you."

"Evelyn." Her father raised his voice, giving his wife a reproachful, exasperated look. "For the Lords' sake."

"Don't you dare!" Evelyn glanced between her husband and her daughter—both her daughters—wildly, then burst into tears, pushing back from the table and fleeing to the kitchen.

Autumn groaned, throwing her head back and looking up at the ceiling. Dammit, she shouldn't be crying, too.

Her father sighed heavily. "If I can come around, she can."

She kept her gaze on the ceiling, on a stain that had been there for at least sixteen years. "*Have* you come around, or are you just trying to stop being an asshole before you kick off?"

"Have to do the one to get to the other."

Autumn dropped her head to look at him, then sighed. "Thanks for trying."

He hauled himself to his feet, grabbing his canes. "Here. Come out to the back yard." He swung himself to the sliding glass doors.

She and Kelly exchanged puzzled glances as they got up, too, Kelly opening the door for her father. Autumn followed behind. "What do you want to show me?"

"Not a thing. I want *you* to show *me* something. You. It's a pretty big back yard. I think we have the space."

Kelly put her hands on her hips. "Oh, you have got—Dad, Mom will flip her shit."

He looked back at the house and grunted. "We all know that ship's already sailed." He waved at Autumn. "So show me."

She swallowed, looking around. There *was* enough space, but she'd be visible around the whole block. Well, word had to have gotten around by now anyway. "Um, okay. You and Kelly should sit down, since there's kind of a big blast of wind that goes along with this." She waited until they had, then walked to about the center of the lawn, closed her eyes, and cast the reversal spell.

"Good Gods," her father said, eyes wide, neck craned back.

She slowly crouched down. "Don't be scared."

"Fat chance of that." He hauled himself back up to his paws. "But I know it's you. I know this is you. And I'm glad I got to see you, Autumn."

Autumn bit her lip, carefully running a finger along her father's side. He gave it an awkward hug.

A shriek came from inside the house, followed by a door slam.

"I suppose knocking on the roof would be a bad idea."

Her father grunted. "Remember I gotta live with her a few more months. I understand if you want to head on for now."

"Yeah, there are crappy daiquiris waiting at Gimpy's with our names on them."

He pointed. "I bet if you stay big and walk down the hill, you can get there in a few minutes. Follow the creek, stay to the open space."

"Three Lords, don't *encourage* her!" Kelly spluttered. "I have my car here!"

"Oh, it'll be easy to carry." Autumn leaned over the house, reaching for it.

"Don't you—oh my God! Autumn!"

CHAPTER 13

Spycraft

SAIDA STEADIED HERSELF AGAINST THE WALL, BLINKING away multicolored stars. Talirend Dynamics advertised their JetNet teleporter beacons as "effortless, comfortable, and near-instantaneous," heavily promoting the idea that the distance between any two beacons was irrelevant. But not only were Saida's two beacons early prototypes, the distance between them was immeasurable. Teleporting between them took anywhere from five to thirty seconds, plunging travelers into a fur-raising limbo: the sensation of falling so fast it felt your bones would snap, while your eyes—if you dared to open them—assured you that you floated motionless in an endless void of bright flickering colors. This trip had been closer to the thirty-second mark, which always left her nervous as hell. Beacon malfunctions were exceedingly rare, but very, very grim.

Straightening up, she sighed, dropped her overnight bag, and poured a cup of water, looking out through the glass doors past her balcony. Her fifteenth-floor apartment overlooked the river running through downtown's heart; at night the view was magical, the lights of the walkways and bridges reflected in the rippling water. When she was younger, she'd dreamed of living in a place just like this.

The other side of the river, the west side, became more residential: buildings rarely higher than two stories, tree-lined streets, and green open parks, all with the forested western hills behind them.

She'd dreamed of living in places like *that*, too, and at times she wondered if she'd made a mistake renting here, paying more for less space. She surely made enough money now to buy a house in the foothills, and her mother had been not-so-subtly suggesting that she was overdue to "settle down" like her brother. Mradhi himself had come as close to suggesting that as he ever would: nothing about family or romance, just offhandedly practical comments about finances.

Truthfully, though, she'd dreamed of living in *lots* of places. That might be why she'd dragged her paws on looking into owning real estate. Maybe she was saving up to travel the world and just didn't know it. Maybe she was just afraid of commitment. (Something else her mother had not-so-subtly suggested.)

What would Autumn make of any of these musings? She'd probably say they were elitist. Maybe that was just the difference between college age and workforce age. She might only be six years older than the rabbit, but those were six world-changing years in most people's lives. Saida had a higher income than either of her parents, but she doubted she was wealthier than her father. Her mother, though, had only become a homeowner again last year, after a decade back in the rental market.

Autumn had gone off to visit *her* mother and father. How was that going? She and her sister would be at home by now, but Saida wouldn't hear anything until she got back to Mensura. From an incredible Friday night to a fraught Saturday night and Sunday morning. What did Autumn look like at Kelly's size? She'd like to know, to tease Autumn about being her little bunny. Although she should be honest with herself: just thinking the phrase *Autumn's little cat* made her ears blush and her heart race, and that was before thinking about being ankle-high to her—

Sighing, she returned to the kitchen, pouring out the rest of the water and swapping it for a glass of rosé wine.

Back in the living room, she flipped on the television. Yet another difference between here and Mensura: flat screen televisions still hadn't overtaken CRTs in the market, and good ones were still deathly expensive. Her plasma set hadn't been cheap, even on sale.

Sunday afternoons were wastelands for TV shows (another difference: here, she had only a half-dozen major channels, and no on-demand streaming to speak of), but maybe she could find something.

She didn't think anything of the soft little knocking sound until she realized it wasn't just joints in the walls expanding from heat, or the air conditioning doing...something mechanical. It was an actual *knock*, with a soft voice calling. "Hey! Hey! Saida!"

Her ears swiveled. What the hell? She turned down the TV, cautiously making her way toward the ceiling-level vent the noise seemed to be coming from.

"Saida!" Definitely coming from the vent. She leaned up to see a Liliren waving at her.

He stood about four inches high, dressed in jeans and a bright pink T-shirt, black hair fashionably cut short on one side and long on the other. Clearly not trying to hide from other Rha, although maybe he didn't need to make an effort. "Tam?"

"Yeah!" He nodded. "How're you?"

"Fine." She'd spied Tam when she'd first moved here, when he'd thought the apartment was still unoccupied. After they'd both gotten over a bit of shock, she'd surprised him by being friendly. Even so, he hadn't hung around much, and she thought he might have moved on. She wasn't clear about his living arrangements, or that of any of the other Liliren in the city. "How are *you?* I wasn't sure if you'd moved out, or the super had done...something." She grimaced.

"Nah. He set a couple traps, but nothing serious."

Her eyes widened. "Goddess Arvya. Traps?"

He waved a hand. "Oh, nothing that'd hurt us if we got caught. Nothing real effective, either. Think he's just going through the motions to convince paranoid tenants he's doing something about the Liliren watching them while they sleep." He wiggled his fingers in faux spooky fashion.

She laughed, folding her arms. "I wouldn't have even thought about that before, but now *I'm* going to be paranoid about it."

"You know we're more interested in watching you when you're

awake." He paused, then added hurriedly, "Not in a creepy way, I mean—"

"To stay out of our way, I know."

"Yeah. Well—we do keep our eyes out for Rha, see you all coming and going. That's what I wanted to tell you. There was someone poking around your place yesterday. And I don't think it was the first time."

"Wait, what? Inside?"

He nodded. "Yeah. Came by with the super. Think he was posing as somebody from the utility company, checking out the water lines."

She lifted a brow. "How do you know he wasn't?"

"Because he didn't come out of a utility truck, he came out of a beat-up car he parked a block away. That's what caught our eye. But that's not all. After the super left him here, he never looked at the water. He was really interested in your big blue egg thing." Tam pointed through the grate.

Saida turned to look. Her ears skewed. While she'd always thought they looked more like oversized flower vases, it was clear what the Liliren meant: the teleportation beacon. "Interested how?"

He shrugged. "Don't know. He looked around it, plugged something into it, looked around your apartment a little, then left."

There was a diagnostic port on the beacon, so someone could technically hack into it that way, but it'd be damn difficult. And to what end? "Did you see the thing he plugged into it? Was it a computer, like a laptop?"

"No. It was a little red box."

That sounded like an official diagnostic unit. She pursed her lips. "Was he a grey tabby?"

He shook his head. "Nah, pitch black."

"Thin?"

"Fat."

Okay, so that let out not only Jonry, but everyone she knew at the office.

She sighed after another few seconds, shaking her head. "All right. Shit." She ran a hand through her hair. "What did you mean when you said you didn't think it was the first time?"

"Asked around. Some of us have seen him here before once, when you were out at work."

Saida narrowed her eyes, tail flicking. "I'll talk to the super. Not sure what I'll say, but I'll figure out something." She snorted. "Maybe I should have you on retainer as a spy. I'm glad you saw all this, but I think I'm also a little disturbed."

Tam laughed. "Might be a lot of disadvantages to being the small ones in a world of giants, but there are some advantages, too. We see a lot more of you than you do of us."

"Definitely a little disturbed. But thanks a lot for looking out. Is there anything I can help you out with?"

"Nah. Nothing right now. I don't think you know how many of my neighbors you helped out with by replacing our food stores after that flood a few years ago."

She opened her mouth, then closed it before she said anything naïve like *but I didn't buy that much.* She'd bought enough dry goods to keep another Rha going for a few weeks, finding ways to sneak it to Tam and a couple other Liliren helpers of his. Technically, that violated her lease—the Liliren were, legally speaking, pests, not residents or guests. But their secret subways and warrens wouldn't have been flooded along with two lower-level apartments if the maintenance department had been doing their job, so she didn't feel at all guilty about a bit of subversion. "Oh. Ah. You're all welcome."

"So do you know what you're gonna do about your spy guy?"

"No idea." She sighed.

"Hmm. Okay. If I see or hear about anything else weird going on around your place, I'll let you know."

"Thanks."

Tam quickly vanished. Sighing, she picked up her briefly forgotten—but now even more desperately desired—wine, took a long sip, then started walking around the apartment. Was anything else out of place? Would she be able to tell? Her personal computer was password-protected, at least, but she didn't know how much security that was in practice. The clunky PCs here weren't like

Arilin's sleek touchpad, data encrypted and inaccessible when locked. Well, she wouldn't be surprised if Mradhi's was encrypted. He was that kind of nerd.

But was he the kind of nerd who would hire someone to spy on his own sister? If she was right, and her apparent intruder *did* have an official Talirend Dynamics diagnostics unit, that had to mean two things. One, he—or his employer—was interested in pulling the logs off *her* unit for some reason. And two, he or his employer had some connection to the company. They might have managed to steal a unit, but she'd likely have heard about it, unless the theft hadn't been noticed yet. Somehow that didn't feel as likely as the first possibility.

She sat down, swirling the wine moodily. What data would be in those logs? Little someone who wasn't a technician would care about —but it'd record the times and dates she'd used it and what beacon it was connecting to. And while the telemetry data couldn't show where that other beacon was, the power profile might well show it wasn't anywhere in Stravell.

That might rule out Mradhi. He set *up* that other beacon; he was the only one who knew his sister took cross-world jaunts, let alone the circumstances of hers.

She didn't want to leap to conclusions and point her nose at Raiben. Yes, she resented him, but she hadn't seen any signs he wanted to dig up dirt on her, to push her out. Yet the suspicion was hard to dismiss.

And, of course, Mradhi had brought in Raiben.

Downing the rest of the wine, she snapped off the television and got up to get a second glass. She needed a plan, but it'd have to start with figuring out just what the hell she had to plan *for*.

CHAPTER 14

That Doesn't Count

"Watch out for the—"

Saida sat down before Autumn finished her sentence, then made a funny face.

"—bench." She laughed, shaking her head.

The Rha lifted herself off the grass, knocking the bench out of the way with an irritated claws-out paw swipe. "Dammit, who would put one of those there?"

Autumn opened her mouth in shock, then laughed again in spite of herself. "The Parks Department. Congratulations, though. It survived a giantess *sitting* on it, and you just broke it anyway."

"I didn't—" Saida looked at the bench, clearly realizing she'd ripped it out of its concrete foundations. "Dammit."

She sipped her coffee, stretching out her legs across the field. "I'll tell them where to send the bill."

"That's a stupid place to put a bench," Saida insisted. "The nearest walking path is nearly a hundred feet away."

"Someone might like to sit off the path, like we are."

"They can damn well sit in the grass, then, like we are." The cat sipped at her own drink—some kind of ridiculously flavored latte, like turmeric vanilla. "Okay, so you've been keeping me in suspense since I got here. How did last weekend go?"

Autumn sighed, drumming her fingers in the grass. She hadn't expected to be telling this story so soon, but she hadn't expected Saida *back* so soon, either. The Rha had suggested she'd be back every two or three weekends, and she'd mentally adjusted that to mean "every three or four" to stave off disappointment. But here it was, just a week after the last visit—after the wonderful dinner at Chimayo, after the *amazing* night afterward, after the unexpectedly aborted day of carrying around a doll-sized Rha. "It went better than I guess I expected it would, which isn't the same as saying it went well."

Saida wrapped her smaller hand around hers as best she could, looking expectant.

She took a deep breath, and outlined her visit, from Mom's strained greetings, through Dad's unexpected attempts at reconciliation and her mother's multiple freakouts during dinner, to her even more unexpected return to her correct size at her father's request.

"And you seriously walked to the bar as a giantess, carrying Kelly's car?"

She grinned. "Yeah. It came through fine, but Kelly was *really* pissed off with me until she hit her second watermelon daiquiri. By her fourth one she was telling me having a giantess for a sister was 'fucking awesome' and kept trying to give me a list of people I should, quote, 'stomp flatter than bad root beer.'"

Saida laughed. "It sounds like it went *kind* of well, then."

"Yeah, we'll stick with 'kind of.'" She shrugged, crossing her paws at the ankles. Two joggers going past on the walking trail, at that point still a good twenty feet from her paws, smacked into one another. She flashed them a raised-brow look, and they hurried on. "I don't know how much Dad really accepts, but he doesn't want to die with us on bad terms, so that's something. But mom? I'm not sure we're any farther apart after that wreck of a dinner, but we're not any damn closer."

Saida squeezed her hand and nodded. "I hope you can reconcile with...well, both of them."

Autumn clenched her other hand more tightly around the coffee cup. Where was a pinecone to toss moodily when you needed it?

Lords knew what damage she'd do by throwing a giant pinecone, though. "It'd help if I was a normal kid, huh?"

"You're a beautiful kid. It's not on you if they can't see that."

She tried to think of a deflecting joke, maybe needling Saida over using *kid*, but it had been her word, not the Rha's. Maybe she should just shut up and take the compliment. "Thanks." She took a longer drink of her coffee. "We never finished your tour of the campus as a little, did we?"

"No, you were interrupted mid-lick, which was all for the best as far as my composure's concerned."

She grinned, sticking out her tongue just enough to show off its stud. "You have an adorable submissive streak."

Saida stiffened, ears going back. "I do *not* have a submissive streak. I'm a company director. I hire and fire people."

All right, that was an unexpected reaction. "I don't..." No, maybe not the time to say *I don't think that rules that out,* even if it was true. Weren't corporate execs the ones most likely to furtively slink off to leather clubs and find someone of their preferred gender who would glare down and step on them, anyway?

An image of slipping Saida into her sandal—or maybe just patiently telling the little cat to lie down in it over and over until she obeyed—came into her head and stuck there, and she felt herself flush. Okay, maybe *she* had a streak she hadn't fully recognized in herself. "Um, I don't, uh, mean that in a bad way."

Saida was frowning at her, as if reading her mind, but sighed after a few moments, looking down. "Sorry. I *may* be a little on edge about work."

"More problems with your new boss?"

"I think he's spying on me."

"What? At the office?"

"No. Well. Yes, probably there, too. When I got home early on Sunday, a Liliren in my building told me—"

"There are Liliren in your building?"

"Some."

"Like, renters? You built space for them?"

"What? No." Saida gave her an expression that clearly read *don't be ridiculous*. "In the walls and spaces between the floors."

"So they're little squatters stuck in weird creepy spaces that Rha build unintentionally?"

"Look, a family of Liliren could build a home on my coffee table, have proportionately more living space than I do, and still leave me enough room to set down some drink glasses."

She briefly pictured a nice apartment with a dollhouse full of mice on the coffee table. Then the image shifted to a smaller dollhouse with no roof sitting on a nightstand, and a blushing little Saida in lingerie looking up at her from inside.

"—dessert?"

"Huh? What?"

Saida gave her a suspicious glance. "You're almost drooling."

Lords, she was going to have an interesting talk with her therapist next session. She cleared her throat. "So the Liliren in your building told you..."

Saida went on to describe the conversation with a Liliren named Tam, about how some other random Rha had snuck into her apartment while she was gone to collect data from the teleportation beacon.

"Shit. He was a coworker?"

The Rha shook her head. "It doesn't sound like it. I think he was a hired investigator."

"And you think what's-his-name—"

"Raiben."

"—Raiben hired him."

"I can't think who else would have."

"It couldn't be a competitor? Corporations do that sort of thing all the time, don't they?"

"No. I mean, they *do* do that sort of thing, but it's usually more opportunistic. Supply chain leaks, bribable disgruntled employees, like that. And a competitor would be snooping around the company. This is targeting me."

"Have you talked to your brother the CEO about it?"

"No." Saida shook her head. "And I don't know what I'd say. I mean..." She trailed off, expression clouding over in a hard-to-read way. Unless—

"You don't think he's in on it, do you?"

"I don't. I'm just not sure what to think."

Autumn frowned. She could tell from Saida's expression that despite her words, she'd at least considered CEO bro *might* be in on it. "I'd be thinking about another job."

Saida recoiled. "What? No. I wouldn't...that would be a hell of an overreaction."

She set down her coffee and crossed her arms. "They've hired people to break into your fucking house. How does that environment get any more toxic without them spraying actual poison in your face?"

"Come on. It's bad now, but that doesn't mean it's going to stay bad. It was great for years."

"We nearly stopped seeing each other after our first date because your new boss overloaded you with work. Literally the first weekend you came back, he hired a private eye to check out the teleporter thing you use to get here. You can't seriously tell me you don't think this guy has it in for you."

"So you're telling me to let him win?"

While that wasn't what she meant, it did sound that way, didn't it? She tugged on one of her ears, thinking. "No. But how can it go back to the way it was now? I mean, even if you get him to stop harassing you, if he's still there, you still have an enemy as your direct boss. Same if he's not really behind this but he thinks you think he is. And if he is behind it and you *don't* get him to stop..." She spread her hands.

"And if I somehow get rid of him, I'm the bitch who drove out the new boss everyone *else* seems to love." The Rha looked like she was the one hunting around for a giant pinecone to throw now.

"Oh, great, so it's a misogynistic office, too."

Saida looked like she was about to object again, then sighed. "Most are."

"And here I was hoping your world was more enlightened than ours, other than apparently everything with Liliren."

"I don't think we have *more* misogyny than you do here, and we've had gay marriage for decades. Well, technically marriage in Stravell is strictly a religious ceremony, and the legal equivalent is 'partnership.' They just go hand-in-hand as a matter of practice. But you and I could be partners there, and some churches would marry us. The only sticking point would be you being a seven foot tall alien."

Autumn smirked, poking Saida in the side. "You're changing the subject. Why can't you just get another job?"

"Because—" Saida stopped and took a deep breath, looking away. "Because this is all I know how to do and the only place I've ever worked at." Her voice grew softer and more hesitant. "And I don't know if I *could* get a job anywhere else. I don't know if I'm honestly qualified for *this* one."

"Hey." Autumn pulled the smaller cat against her lightly. "You're smart, you've got a head for numbers, you've got management experience. You could get a job anywhere."

Saida sagged. "I don't think that's true. And I want to keep this one."

"Well, there's only one thing to do." Autumn picked up her coffee again. "Put his name on my list so I can stomp him flatter than bad root beer."

She laughed, relaxing against the rabbit. "Stop it."

Autumn grinned down, then nosed the Rha's ear. "I still want to learn more about how you have Liliren neighbors, illicit or not."

Saida squirmed at the nosing. "I don't know if there's much to say. The building super knows about them but mostly looks the other way, and they avoid Rha residents as much as they can. I only met Tam by dumb luck."

"But you know him well enough. Do you know any other Liliren by name?"

"A few."

"Ever date any?"

"No!" Saida poked her back.

"Don't say you haven't thought about what a giant cat could do with a little rat." She lowered her voice to a whisper, lips against Saida's ear again. "Or a giant rabbit with a little cat."

The Rha shivered, eyes closing and tail flicking. "My curse doesn't count as a submissive streak." Her tone was simultaneously wavering and warning.

She pulled back, smiling down curiously. "I didn't say it did."

Saida sighed. "Sorry. Maybe I should try to see your friend Professor Snep about this whole thing. The curse, not Raiben."

"'Friend' might be too strong a word. But I've mentioned you to him."

"And?"

"He was, um." She searched for a word. "Skeptical."

"That he could do anything?"

"That it was really a curse."

Saida's ears went flat. "Great."

CHAPTER 15

This May Hurt

EVEN THOUGH SHE'D TOLD AUTUMN THAT THERE'D BE NO problem with her staying an extra day to "work remotely," Saida worried she might be lying. By not coming into work, she might be giving Raiben—or whoever was behind this—more ammunition in whatever game they were playing. On the other hand, after he started pushing her to be "in the field" more she'd spent as much time out of the office as in, so it might not even be noticed. When she got back home later tonight she'd wipe the teleporter beacon's logs, just in case. Assuming she could remember how.

Autumn was leading her down a hallway in the college of magic. It looked at least a century older than it could possibly be: stone floor, walls, and ceilings, archways that had to be a hundred-thirty feet high at their keystones. The railings and balconies present in some buildings for little students were absent here, replaced—so she'd been told—by hidden pedestrian subways.

"You're sure he's not going to mind?"

Autumn glanced back over her shoulder. "It's open office hours."

"For student questions, not consultations."

The rabbit laughed. "I said I mentioned you to him before. He's interested in you."

"But you said he didn't think it was a real curse."

Autumn slowed down, stopping in front of a closed, solid wooden door. A small wooden sign with neat letters burned into it read, simply, PROF. ALTUS SNEP. "That doesn't mean he didn't find you interesting." She rapped on the door.

Saida flicked her tail. "'Interesting' comes across as ominous in this context."

It took several seconds for a reply, of sorts: the door unlocked with a heavy clack. Autumn pushed it open.

Floor to ceiling shelves lined every wall of the room they stepped into. Most held musty hardbound books, but others brimmed with knickknacks both mysterious and mundane: vases, charts, subtly glowing vials, wooden figurines, frightening-looking skulls, and along one whole shelf, little bookshelves filled with little books— several times more volumes than ones on giant scale. Amber light shone from oil lamps in each corner and over a huge, cluttered black wooden desk.

Behind the desk sat a tall, lean snow leopard, with ice blue eyes that so far hadn't moved from the paper he was writing (with—of course—quill and ink). Long, thin black hair fell in a neat cut to just below his angular cheekbones. While she wouldn't have been surprised to see stereotypical wizard robes, his outfit was more forlorn romantic poet: black slacks under a ruffled white shirt.

It took a full five seconds before he spoke, still without looking up. "Miss Caligo...and friend." The words came so deliberately paced she could hear the ellipsis. His voice reminded her of ash in an abandoned fireplace.

"This is the woman with the curse I told you about, Professor."

Snep didn't reply, finishing the sentence he was writing before returning the quill to its holder. Then, finally, he looked up, eyes first on Autumn, then on Saida, expression unreadable. "The one who claims to have a permanent resurrection spell cast on her that she wishes to have removed."

"Um, yes. That's me. I'm Saida. Saida Talirend."

He remained motionless.

She cleared her throat, willing her tail not to flick. "Autumn had kind of the same reaction to me calling it a curse. I know. But, I mean —I didn't ask for it."

He lifted a brow fractionally. "No one asks to be born into wealth, but those who are rarely regard it as a problem to be corrected." He looked back to Autumn. "I trust you haven't...misled your friend into believing I can snap my fingers and lift a curse."

"No." The rabbit shook her head. "I just said you might take a look."

The snow leopard's expression remained frozen for long seconds. Then he leaned back and crossed his arms. "Tell me about this 'curse' in your own words, Miss Talirend."

Saida bit her lip, then sketched out what she'd told Autumn in as minimal detail as possible—at least, as little as Snep let her get away with. He made her describe Kenley the stag and what he did in detail, particularly what she felt both when he shrank her and when she died that very first time, although he impatiently waved her past the more prurient aspects.

"So you never saw him cast a spell."

"No. But I didn't see him all the time, and I don't know if I'd know what I was looking at." She lashed her tail in spite of herself. "I'm not making this all up."

Snep got up from his desk, moving to a bookshelf set against the far wall and running a claw along the spines. "The question, Miss Talirend, is whether you are *understanding* this 'all up.'" He stopped at one book, relatively slim and small, and pulled it down from the shelf.

Autumn tilted her head. "Are you saying it might not be a curse?"

"I know it's real," Saida protested, shaking her head. "I've been— I've been eaten since then."

He looked up from the tome as he opened it. "If I believed you were delusional, I would say so. Your knowledge of your condition comes only from your own experience and from the...gentleman... who afflicted you with it. He is malicious and likely unreliable, while your experience is subjective and likely uninformed. Miss Caligo, do you recognize the book I've chosen to consult?"

"No, sir."

"Garwick's *Abductive Metamagic*. It's less a book of theory or practical magic than a book of diagnostic tools." He looked back to the Rha. "I need to cast several small spells. They may hurt."

Saida bit her lip again, then nodded. "Okay."

The snow leopard motioned for her to stand. She did. Then he traced an intricate pattern in the air with a claw tip, leaving glowing lines behind, shimmering between orange and blue. He finished by tapping that claw to Saida's forehead.

Abruptly it felt like string had been laced throughout her body, being pulled out slowly through unseen openings in her hands and feet. She started to scream, but as soon as she opened her mouth, the strings filled it, and the scream came out as a gargled choke.

Snep traced a pattern with his other hand, and touched the back of her neck. All the string lit on fire. This time when she tried to scream, her body simply didn't respond.

The wizard stepped back, then held his hands in front of his chest and slowly spread them apart. A blue sphere formed in the air, multicolored lines forming on its surface. "Do you recognize this, Miss Caligo?"

Saida tried to smile reassuringly, but it was clear from Autumn's horrified expression it wasn't working. "Y-yes, I think so," the rabbit stammered. "Just from books. It's showing...residual magic." Her brow furrowed as she moved closer.

"And what do you see?"

"Nothing." She sounded puzzled. "How is that—does that mean she *isn't* cursed?"

He spun the sphere around slowly with a hand. "Now what do you see?"

"Just the standard traces of mana that non-magical living beings have. I mean, it's not exactly like mine or yours, but she's from a different world. Could you let her—"

"Look *harder*, Miss Caligo. You've surely researched resurrection magic."

Saida's vision had started to blur with tears of pain. Whatever

Autumn was supposed to see, she sure hoped the rabbit saw it soon. Being a living magic lesson sucked.

Autumn swallowed, eyes flicking back to Saida, then back at the globe. Her eyes, then her fingers, traced the lines, moving frantically.

"The orange pentacle. What is it?"

She leaned forward. "It's..." She zoomed the sphere in, eyes moving back and forth. "Like a resurrection spell coupled with trans-mutation...to bring someone back from virtually nothing. That's crazy complicated. But how can it be *there?*"

Snep snapped his fingers, and the sphere dissipated. Saida felt the fire and the strings vanish in the same breath, and she stumbled. "How indeed, Miss Caligo."

"Spells like that should be overlays, bindings, not intrinsic." Autumn ran a hand through her hair. "Shouldn't they?"

Saida steadied herself on the desk. "Could...uh." She wiped a line of drool away from her muzzle. "Could somebody please explain things in small, non-wizardly words?"

Snep looked to Autumn expectantly.

She took a deep breath. "It looks like—like it's all *you*. Your natural magic."

"I don't *have* natural magic!" Saida straightened up, tail lashing. This was insane. "There's no magic in my world. We don't have wizards or faeries and all this—" She waved her hands around. "All *this*. Kenley didn't somehow wake up power I already had. He changed my size, he changed his own size, *he's* the magician, not—"

"Miss Talirend." Snep's voice was resigned but gentle. "You said this Kenley disclaimed being a magician, and that he used the phrase 'bending the framework of the universe.' I don't think he cursed you in the sense that mages use the term. He changed what you are."

Her tail lashed. "So...so you can't remove it."

"With sufficient time and study, I might be able to. But there are no guarantees, and the change in and of itself is not harmful."

She gritted her teeth.

Autumn took her hand. "Maybe you don't beat this by removing it, you beat it by...making it yours."

"What about the chance that every time I die, there's a chance I won't come back from it? *That's* a curse, isn't it?"

"I saw no evidence of any curse beyond that of mortality, Miss Talirend. You are doomed to eventually join the rest of us in staying dead." He arched a brow. "Your habit of dying more often may take a few years off your life, but so would many more...common vices."

Saida ran a hand through her hair. "That's..." That's not what Kenley had said, but he would just point out again—correctly—that the stag wasn't trustworthy. She cleared her throat hesitantly. "And the spit thing?"

"The 'spit thing,'" Snep repeated slowly.

Autumn grimaced. "I hadn't mentioned that," she muttered.

Shit. Well, too late now. "Part of the curse is that I'm kind of, um, turned on by, um, spit. And I know maybe you didn't see it but it's definitely there." Her ears burned by the time she finished.

Snep stared at her with an unreadable gaze for an uncomfortably long time. "Are you asking me to test if that is truly part of the curse as well, Miss Talirend?"

"Will this hurt, too?"

"It will not."

She felt self-conscious, but nodded.

The snow leopard stepped forward, took her hand, tilted it so the palm pad was facing up, and then spat in it.

Saida's ears went back. "Ewww!" She jerked her hand back with enough force to get it free, and wiped it frantically on her jeans.

"Do you feel...turned on?" His face remained studiously blank.

"No!"

"Let's mark this as 'not a curse,' then. Will there be anything else, Miss Talirend?"

Autumn covered a giggle.

A Different Side

"WHY, THAT ALMOST MAKES IT SOUND LIKE YOU LIKE being loomed over." Judy grinned down at Kim.

The raccoon woman and Autumn sat around a table in the dorm's common area, with Kim—the goat barista from Higher Grounds—sitting on the table between them. All three had coffee drinks Kim had brought with her; Autumn had enlarged hers and Judy's. Judy had just suggested Kim let Autumn enlarge her, too; the goat had, as she always did, demurred, saying, "I like it down here."

Kim snorted at Judy's teasing, sipping her own drink—a simple Americano rather than the rabbit's cappuccino or the raccoon's white mocha. "I'm not a macrophile. You think I'm just down here to stare at your tits?"

The raccoon set her coffee down and slowly leaned over until her head was right over the goat's—letting her sizable-even-in-scale chest hit the table's surface.

Kim's eyes got very, very wide.

Judy lowered her voice to a sultry whisper. "Why, you don't have to just stare, sugar." She traced a finger down from her collarbone.

Autumn snorted. "Stop trying to make the goat burst into flames."

"Not a macrophile," Kim got out between unsteady breaths. "Back me up, Autumn."

The rabbit raised her hands. "Look, I wanted to talk to *both* of you and it'll be tough if you turn Kim's brain to mush first."

"Fine, fine." Judy sat up, picking up her drink again.

"So—" Autumn stopped, feeling her phone buzz in her pocket. "Uh, hang on." She fished it out, taking a look.

Talking to an acquaintance who'd know about this kind of work makes me pretty sure I was right: that guy was a private investigator, of the sleazier kind. Since I haven't found him, I can't find a paper trail back to who hired him, but the connection to the beacon limits that pretty sharply.

Nobody's directly confronted me at work about this yet, but it has to be Raiben or one of my direct reports who thinks they can get me fired by getting dirt on me and going to Raiben with it. I'd like to think Mradhi would be some kind of shield, but he positively grilled me about the extra day I took with you to visit Snep. I told him as much as I was willing to—he already knows I'm going to Mensura, after all—but he made some unsettling comments about how it was getting harder to keep my two beacons "off the books." The one in Mensura has never been on the books.

Anyway, I'll keep you posted. I doubt I can get back next weekend, and I'm sorry to push the next visit to three weeks away, but all things considered I don't want to push my luck. At least we have the email gateway set up. Keep writing!

Love, Saida

She tapped back a quick reply before putting her phone away: *Keep me posted. I'll write more later. XXX*

"How often do you email that cat?" Judy said, smiling.

"Every day. That's—sort of what I want to talk about. How to handle a long-distance romance. She won't be able to visit again next weekend because her work is getting crazy. Not normal office crazy, but spy intrigue crazy. I'm worried they're looking into her traveling here."

"They don't know she's traveling between worlds?" Judy sipped her coffee, setting the paper cup down in just the right position to let her fingers land within a couple feet of the goat.

"Her brother does. He's the CEO. But nobody else."

Kim gave Judy a suspicious stare, then walked over to the raccoon's hand, leaning her back against it with an almost challenging expression.

She leaned forward over Kim. "If you want me to pick you up, just ask."

The goat's ears splayed. "I've been picked up by giants before. Well, by Autumn."

"Autumn's nice. So you might not think about how a giantess who picks you up can do absolutely anything she wants to you." Judy dropped her voice to a more seductive register. "Or how she could do anything *you* want to you."

Kim stared up, frozen, for several long seconds. "Stop trying to make me flustered," she said weakly.

"Oh, you sweet little thing. I'm barely trying yet." She fluttered her eyelashes. "But, yes. Autumn. Your crazy sci-fi romance. That gives new meaning to 'long distance.'"

Autumn nodded and sighed, leaning back in her chair.

"I don't know if I have *good* advice. I tried once, with my high school sweetheart, after I went off to college and he stayed home to work on his family's farm."

"Seriously?" both Autumn and Kim said at the same time.

The raccoon laughed. "Neither of you know much about giant lands, do you?"

They both shook their heads.

She nodded, smoothing down her dress and taking another sip of the coffee. "They're...provincial. Different species rarely mix except in the city, and when I say 'the city,' I mean the one, singular city. *Maybe* sixty thousand people. We thought of it as a huge metropolis, and the towns of fifteen or twenty thousand as big city life. I think there's *maybe* half a dozen of those. So, yes, there's a lot of small towns, a lot of farmers and ranchers."

"A city of sixty thousand giants." Kim stared up. "And there are farm animals on your scale."

"Of course, dear." Judy laughed. "There are animal goats and people goats—and raccoons and rabbits—on *your* scale, so why wouldn't there be on ours?"

"It's just kinda terrifying to think about from down here. Anyway, Autumn, it sounds like you and Saida are doing the right thing—staying in touch every day, planning regular visits. That's what I was doing with Rachel."

"But you and she broke up." She glanced at Judy. "And you didn't stay hooked up with your high school crush, did you?"

"No, and we're both happier for it." The raccoon waved a hand. "He didn't see the appeal in mixing sizes at all. My ambitions and appetites were bigger than his."

"For me, as we both got busier we stopped planning regular visits, and our every day chats became every few days, then every week or two, then..." Kim shrugged. "Then after a couple months with no contact, Rachel emailed me to talk about her new boyfriend. I emptied a bottle of tequila fantasizing about head-butting both of them to death, then sent back 'Great' and deleted her contact."

"Well, this all puts my mind right at ease, you two. Thanks a bunch."

Judy leaned over the table—letting her chest slide more toward Kim, who let out a dismayed bleat—and put a hand on Autumn's. "We can't tell you this is going to be easy if it won't, dear. Tell me this. Where do you see your relationship with Saida after college?"

"I don't know."

"Think about it."

Where *did* she see it going? She'd had that first night and two weekends with the Rha, and a handful of emails. It wasn't a hell of a lot to build a lasting relationship on. The times their conversations had touched on economics, they hadn't seen eye-to-eye, so how compatible were they politically? She got the impression Saida was progressive by Rha standards, but that might just be her projecting. She didn't *know* Rha standards.

"I know it's going to be...hard," she finally said. "I think there's more here than just physical attraction. But I literally *can't* move to

Stravell, and she's a rich executive there, so I can't ask her to move here. Do we still just see each other every other weekend?"

"If it works for you." The goat hadn't been bowled over by Judy's prodigious chest, although she hadn't stepped back from it, either. "I know it sounds sappy, but if it really *is* what you think it is, you'll hammer it out."

"And the physical attraction doesn't hurt," Judy added.

Autumn sighed, slumping down in her chair and sipping more latte. "I mean, yeah, it's totally there, but it's like—I want to—to—urgh." She rubbed her face.

Judy leaned forward, brows lifting. "You'll have to be a little clearer, sugar."

"She brings out a side—I'm not—a side in me I didn't—I am so lost explaining this."

"Hmm. Well, this is a stab in the dark based on what you're saying now, what you're *not* saying now, and just from knowing you." The raccoon moved to rest her elbows on the table, chin in her hands. "You want to see her in nothing but a cute little collar with a nice leashable D-ring."

Autumn spluttered, staring at the raccoon.

"Or *maybe* wearing just that collar, shrunk down to our adorable little goat's size, kneeling in your hand and calling you," she finished in a breathy tremolo, "mistress."

The rabbit's ears had started to burn. By the time Judy finished, she'd nearly sunk under the table. "I..."

Kim's stare didn't help, equal parts shock and amusement. "Holy shit, Autumn."

"Hey." She swallowed, giving the goat a glare. "You've talked about clubs you've been to."

"Yeah, but..." Kim rubbed one of her horns, sighing. "Yeah. I guess it's the size aspect that makes me go 'holy shit.' But you always did have a dommy vibe for a bunny."

Autumn rubbed one of her ears. She did?

"Mmmm." Judy sipped her coffee, looking highly amused. "What does Saida think of this?"

"We haven't talked about it. She's insistent she doesn't have a submissive streak, but..." She cleared her throat. "I kinda think it's more that she's scared she does. So I'm not sure how to go there. Or even if."

"Obliquely, dear." Judy smiled. "Give her a safe space to think about it. You know I have dates with littles, and there's always an element of submission and dominance there."

"Always?" Kim stared up at her skeptically.

"Always," Judy repeated, looking back down at Kim with a mischievous grin. Then she looked back to Saida. "If these thoughts are bouncing in little Saida's head as much as they are in yours, she'll let you know, if she feels she can do it safely. Set up safe words. Let her be the one who decides she wants to be helpless with you. Navigating this might just be easier than who lives with who if you're still together in five years."

I'll have a place of my own and she'll have a dollhouse. Autumn felt herself blush again at the thought, and she just nodded slightly.

"I guess I didn't really think about dom/sub this way. I mean, with all the size...stuff." Kim furrowed her brow. "But yeah, I think Judy's right."

"Thanks." Autumn sighed. "I'm not sure I know where I'm going with this, but talking about it helps. You want me to give you a walk back to town?"

"Sure."

Judy smiled, downing the rest of her coffee and licking her lips. "Oh, I can do it if you'd like." She rested her hand on the table by the goat, palm up.

"I..." Kim stared at the giantess's palm pads. "Right after all the conversation about how if you have me in your hand you could do anything you want with me?"

"Why, all I'm offering is a pleasant, perfectly safe walk back off campus." Judy winked. "Anything else is up to you."

Kim grumbled. She finished her own coffee, took a deep breath, and then climbed on all fours onto Judy's hand.

Autumn smirked, shaking her head. "And she converts another one."

Judy slowly lifted her hand up into the air, even as Kim turned to give Autumn a glare.

The raccoon giantess stood up, then set Kim down on her collarbone. The goat's eyes got wide again, mouth dropping open. She sank into the raccoon's plush fur, clutching at it as she looked down into Judy's cleavage, then back up at the muzzle right overhead. She managed a weak, breathy bleat.

Autumn patted the raccoon's shoulder as she got up. "She's my favorite barista. Please don't break her."

CHAPTER 17

Tough Woman

Jonry's tail lashed as he glared across at Saida. "Why are you coming down on me for doing my job?"

"I'm not. I'm coming down on you for taking two of Windswept Realty's VPs out to a titty bar."

The office personnel manager, a quiet but polite woman old enough to be Saida's mother, winced. Apparently, Jonry hadn't figured out what Karelle's presence meant yet.

He rolled his eyes. "It's not politically correct. I get it. But deals happen at places like that all the time."

"The deal happened when they signed the contract at their office."

"You know what I mean."

"What I know is that this is not the first time, and that I've given you *two* warnings about this behavior before. One of the three Windswept executives they sent out here for this deal was a woman. How do you think she felt about your choice of dinner restaurants?"

"We didn't take her." His ears lowered. "She complained to you?" He didn't finish with *that cunt*, but she could hear it in his tone. She'd overheard him speak of female clients that way in the past, when he thought she was too far away to hear.

"No, Jonry, she complained to Windswept's CEO, Mikka Taversi, and *she* complained to me."

His ears splayed. "Mikka's not a woman's name."

"It's a unisex name, and she's been profiled in a half-dozen business magazines as a feminist icon. Which you should have known, since that's basic client research. Because you closed that deal at a 'gentleman's club,'" she made air quotes with her claws extended, "I had to spend two hours on the phone with Taversi and her junior exec."

He squirmed in his seat. "Sorry, but look. That's kind of a freak one-off, isn't it?"

"I don't *know* whether it's a freak one-off. I looked at your expense report, and that club isn't on there. Maybe you've buried it somewhere in your strangely high 'miscellaneous' figure, maybe you're paying for it out of pocket, I don't know. But I have no idea how often you've been doing this, so I don't know how many deals you've closed this way. I also don't know how many deals you've *lost* by being a retrograde lounge lizard. You can close deals at a steakhouse or any number of other expensive clubby places that *don't* risk having our company held up as an example of 'rich assholes behaving badly.'"

His tail lashed again, but his ears had lowered. "Did you save the deal?" he muttered. He sounded less hopeful than resentful, as if he expected this to become another lecture about how she cleaned up one of his messes.

"Yes, with a promise that we were going to have a serious talk."

"By 'talk,' do we mean, like, 'talk about not doing this again' or 'talk about you cleaning out your desk?'" Jonry smiled nervously.

"I'm sorry, Jonry, but we can't keep doing this."

His ears flattened. "What? You are *not* telling me you're throwing me under the bus." He pulled his lips back in just the barest hint of a threat.

Oh, do *not* pull that shit. She kept her voice perfectly level. "Jonry, I haven't thrown you under a bus. I've been trying to stop you from running in front of buses screaming 'I dare you,' and you've refused to listen."

He opened his mouth, but thought better of what he was going to say, just sinking down into his seat with a scowl.

Saida nodded to the personnel manager, who handed Jonry a folder that she'd already prepared. "Review this and we'll sign it in my office. Assuming you accept the terms, you'll get a generous severance package, and we'll classify this separation as a layoff rather than termination with cause."

He took the folder and nodded slightly, looking sullen.

"Do you have any questions?" Saida said.

He shook his head, just as slightly.

"All right." She nodded toward the meeting room door. "Good luck in the future, Jonry. If I can offer a piece of advice, consider treating women more like actual people than decorative furnishings."

That just made his scowl deepen. He pushed back from the chair, standing up, and slunk quickly out of the conference room.

"You're a tough woman, Ms. Talirend," the personnel manager said quietly, tone admiring rather than admonishing. She flashed a small smile and left as well.

Saida got up, closed the door, walked around to the chair she'd been sitting in and dropped into it heavily.

She'd never fired anyone before. She'd come close, with a kindly but none-too-talented older salesman, but he'd seen the writing on the wall and left on his own. This was the first time she'd had to draw up termination papers.

In movies and television shows, bosses were always the villain. Bureaucrats who couldn't handle their employees thinking outside the box. Gleeful jerks who enjoyed power games. Nobody in those stories ever *really* deserved to be fired.

Goddess, was she crying? She was. She felt nauseous. She felt like throwing up. And she knew nobody would have a damn bit of sympathy for her. It didn't matter how much Jonry deserved it. She wasn't the one whose life had just been upended. Bosses were always the villain.

About fifteen minutes later, she felt composed enough to step out of the room, and headed to the break area for some coffee. Jonry was gone. The two remaining salespeople studiously avoided looking at her.

"Saida."

She paused on the way back to her desk. Raiben had poked his head out of his office and was motioning at her. "Yes?" she crossed over, standing by the taller orange tabby in his tailored casual suit.

He didn't invite her into the office. She'd realized a few weeks ago that this was one of his power moves: "friendly" hallway conversations that made it possible, even likely, for other staff to overhear what was being said. "How'd it go with Brakar?"

"I suppose as well as you'd expect."

"Firing is hard. It's a shame to have lost him. He was a good performer."

"Performance wasn't the issue."

"I know. It's just—are the numbers from this contract so good they back up saving it by letting him go?"

She struggled to keep her tail from lashing. "Windswept's talking about not just equipping their offices but their boutique condo units worldwide. So, yes, they do. It could become our biggest contract to date. But with all respect, Mr. Raiben, again, that wasn't the issue. Jonry was lying on expense reports and exposing us to a host of potential harassment lawsuits. You saw the memo the personnel office drew up."

He nodded. "You're his manager. It's your call. Speaking of reports, though, I don't think you've completed all of your asset inventory spreadsheet, have you?"

If it's my call, then why are you not-so-subtly questioning it? "I emailed it back last Friday."

"You included all the information about the beacons you're using? Second sheet of the file."

"I...yes, I'll check." Her tail-tip twitched in spite of herself.

"Good. Thanks." He ducked back in his office.

She walked back to her cubicle, setting down the coffee and opening the asset spreadsheet again. *What second sheet?* This hadn't had a second sheet last time she filled it out.

There it was, though. Asking for the serial numbers of all beacons she'd been given by the company, their installation locations, their primary use cases, if any non-employees had access to the network through the beacon and, if so, who.

Her ears lowered. It all seemed blandly straightforward, with suggestions for use cases like "work commuting" or "second home" and notes that they only had to put down cities, not street addresses. But before when they'd done inventory they'd just listed beacons along with everything else on the first page. The second home example made it clear enough: if you had two homes, which she doubted more than two employees counting herself did, you needed to list both of the beacons. This was a fishing expedition about *her* beacon usage.

The one in Mensura, though, didn't even have a serial number, just an identification tag, something like "EVT-2." That was back from when the company was just her and Mradhi, no offices, back when it felt more like her brother's crazy science project. She'd never listed it on an asset report before, and what location could she list for it, anyway?

Finally, she just copied the information about her home beacon from the first page to the second, simply entering "travel" as the use case. Exceedingly nondescript, but not lying, either.

Saida stayed around her cubicle the rest of the day, taking lunch alone at a nearby deli, and left to head home precisely at the office's official closing time, teleporting rather than walking.

After pouring herself a glass of wine, she sat down and tapped out a quick message to Autumn, mostly ranting about the day. *I know I didn't make a mistake firing him*, she wrote. *But that doesn't make me feel any better about it. And I'm positive Raiben is up to something. I just don't know what.*

After sending it off, she turned on the television, switching to a game show. She didn't think about the email until her phone beeped about a half-hour later with a reply.

Or, at least she thought it would be a reply. Instead it was a cryptic error message:

warning: gateway connection refused
status=deferred (mail transport unavailable)

Setting down her wine, she got up and crossed to the corner, checking the beacon's status lights. It seemed to be fine.

Gateway. Did it mean the hack that Mradhi had set up years ago to get messages and email between here and Mensura, using the beacons as a bridge? The data line between the beacon and her home network was still connected, and the light by its port showed a good connection. And...that was about as much troubleshooting as she knew how to do. She was fairly tech-savvy, but this was well beyond spreadsheet power user level.

Biting her lip, she picked up her phone and gave Mradhi a call.

"I didn't know you were still using that," he said after she described the problem.

"Yeah, I am. Doesn't whatever you set up to convert currency between here and Mensura use the same system?"

"It does." He hesitated. "I'll get the system back up later, but there are some outside security consultants running checks on our company's IT infrastructure this week."

"This is something the new IT guy wanted to do, huh? But this isn't part of our 'company infrastructure.'"

He started to sound agitated. "No, it isn't. It's an undocumented, unauthorized server tunneling over our company's proprietary infrastructure from a high-ranking executive's personal network to an undocumented beacon, and it's in your best interest not to call any attention to it."

Her ears lowered as he spoke. "You're the CEO. Can't you just— sign off on this?"

"No," he said curtly. "How did you document your beacons on your asset report?"

"I only mentioned the one I have here, and I said I use it for travel. Mradhi, what is going on?" She nearly mentioned the private investigator, but drew herself back. If he didn't know, maybe she should tell him, but if he *did* know...

"I suppose we're growing up as a company."

She grunted. So emailing Autumn was out, and she'd have no way of explaining it to the rabbit until she could get back to Mensura.

When they hung up, she poured out the rest of the wine and poured herself a glass of *ulvi*—a colorless, high-proof herbal liquor—instead, turned off the television, and sat drinking in silence.

CHAPTER 18

Testing

WHILE SAIDA USUALLY LOOKED CUTE FLUSTERED, tonight she looked more angry flustered as the rabbit waved to her. Still cute, but with a manager-slash-predator edge to it Autumn rarely saw her show.

"I'm sorry. Again. Arvya's sake, this has been a shit week." The cat pulled the chair back from the table at the Beanstalk and dropped down into it with a groan.

"You explained already. I'm not upset. I knew it was some kind of technical error when I saw the 'mail transport unavailable' message." She'd gotten the same quasi-secluded corner table she'd been sitting at when she'd first met Saida months ago; it had always been her table, when she could get it. Now maybe it'd be their table.

"*I'm* upset. The gateway going out at the same time they're doing this 'asset inventory?' That's not a coincidence."

"And you think it's, what's his name, Raiben?"

"Absolutely. The pretext is that our new IT manager is trying to get a firm handle on the situation he's coming into, but guess who brought that new manager in?"

"Raiben got your old IT manager fired?" She didn't know much about internal company politics, but that sounded brutal.

"We didn't have an old IT manager. Raiben convinced Mradhi that we needed one. He got the director of *marketing* fired to bring on another executive from his old company, though. I mean, technically he became her boss, then let her go."

"Just to bring in one of his cronies? And your brother's okay with that?"

"It's part of 'growing up' as a company." If the Rha's tone had been any more acidic it would have burned through the table.

"Three Lords." She took a sip of her beer. "You think he's in on it? With Raiben, against you?"

Saida shook her head, then paused, sighing and slumping back. "I don't know. I don't think so. But he's gotten even more cryptic than usual lately."

Clearly a *yes, I'm worried he's in on it,* but encouraging her girlfriend's anger wouldn't help. "Relax. Forget about it for the weekend."

The cat sighed. "I'm going to try."

"Take it as an order, little cat."

"I wish it worked that way." Saida snorted. "I should get a beer."

"Yeah." Autumn finished hers in a gulp, flashing back to the talk with Judy and Kim. It *could* work that way, maybe, if Saida let it, but damned if she could see how to bring that up. Maybe...hmm. "Get me one, too." She slid her empty glass across the table.

"Sure." Saida stood up and took the glass. "Which one?"

"The raspberry wheat. You get it, too. It's about dinner time, too, right?"

"Yes."

"Let's split a small pizza. Half sausage and mushroom, half pepperoni and pineapple."

"Pepperoni and *pineapple*? Really?"

"You'll like it."

The Rha looked skeptical, but headed off to the counter.

Autumn let out a deep breath. Promising start. This might just work.

Shortly the cat returned with two glasses, setting Autumn's down before she took her own seat. "Raspberry wheat, huh?" She took a cautious sip. "That's good. I don't think I'd have ordered it on my own."

"You like rosé wine."

She hmphed. "Hardly the same thing."

"It was an educated guess." *By which I mean "lucky," but we'll leave that out.*

The cat smiled, leaning back. "You're back at full goth look tonight, aren't you?"

"It's what I was wearing when we first met."

"And you'd still catch my eye from across the room."

Autumn tried not to too obviously melt into a happy puddle. That'd undercut the experiment. "You'd still catch mine."

The pizza came out quickly, barely fifteen more minutes. The server was the same retriever who'd been there the first night they'd met, too. "Here you go, ladies." He set the pizza down in the center of the table, then set down two plates.

"Thank you." Saida flashed her bright smile up at the dog.

"You're welcome." His tail wagged as he walked off.

"All right." Saida started to reach for one of the sausage and mushroom slices.

Autumn reached out and guided her hand toward the pepperoni and pineapple. "That first."

Saida sighed theatrically. "Fine." She worried the piece away from the pie, dropping it on her plate and licking at her fingers. "It's too hot to eat yet, though."

Autumn picked up a piece, looking levelly down into Saida's eyes, and took a bite. Crap, the cat was absolutely right, it was molten lava. She managed to keep her face expressionless.

Saida smirked. "Okay, you're somehow making eating pizza look all sexy-aggressive, but you are burning the shit out of the roof of your mouth right now, aren't you?"

She swallowed. "Yes. Fuck, that was really stupid." She took a huge gulp of beer.

Saida laughed, and picked up her own slice, blowing on it a little, then took a far more careful nibble, then another. "This is pretty good," she admitted.

"Of course it is. Giant goths know their pizza."

"I can say with certainty all the ones I know do."

Autumn grinned, eating her own slice, this time more carefully. "So. I want to get your mind off your office situation. Tell me if the best way to do that is to try and work through it with you, or keep doing things that keep you from thinking about it at all."

"I don't know how you can work through it with me any more than we have."

"You're always 'on' at the office, right?"

"What do you mean?"

She waved the pizza slice—just crust, now—around. "The stereotype here is that women have to work twice as hard to get half the recognition. It's changing, but there's a way to go."

Saida shrugged, sighing. "I guess I'm just used to that. If I act like the male executives I've met—hell, if I do what Mradhi tells me I should, half the time—I get accused of being shrill and aggressive and demanding." She waved a hand. "There are some ways Stravell feels more progressive than here, but a famous line from a feminist scholar was 'we put women on pedestals, then beat them if they try to step off.'"

"So what do you do?"

"Just like you said. Work twice as hard. I may be self-taught, but I've studied a *lot*. Maybe I'm a tough taskmaster, but I know how good our sales department is under me." She slumped. "Except for Jonry."

"You got rid of him, though, when you had to."

"And that might be more ammunition for Raiben."

Autumn picked up her second piece of pizza, this time switching to the sausage. "Okay, let's try the 'do things that keep you from thinking about it' instead."

Saida laughed. "Let's."

They made small talk as they finished the pizza, Autumn trying to guide the conversation: her classes, how friends were doing, people she should introduce Saida to sometime. Leading like this wasn't something she was used to, but it came more naturally than she'd expected.

"It's still an early evening. What do you do around the college for fun on weekend nights?"

Autumn laughed. "There's an outdoor concert tomorrow we can go to. Tonight, though...a movie at your place."

"Anything in mind?"

"Something you won't mind missing parts of if I keep you distracted."

Saida laughed. "That makes it an even better offer."

They held hands as they walked back. Autumn led them on a less direct but prettier route through some of the college's open space preserve.

When they got to Saida's little suite, Autumn headed to the sofa, slipping off her sandals. "Why don't you get us both glasses of rosé." She kept her voice casually light, but made sure it wasn't a question. Keeping this up while trying to keep it from being obvious was like walking a tightrope.

"Since when did *you* like rosé? Isn't that against the goth code?"

Autumn leaned forward. "Now I'm just going to be insistent about it, little cat."

Saida smirked, shaking her head. She went to the kitchen and returned with two glasses, handing one to the rabbit, then starting to take a sip.

"Don't we wait until we clink glasses?"

The cat stopped, giving the rabbit an exasperated but amused look, and held out her glass.

Autumn waited until it felt like it was just past a comfortable delay, then clinked her glass to Saida's and took a sip of the wine. Honestly, pink sweet wine probably *didn't* fit the image, but not following arbitrary rules—like "goths don't like rosé"—did. And while she knew next to nothing about wine, she could tell this was good stuff.

"All right." Saida picked up the remote control, turning on the TV and starting to flip through channels.

"That one," Autumn said after a few seconds.

"What?" She paused. "What is it?"

"It looks like the start of 'Slow Lane.' It's a rom-com from about ten years ago about a fox from a big city who moves to a small town in the South and falls in love with...somebody. Honestly, I haven't seen it."

"But you've wanted to." Saida sounded uncertain.

"I do tonight."

Grunting, the cat set down the remote and leaned back. Autumn put her arm around her shoulders, pulling her smaller girlfriend close.

Liking the movie also wouldn't fit the goth image. Fortunately, she didn't. The acting was fine, the fox and coyote leads had great chemistry, but it fell into that long-standing facile narrative about simple country folk being more "real" than shallow hipster urbanites. Her suburban hometown had embraced the same notion, leaning hard into its rural self-image. And it had mostly been hell. Her dysphoria hadn't made it any easier to fit in, but she'd had more than one straight cis friend who'd been made nearly as miserable.

About twenty minutes into it, Autumn figured it might be time to push a little more. Her nose wiggled as she considered a moment. "Hey."

"Hmm?"

She gave Saida's nose a kiss, then pointed down. "Rub my paws?"

Saida blinked, looking down at the big bunny paws. Yes, there was a bit of that fluster in Saida's expression. Good. She wasn't *quite* sure she'd seen that look in the Rha's eyes when she was shrunken and staring at Autumn's "huge" paw, but she'd had a definite suspicion.

"Okay," the Rha said. "Lift them up." She waved her hand.

"You just sit down there." She pointed at the floor again.

Saida's ears skewed. "That seems..." She slid off the couch, sitting on the floor by the rabbit's paws.

"Yes?"

The Rha looked up. "Like you're testing me." She flashed a somewhat reproachful smile. "I told you I'm not submissive. More than once. And half our conversation tonight has been about me being the aggressive bitch boss. I'm used to giving commands."

Autumn leaned over, cupping her hand under the Rha's chin. "And I'm sure you're great at it," she said softly. "But if you want to

get away from that, maybe you should take commands for a while."
She took a deep breath. "Like you have been."

Saida stiffened. "What?"

"All this evening." Autumn kept her voice soft. "I didn't ask you
what kind of pizza you wanted, or what kind of beer, or what you
wanted. I just kept telling you what to do. And now you're sitting on
the floor at my paws."

Saida's eyes unfocused, and she let out her breath unsteadily.

Autumn kept her eyes on the Rha's expectantly.

After several long seconds of stillness, Saida abruptly scrambled
to her feet. "I think you should go."

Oh, shit. This wasn't—

"I'll call you tomorrow. I promise." Saida took one of the rabbit's
hands in both of hers. "I'm not—I just—have to think. Alone."

Autumn felt her face fall. Part of her wanted to give Saida a
sharper order, a forceful *sit down*. But she couldn't risk that. "Saida,
this isn't—this isn't bad. This isn't weak of you."

"I didn't say that. I just—Autumn, just give me a little space
tonight to...process. Okay?" She closed her eyes. "You might think
I'm asking a lot, but...so are you."

Letting out a shaky breath, she nodded numbly, getting to her
feet. "I'm sorry," she mumbled. It's not like she'd suggested shrinking
her yet, suggested some of the things in her head, but maybe she'd
still pushed a little too hard. Maybe she should have denied she was
doing it and just dropped it.

Saida gave her a hug, at first awkward, then tight, giving the
rabbit a kiss—but on the cheek, not the lips. "I'll call tomorrow."

She looked down into the Rha's eyes. "Promise." She swallowed.
"Please?"

"I will."

Outside the Rha's door, she took a few steps, then stopped,
looking up at the clear, cold night sky. "That could have gone
better," she said aloud.

CHAPTER 19
Daiquiris

Saida had assumed all the condos in the staff housing block were identical to her suite, but this one wasn't just bigger—a true one-room apartment rather than a studio—it felt less like a hotel than like the home it was. From lean, modern metal and glass tables to dark blue sofas, brimming bookshelves, even a small dry bar near the kitchen, it had the tasteful but slightly eclectic style of her cousin. Arilin stood at that bar, pouring from a tall shaker into two martini-style glasses.

"When did you become such a bartender?"

She chuckled, walking over and holding out one of the drinks. "I've picked some skills up over the years."

Saida took a sip as the other Rha sat down by her. "This is a great daiquiri."

"It's only three ingredients, and it's been firmly impressed on me that the quality of those ingredients matters." She sipped her own drink, then set it down, readjusting her glasses and leaning back. "So. Let's talk."

She cleared her throat, fidgeting. Once she'd told Autumn that she hadn't been very close to Arilin in Stravell, and that was absolutely true. They were fifteen years apart in age, and she'd still been young when Arilin had been presumed killed along with her parents in the war. And the family whispers about her cousin, even after her "death," hadn't been very kind.

Since Saida started coming to Mensura, they'd become friends, but frankly, Arilin could be intimidating. The older Rha had an elegance, an assured ease, that sometimes Saida felt jealous of. A few years ago she'd started to consciously model her office fashion sense after her cousin. Even now, in a casual weekend meeting, she felt a little underdressed.

Well: not that casual. Less than an hour after Autumn had left, she'd called Arilin, asking if she could come over for advice.

While she'd intended to talk about the rabbit, maybe she could ease into it after the drink. Instead, she sketched out the outlines of her office problems, from Raiben's displacement of her to the spying, culminating with the mail gateway being shut down—and Mradhi's unsympathetic response to it all.

"So you think this Raiben fellow is trying to find a pretext to get you fired."

"Technically, I don't know if he *needs* a pretext. He's my boss now, and he's already fired one other executive just to bring in his own crony."

"But that other executive wasn't the CEO's sister."

"I know. So he has to get Mradhi on his side if he's going to get rid of me, doesn't he?"

Arilin didn't give her the nod of agreement she expected. Instead, the other Rha leaned back, tapping her finger against her own glass and looking thoughtful. "The beacon in your apartment is the one Mradhi set up for me here at first. He's brought it up to your company's commercial spec since it's been yours, right?"

"I think so."

"And he set up this mail gateway that's now been shut down, and rigged up the banking between worlds that you're using. I know he made contacts here—and with a bank back in Stravell—when he arranged to get me the inheritance that I would have received. As I recall, that involved a lot of grey areas, since I'm still legally dead back home."

"I guess so."

"So everything you think Raiben might be trying to dig up on you implicates Mradhi, too, and vice-versa."

"I know. Which means Mradhi might have to sacrifice me to keep his own job."

"Maybe." Arilin set her glass down on the end table again. "But when he went through my father's papers and realized my early prototype beacon might have malfunctioned in the lightning storm attack and sent me gods know where, he spent two years figuring out how to make a rescue attempt with no guarantee I was alive, or that the attempt wouldn't kill him, too." She shook her head. "He didn't know that would lead to a business idea, and he didn't even *like* me. Whatever Mradhi's faults may be, I would literally stake my life on his scruples."

Saida sighed, looking into her glass. "You're not wrong. But I don't know how else to explain what's happening."

"Raiben doesn't have to get Mradhi on his side if he gets rid of both of you."

Saida looked up, eyes widening. "You think he's trying to take over the whole company?"

"I think it's a possibility."

She rubbed her forehead. "Goddess. I have even less idea how to fight that."

"Decide what you want to fight *for*. Is it your job? Is it the company as a whole? Is it traveling between here and there?"

"All of it! I'm kind of, uh, in a relationship with someone here at the college."

"Miss Caligo."

She blinked. "You know about that?" Her ears lowered. "Who's gossiping to you?"

"I don't know if I'd say you're the subject of gossip." Arilin flashed a wry smile. "But people do know you around campus. You're 'Professor Thorferra's cute cousin.'" She tilted her head. "Is it your job that's most important, or is it being able to come here and visit, especially now that you have a girlfriend?"

"I can't have the one without the other. And it's the travel here—the beacon here in Mensura, specifically—he's trying to use to push me out. If I lose the job, I lose everything." An unpleasant shiver ran down her tail.

"Talk to Mradhi. See if he has the same suspicions, or if any of this makes sense to him."

"If you're wrong, and he *is* in on this, won't that just make things worse?"

"If he's in on it, you've already lost."

Saida groaned, taking a big swig of the daiquiri, then staring at the ceiling. "I'm so tired of office politics. If I'm not the diamond-hearted queen ruthlessly stomping people under my sandals, I'm too weak to handle my responsibility."

Arilin shrugged. "When I lived in Stravell, I didn't have any responsibilities, and I stomped people under my sandals for fun."

"I can never tell how serious you are when you say things like that."

"A silver lining of being a reformed sociopath is keeping people guessing about just how reformed you really are." She picked up her drink again. "I'd say you come here so you can let go of being the diamond-hearted queen, but I think you'd told me that you come here because you enjoy being a giantess."

"I do. That kind of leads into another problem I wanted to talk about, though." She sighed. "With Autumn."

"I'm not sure I'm the best one to go to for relationship advice."

"You've been in relationships since you've been here. Also you're the only person here I could talk to about this. No, the only person anywhere. Nobody back in Stravell would understand it at all."

Arilin's ears swiveled forward. "So it involves...hmm. Mixed sizes, since nobody in Stravell would talk about Rha-Liliren couplings in polite company. Autumn is a giantess, but noticeably bigger than you or I, so perhaps that counts. But—she's studied transformation magic." She tapped the side of her glass. "She wouldn't want to shrink herself, so she wants to shrink you, perhaps."

"For Arvya's sake, stop playing consulting detective." Saida raised her hands, feeling the blush in her ears. "She wants—she thinks—she thinks I should let go of being the one in charge by, uh, letting her be the one in charge."

Arilin nodded expectantly, clearly waiting for more.

"Really in charge. Like...giving me commands."

"All right." Arilin still looked expectant.

Saida glowered. "What do you mean, 'all right?'"

Her cousin shrugged, leaning back and crossing her legs. "You enjoy being implicitly dominant by being a giantess. Believe me, I understand that. I understand being explicitly dominant, too. But you're clearly exhausted by having to be the dominant one at work, and if this wasn't raising questions in your mind you wouldn't want advice about it."

She crossed her arms. "Are you saying I secretly want to be dominated by a rabbit?"

"I'm specifically asking what attracts you to being giant. The power differential between you and a world where 'little' is normal?"

"I...yes, sure. But that's the opposite of what we're talking about."

"It's the flip side of what we're talking about, but not the opposite at all."

"Okay, fine. But just because I enjoy the one doesn't mean I enjoy the other."

"No, but it doesn't mean you *don't*, does it? It's natural to wonder."

"So back in Stravell when you were..." Saida caught herself, ears lowering. She'd avoided bringing up what she'd heard about Arilin's past there, but let herself rush right into that one this time.

"When I was a Liliren-killing psychopath?" Arilin's tone was amused, not bitter, which was both a relief and a little unsettling. "No, I didn't daydream about being at the mercy of a giant mouse. But after I'd ended up here, after I was...better, I wondered, yes. And I *have* been ankle-high to a mouse or two since then. It may well have been part of the healing process."

"What do you think I need healing from?"

"I don't know. I'm not you." Arilin shrugged. "But you've made enough oblique references over the last year to your mysterious curse that I can't help but suspect it ties in here."

Saida swallowed. "I didn't think we'd talked much about that."

"We haven't. But you've hinted it has something to do with you being made to feel like prey."

When had she done that? "Not just feel like it. Made it, period, and brought back." She sighed, finishing off the daiquiri. "It seems like I've been talking about it more and more lately, and the answers I get aren't the ones I want to hear."

The older Rha had lifted her brows at the first part, but seemed unruffled by the revelation. "What *are* the ones you want to hear?" She picked up Saida's glass with her own and headed back to the bar.

"That when Kenley the mage or god or demon or whatever the hell he is did this to me, it wasn't a damn blessing he tricked me into thinking it's a curse. That I don't really have a secret desire to be shrunken or swallowed whole or stepped on or Goddess knows what else, or wouldn't if it wasn't for him fucking with me." She heard her own voice rising in pitch and speed, as if she were listening to someone else edging into hysterics.

Arilin finished shaking up a new batch of the daiquiris, pouring it into the waiting glasses. "Because if you did have desires like that, it'd mean you weren't a real giantess?" She headed back to the living room, setting the glasses down.

"Because if I like it, it means he won!" Saida shrieked. Her eyes widened in shock at her own outburst, and her voice broke. "It means he won."

She didn't see Arilin sit down by her, she just felt the other Rha wrap an arm around her shoulders, pulling her close. Her cousin didn't say anything. She just held her, purring reassuringly, as Saida closed her eyes, tears starting to run.

CHAPTER 20

Melodramatic

THE MUSHROOM BURGER AT THE UNION FOOD COURT wasn't bad, just a little bland. Fortunately, the condiment bar always had a "sauce of the month," and right now they had a green chili aioli. Autumn could have one of *these* burgers every day.

At least, days when she didn't have a case of nerves like this. She threaded her way through the open space to a table by one of the huge windows—technically, a tile of many little windows, which weren't truly little at all. She usually sought out secluded dark interior areas, but she had a need to stare morosely at the cool gray sky.

As she sat down with her tray, she pulled out her phone again. Just past three o'clock: too late for lunch and too early for dinner. Well, she was a college student, so she had the right to a screwed up schedule. But still no messages. No missed phone calls.

She'd just said "tomorrow," not a specific time. And she'd promised.

Of course, she'd promised after their very first date, and then hadn't gotten back in touch for two months. But their relationship was better now. Wasn't it?

At least until her stupid command and control stunt.

Sighing, she slumped back in her chair, dragging a thick strip of fried potato through a puddle of ketchup. It didn't help much; the grill's chips were notoriously uneven, and today's batch were pale and soggy.

Three Lords, had she read everything wrong? Saida liked being little around her, didn't she? But even if Autumn had made the suggestion, the Rha had come to the decision on her own. This time, Autumn had just sprung it on her. Had she treated their relationship like some kind of taste test? Surprise, you've been drinking the store brand diet soda all along!

She'd gotten lost enough in her thoughts that she didn't process someone calling her name until the third try. "Autumn!"

Blinking, she turned away from the window, looking—oh. Up, at the railing for one of the "little" levels that had a balcony overlooking this seating area. A rat, kind of cute in a ripped-jeans punk way, stood there waving at her.

"Jen. Hey." She waved back perfunctorily. Jen was another MAP student, and thanks to their shared interest in transformation spells —and size spells, specifically—her occasional lab partner. Nice enough, although Jen's frustration with Snep got transferred onto Autumn occasionally. The rat wanted to rush through her spells to get to the "good stuff" as fast as she could, and Snep would have none of it. That Autumn had arguably been allowed to rush through *her* spells to get to the good stuff could be a bit of a sticking point.

"Hey." The rat leaned over the railing in a way that looked precarious. "How are you doing on Snep's combinatory alchemy thing?"

"Fine." She ran a hand through her hair. "Well, I haven't looked at it much, but it didn't look too difficult."

"So you follow the spectrometry bits?" Jen's tone made it clear she didn't.

"Yeah. We can go over it sometime if you want."

"That'd be great." Jen bit her lip. "Hey, are you okay? You didn't look real happy when I walked up."

"Just a lot on my mind about a relationship I'm in, assuming I haven't fucked it up to the point I'm not in it anymore." She sighed. "Sorry, I shouldn't unload on you."

"For whatever it's worth, you seem to have a pretty good head on your shoulders. If you do want to unload..." The rat shrugged. "I know we're not best friends or anything, but I'm a good listener."

"Thanks, but—" She paused, as her phone buzzed. "Hang on." She pulled it out of her pocket hurriedly, then stared at the email she'd just received.

"Autumn?" Jen finally prompted.

"Sorry. Uh. Professor Thorferra wants to see me." She swallowed. "Now."

"Are you even in one of her classes this semester?"

"No." Autumn finished the burger, then got up, looking across rather than up at the rat. "It's, um, complicated."

Jen's ears folded back. "You're not dating *her*, are you?"

"No! Three Lords." She squinted as Jen's ears came forward again and the rat visibly relaxed. "Why?"

Jen sighed. "I might still have kind of a crush on her, okay?"

"Hey, I'm not standing in your way." Autumn grinned wryly, then tilted her head. "You're okay with mixed-size couples, huh?"

"I'm dating somebody else now. But yeah, I've thought about it..." She trailed off, then turned away, ears coloring. "...a bit. The SO you're having problems with, uh, they're not a little, are they?"

"No. Well, actually, that's complicated." She shook her head. "I have to get going."

"Okay. If you need to talk, though—call."

"I will." She took a step away, then paused, looking back with a half-smile. "Hey, I shouldn't ask this, but I can't help it. You like giant women, but..." She waved a hand at herself. "I guess I'm not your type?"

Jen stared down, silent for several seconds, then crossed her arms. "Apparently I was being *way* too subtle the first semester we were working together."

Autumn swallowed and smiled a bit sheepishly. "I was pretty... focused back then. Sorry."

The rat shrugged. "It is what it is." She made a shooing motion. "You don't wanna keep Thorferra waiting."

Autumn cleared her throat. "Right. Gotta go." She hurried away.

The humanities college lacked both the oversized gothic castle look of the magic arts college and the clever mixed-size modern architecture of the Student Union. Instead, it looked like any generic institutional building. On a grand scale, yes, and she knew there were subways for littles under the floor. She still remembered walking through them, listening to the steps of giants as they passed by above. But the building was far more function than form.

Professor Thorferra's office was toward the end of the hallway, marked by her name on a frosted glass window. A matching door at little scale stood near Autumn's paws, protected from accidental (or deliberate) misstep by a steel frame. Biting her lip, she knocked on the door.

After a moment, it opened. She'd forgotten how much family resemblance between Ms. Thorferra and Saida there was; the older Rha wasn't her cousin's twin, by any stretch, but if you stood them side by side, at first glance you'd only tell them apart by the different color palette: snow white fur rather than egg cream, blue eyes rather than green. And, of course, the suit. Ms. Thorferra looked like the high-powered executive Saida actually was.

"Miss Caligo." The Rha stepped out of the office, pulling the door to. "Let's walk, if you don't mind. I wanted to talk briefly, but don't want it to feel like a teacher-student conference."

"Okay." She ran a hand through her hair. "Is this about Saida?" She followed the Rha down the hall to a back exit and out onto the sidewalk.

"Yes, although it's not...hmm. I was going to say it wasn't as melodramatic as you might be imagining, but I don't know what you're imagining."

"That she's breaking up with me and couldn't face me herself, so sent you instead." Autumn tried and failed to keep her voice light rather than filled with dread.

Ms. Thorferra readjusted her glasses and smiled wryly. "Good news, then. It's not as melodramatic as you're imagining. She went back home to Stravell this morning, though."

"So the not being able to face me and sending you instead is right."

"Blame me for that, Miss Caligo. Autumn. I suggested she go home and let me apologize to you on her behalf for not calling today. She has a lot to process."

Autumn sighed, thrusting her hands in her pockets and slumping as they walked. "How much did she tell you? About, uh, what she's processing?"

"Enough. Arguably, more than enough. And I know more about her curse now than she'd been willing to share with me until last night. I assume she's shared details of that with you."

"Yeah." She nodded.

The Rha nodded, too, and looked like she was gathering her thoughts. "There are wounds there that haven't healed."

"I know. I'm trying to help, not hurt. Mostly with her fucked-up work situation. But I think she's...this is really awkward to talk about with you, Ms. Thorferra."

"If you call me Arilin, will it be less awkward?"

"No." She half-smiled, then lowered her voice, as if she might be overheard. "I think Saida likes being submissive. At least with the right people."

"You being one of the right people."

She nodded.

"Then don't try to trick her into going there."

Autumn felt the blood drain from her ears. "I wasn't!"

Arilin readjusted her glasses. "Autumn, you may be *the* right person. But think about Saida's first experience with being turned on by being at someone else's mercy."

"With Kenley, the guy who gave her the curse." She sighed. "And I imagine the times she's been eaten since then haven't been a lot better."

"I didn't pry for details."

"But I'm not like that. I'm not even sure I want to eat her!" She sighed, frustrated. "Three Lords, this is a weird conversation. I mean, I wasn't trying to make her feel trapped or something. I was trying to make her feel safe in giving up control. That's all."

"That's a lot." Arilin tilted her head. "She has to untangle her feelings about being helpless, even with you, from her feelings about being humiliated by Kenley. And I don't think she can do that if you take control from her without her consent."

"I'm not *trying* to—" Autumn cut herself off, closing her eyes. She wasn't, but that might not matter.

"I know." The Rha reached up to touch her shoulder. "I don't think your instincts about Saida are wrong, either. She's always had a fascination with powerful beings." Arilin waved her other hand. "Magicians, seemingly mythical creatures, giants far larger than you or I. And I know she's quite head over heels for you."

Autumn felt her ears flush, but she just nodded, looking aside and down at the professor. "You sound a lot more like a therapist than I'd expected."

"I've picked up some of the patter."

Arilin had led them in a circle around the building and up to the front door again, where she stopped, facing Autumn directly. "Again, you can blame me for sending Saida off without saying good-bye. I expect she'll be back next weekend, assuming her office troubles don't impact that somehow."

The rabbit grunted. "I forgive you, but that makes me worried. I mean, if she loses her job, or they suspend her and confiscate her beacon thing, she's not going to be able to get back here."

"That's a possibility, although I don't expect they'll move that quickly. And whatever our faults are, we're a resourceful family." Arilin pushed her glasses up again, and fixed Autumn with a sharper gaze, tempered by a slight smile. "Be gentle with Saida's heart, Miss Caligo. I'm more protective of her than I think she knows."

"Yeah, I've picked up on that. I will be. Thanks." Mostly thanks, at least.

After Arilin stepped inside, Autumn headed back toward the Union. She didn't blame Professor Thorferra for shooing her distraught cousin away from the girlfriend who made her distraught, but with the message gateway down, she was back to where they'd been right after that first date: waiting for Saida to get in touch with her.

As she headed to the Beanstalk for a sorely needed beer, her phone buzzed again. A message from her sister Kelly, just a single word: "Call."

When it rained, it poured. She hesitated, then put the phone away. She'd call, but she'd be on her second beer before she did.

CHAPTER 21

Coup

WHILE THE AFTERNOON WAS WARM—POSITIVELY HOT compared to the temperature back in Mensura—it was pleasant enough on her balcony that Saida was glad she'd taken her breakfast out here. Late enough to be lunch, yes, although it didn't feel fancy enough to be brunch: sausage, egg, and fried bread, the latter two cooked in the fat from the sausage. As she finished the last bite of sausage, she watched a boat go by on the river below. It was common for littles to say they could get a giant's-eye view of the world by looking out a high building, but it wasn't the same thing. The boat below looked small in the way something a great distance away did; a boat sailing a river by the college looked small in the way something, well, small did.

After shuttling between Mensura and Stravell, it was hard not to wonder how it all *worked*. Was this world all giant, or was theirs tiny? Or was the change somehow an artifact of the teleportation system? Would the magic in Mensura let them build something like this apartment building? At eighteen stories, this was one of the taller residential structures in the city, but not what anyone would call a skyscraper. But if it were transplanted to Mensura it would massively dwarf the tallest building in their world--without adding hundreds of extra feet by sticking on spires or masts. The campus didn't have a single multi-story building on a giant scale.

What attracts you to being giant?

She wasn't giant. She was just five foot seven, with a six foot nine *(one hundred foot)*

tall girlfriend in a doll-sized world.

What attracts you to being little?

Sighing, she took her plate inside, finishing the last of the pomla juice.

If you want to get away from that, maybe you should take commands for a while.

But she couldn't, not yet. The more she'd thought about it, the more she suspected Arilin was right: Raiben was going after the whole company, one way or another. Maybe he'd convinced Mradhi that all the execs below CEO level needed to be replaced with "more experienced" people—his cronies. She was clearly next on the chopping block. If Mradhi objected, maybe Raiben would back down. But maybe he'd threaten to go to the board. And maybe Mradhi wouldn't object. Either way, the only way to save *her* job would be to go after Raiben first—and she'd need Mradhi's support to do it.

She dialed Mradhi's number without knowing what she would say when he picked up. Well, she'd always liked to think she could argue well ad hoc.

The voice that answered, though, wasn't Mradhi's. "Hello, this is Rinni."

His wife, of course. "Hi, Rinni. This is Saida."

"Oh. Hello."

Saida's ears lowered. She'd considered Rinni at least a casual friend; they'd met when Mradhi was still dating her, and they'd even gone out shopping a together a couple times. But her voice had dropped from cordially warm to freezing. "Um, I need to speak to Mradhi. Is he around?"

"No. He's at a company board meeting."

"On Sunday?"

"It's some special meeting they've summoned him to."

Saida couldn't miss the slight emphasis Rinni put on *summoned.* "That sounds..." She flailed for an appropriate word, then settled on the honest one. "...ominous."

"I'll let him know you called." Her voice remained icy.

"Rinni." She spoke more softly. "Please tell me what's going on."

A long silence followed. Finally, the other Rha spoke in a voice less frigid but more miserable. "They told him it was about 'reviewing improprieties relating to running the corporation as a family business,' and when I asked him if that meant me he said no." Her voice sharpened again. "When I asked if it meant you, he didn't say anything."

"Raiben's making his move." She sighed, running a hand through her hair. "Do you know where they're meeting?"

"For Goddess's sake, Saida, you think barging into an emergency board meeting is going to make things better?"

"Do you honestly think it'll make things *worse*?"

Another long silence and a thin sigh. "It's at the office of one of the board members. That's all I know. What does Raiben have to do with this?"

"I think everything."

After they hung up, she hurried over to her computer, pulling up the company's own web site. Mradhi was one of the five board members, and two of the others were wealthy early retirees. Technically they *could* be meeting at some million-dollar mansion, but if Rinni was right about it being an office, that left the two working executives: Leegan Brossi and Zya Wilamin. The chances were the meeting would be at the office of whichever one was friendlier to Raiben.

She'd met both a couple times, but only in passing; she didn't have much sense of their characters. But Raiben had gotten rid of the company's other woman executive, seemed to be out for her, and every crony he'd brought on was male. If he was going to recruit an ally on the board, it'd be a guy. Brossi it was.

With flat sandals, shorts and a tee shirt, she wasn't dressed for a showdown, but she had no time to change outfits. At least it was a designer tee shirt. Grabbing her keys, she hurried out into the hallway to the elevator.

Time. How much time *did* she have? When had they started? Would they still even be there when she made it there? Swearing, she dropped into her car, a sporty little red convertible she didn't drive for fun nearly enough. Punching the name of Brossi's investment company into the GPS, she pulled out of the garage fast enough to make the tires squeal.

Twenty-two minutes. She gritted her teeth and turned on the radio, hoping it'd distract her. It didn't. Cars in Mensura would have streaming radio by now, wouldn't they? Or she'd be able to just plug her phone in, or have it connect wirelessly, or something. That would be so much better.

Except that she'd be carrying the car around in her purse. The image made her giggle in spite of herself.

Talirend Dynamics was on the other side of the city from her apartment building; Quadrangle Capital, though, sat across the river, a few miles northwest, nestled in the foothills. At first glance, the upscale office park looked like a continuation of a luxury resort right across the street. A couple of customers had met her to discuss sales contracts in the hotel's lounge, a sleek brass and wood affair that made decent ten dollar cocktails it charged fifteen dollars for. In the past couple years this neighborhood had become ground zero for a fledgling technology boom, one Talirend had been in the vanguard of. The tech companies didn't put their offices here—the venture capitalists they wanted to get money from did. VCs like, presumably, Leegan Brossi.

She did a circle around the office park's lot, looking for—ah. Yes, that was Mradhi's car, a high-end exotic masquerading as a sedan. It could leap twice as fast as Saida's off the starting line, but its relentlessly pragmatic owner rarely drove more than five miles over the speed limit. If he hadn't married Rinni, he'd own an economy hatchback or something. Saida pulled in a few spaces down, then dashed toward the building.

It took another three minutes of checking directories and sprinting down tastefully appointed hallways to find the Quadrangle office. Locked. Had she guessed the wrong location?

Buildings like this—shared offices—sometimes had shared conference rooms. Maybe they'd reserved one of those. Had they been marked on the map by the reception area? Swearing, she doubled back.

As she passed by the restroom, she nearly ran into someone stepping out. "Sorry," she mumbled, hurrying past, then stopped, doing a double-take. She knew that face, that tan-to-charcoal fur coloration, that frumpy business suit. "Ms. Wilamin?"

The older Rha woman stepped back, muzzle slightly open. "Ms. Talirend? What—why are you here?"

"Board meetings are open, aren't they?" She couldn't keep the hostility out of her voice.

"They called this one as an emergency."

She'd expected Wilamin to sound more shocked or affronted by her presence, but she just sounded tired. Defeated. With a slight start, Saida realized the older Rha had been crying. "And what was the emergency?"

The woman's ears lowered. She shook her head, then took one of Saida's hands in both of hers. "I was one against three, Saida. I'm sorry."

Saida's ears lowered, too.

Wilamin cleared her throat, dropping Saida's hand, and hurried away.

It took another three minutes of walking—in a slow daze, until urgency overtook her again—to stumble on the conference room the meeting must have taken place in. The door stood open, but the room was empty except for Mradhi, who sat in a chair facing the window, turned away from her. For a moment her mind filled with overdramatic, absurdly awful possibilities, that she'd find him dead through treachery or by his own hand. But she could see his breathing, see his ear flick when she slowly stepped in and took a seat.

He didn't speak for at least a minute, although it felt like ten. When he did, he didn't turn to look at her. "You spoke to Rinni."

"Yes."

"I hope she wasn't too angry with you."

"Maybe she was right to be."

He shrugged fractionally. "The company has always allowed

employees to have personal beacons. It's just...your second one can't be explained to the board without me sounding like a madman. 'It's a gateway between worlds that we're just keeping our little family secret.'"

She lowered her voice, although it didn't keep the edge out of it. "We always said we *had* to keep the beacon in Mensura out of the records. Was that wrong? Did we—did I—screw up?"

He shook his head, finally looking at her. "No. You didn't do anything wrong."

"Then neither did you!"

"This wasn't about whether I did anything wrong. It was about sowing doubt in my judgement." Mradhi steepled his hands on the table, leaning forward to rest his chin on them and stare into space rather than at her. "The board decided they lacked confidence in my suitability to lead Talirend Dynamics to the next stage of growth. So I'm being asked to step down."

Saida's tail bottled out, and she felt her claws come out involuntarily. She didn't know what she'd expected, but this— "It's your fucking company!"

"We—they—have investors, and..." He trailed off. "They'll start a search for a new CEO, but they're appointing an interim one starting tomorrow."

"Raiben." She couldn't keep herself from baring her teeth.

He looked down at the table. "When I brought him in, I told you I didn't think you'd make a good VP. I'm sorry for that."

"What? No. You were right." She sighed. "You're only reconsidering now because you brought in a snake."

He gave his little shrug again, still looking down. "You would have grown into the role, faster and better than I grew into a CEO. At heart, I'm an engineer. I'd been thinking about bringing in another CEO in another couple of years and stepping away. It should probably have been you."

She reached across the table and touched his hand. He let her take it, and they both stayed silent another minute or so.

"We should both get generous severance packages," he said. "A year's salary."

A chill ran down her tail. "What about our beacons?"

"We'll have to start paying service fees on our own if we want to keep them. And they want your prototype returned."

Her ears folded flat. "I can't give it back. I mean—that's literally true, isn't it? We'd need another beacon in Mensura to get the first one back." You could only teleport between beacons; only the fluke of Arilin's accidental teleportation there with an even earlier prototype solved that chicken-or-egg problem, and that flaky, dangerous early model had long since been decommissioned.

"Yes."

"So what do I do?"

"I don't know."

They both fell silent again.

CHAPTER 22

The Wrong Corner

SOMETHING TINY BUT HARD BOUNCED OFF AUTUMN'S paw. She blinked, realizing she'd started to drift again, and looked down to see her sister standing a few yards away from where the giantess sat cross-legged. "Did you just throw a rock at me?"

"I threw *three* rocks. This is the first one you looked down at."

"Oh." She frowned, rubbing her paw, although it didn't hurt. "You could have just called me."

Kelly put her hands on her hips, glowering up. "Did that twice, before walking out trying to find you. Fortunately you made yourself visible from space again."

"Sorry. I'm..." She sighed, then just let herself fall down to the grass, staring up at the sky.

Kelly yelped. "Being a hazard."

She stretched out her legs. "I'm not blocking any paths. I found a big field. I go to the park all the time."

"You go to the park back in Mensura where people aren't freaked out by having a giant goth girl loom over them. This is *not* Mensura. This is a town where we almost never see giants on the news, let alone in real life. Also, you're lying on the damn soccer field."

Autumn closed her eyes. "There's no game going on."

"No, there's not." Kelly's voice rose in volume. "Because the field is being taken up by a *giant goddamn rabbit.*"

"They'll reschedule."

Kelly sighed theatrically. After a moment, Autumn felt something against her side—then climbing up her.

She opened an eye and raised her head so she could look down the length of her body at her sister as she scrambled up to her stomach. "What are you doing?"

"I was climbing up to punch you in the nose, but it's seeming like less of a good idea from here."

"Yeah, probably not your best option."

Kelly grunted, and sat down where she was. Autumn lowered her head back to resume cloud-watching.

A few minutes passed in relative silence. Wind in the trees, cars in the distance, people playing games in other fields. And more than a little conversation about the giantess. *Three Lords, is that real? Is it dead? Is it allowed to be here? It won't hurt us, will it?* She fantasized about abruptly sitting up and roaring, but she didn't want to topple her sister. Much.

"So how's Saida?"

Autumn lifted her head again. "What, now we're making small talk?"

"You're not giving me much else to talk about."

"You saw how mom looked at me when she saw me. She didn't call me, you did, and I bet she didn't want you to. She doesn't want me here. She doesn't want my help at the house. She doesn't want me at the..." She found herself trailing off, and she didn't know why. She hadn't cried since she'd returned Kelly's call yesterday back at the college, gotten the news—the only news it could really have been. So it was odd the word *funeral* stuck in her throat. It was odd she hadn't cried yet, too. Wasn't it?

"She didn't say any of that. You're just reading into things."

"I don't have to read into them real deeply." She rubbed the back of her neck. "I'm going to sit up, because holding my head this way is killing me."

Kelly scrambled back to sit on her thigh, and she pushed herself up.

"I don't know what she wants. I don't know if *she* knows what she wants right now. I told her I was coming out to find you and bring you back and she didn't object." Kelly tilted her head back to look nearly straight up. "It might help if you weren't baiting her."

"How the fuck am I baiting her?"

She waved her hand up and down to indicate Autumn's giant form, making full sweeps with her arm to emphasize the point.

"Oh, come on. Me going back to being little isn't going to help. I'd still be wearing 'those clothes that make you look sad.' I'd still be attending a college both she and dad disapproved of. And, oh yeah, I'd still be a girl." She pointed a finger at Kelly accusingly. "And don't say I could change that back, too."

Kelly flinched, either because she'd been thinking that or because Autumn's claw looked like a curved obsidian dagger. "I wasn't gonna." She swallowed, then leaned forward, touching a finger to the giant claw. "You need to take better care of your nails. This is kinda pitted."

"It's fine." Autumn lifted her hand away. "You're just at a tiny scale."

Kelly snorted. "So are most of the people who are gonna be looking at you, and most of them are gonna see your claws. Especially those." She pointed at Autumn's toes. "Shrink your girlfriend down and give her a rotary sander, maybe a 320-grit disc..."

"Stop it." She hoped she hadn't blushed at the image; if Kelly noticed that, she'd never hear the end of it. "Look. I guess Dad was about as there for me in the end as he could get. I'm not going to be able to be there for him the same way, and that sucks, but it's the way it is."

"That's it?"

"I don't see Mom changing her attitude any time soon."

"Give her a chance."

"Dammit, Kelly, I've been giving her a chance for years. What else am I supposed to do? I can't meet her halfway beyond shrinking to fit in her dinky little house."

Kelly hunched down and fell silent. That might have been a deep cut; *c'mon, meet me halfway* was Kelly's favorite exasperated appeal in high school.

Sitting quietly—now with eyes open—made it painfully clear how right her sister was about this town and giants. People didn't even try to hide their stares, unless she let her eyes fall on them and they hurried off. More than one kid had run away screaming in the time she'd been sitting there; a few others had approached before being steered away by frightened moms. Back in Mensura, kids—and parents—didn't care so much. They'd even come up to Saida when Autumn was sitting with her and ask if they could climb her. Kids didn't do that with *her*, even though Saida was ostensibly the giant predator.

"I don't know how Saida is."

"Huh?"

"You asked how she was. I don't know."

Kelly's brow furrowed. "Shit, you didn't break up, did you?"

"No. I mean...I hope not. We had a fight a few days ago, and she went home without speaking to me, and because the thing that was somehow sending email between dimensions isn't working anymore I'm not gonna hear from her until she gets back in touch. If she does."

"You have a really complicated life," Kelly said after a few seconds.

"Don't I know it." She let out a long breath. "So should I let you drag me back?"

"As if."

Autumn grinned a little. "Hop down and I'll get small again." Kelly did as requested.

While she stood up slowly, it still caused more commotion among the park-goers. For the Lords' sakes. This time she couldn't resist: she leaned forward in a crouch, raising her hands over her head, claws out, and belted out her best roar.

Screams erupted from little crowds and pedestrians, and dozens of people—none of whom were very close to start with—started stampeding away.

Kelly threw her hands up in the air. "Goddammit, Autumn!"

She laughed, straightening up and casting the size-shift spell. "Oh, come on, it was funny."

"It was not—holy hell, you're seven feet tall!"

"Six foot nine." She shrugged. "It's what Saida said I'd be relative to her in her world."

"This isn't her world!"

"No, it's a world I'm a giantess in. This is as halfway as I plan to get from now on."

Kelly shook her head, trudging back toward the house, a ten-minute walk away. "You're insufferable."

"You're just pissed off 'cause your little sister's a foot taller than you are."

"I can still kick your ass."

"I can shrink you."

"Do it and I'll break each of your toes one by one." She mimicked bear-hugging one.

Autumn grinned.

When they reached the house, they glanced at one another. Knock, or just go in? Kelly made a decision before Autumn could ask out loud, though. She unlocked the door with her own key and motioned her sister inside.

The house smelled gaggingly sweet, the artificial cinnamon and sugar cookie room sprays her mother favored applied with a far too heavy hand. Otherwise, the only difference from the last visit was her mother, and only a difference someone who'd grown up with her would notice: she sat in the wrong corner of the couch.

For as long as Autumn had been alive, Evelyn Caligo had sat in the corner closest to the kitchen, her newspaper section—the one with the comics and the crossword—and her never-completed needlepoint on that side's end table. Jasper sat on the other side, with the rest of the newspaper—not that he'd ever seemed to read anything but the headlines—and the television remote. But tonight, her mother sat where her father normally would have been, hands folded in her lap, looking blankly at the dark television set.

It took her longer than usual to look up when Kelly and Autumn entered. She smiled, a smile so normal and broad it looked unsettling—as if her husband of decades hadn't passed suddenly due to a post-surgery complication, as if the daughter she refused to recognize wasn't standing there at all, much less at a truly ridiculous size. "Dinner should be ready soon."

Kelly took a seat by her mother. "Mom, you don't have to—"

"Yes. I do."

Autumn took a seat in an easy chair facing the other two rabbits.

Evelyn looked at her, pointedly raising her eyes from where she expected Autumn's eyes to be up to where they really were, although she kept a slight smile. "You want to remind me you're really a giant, I see."

"Mom—"

She raised a hand. "It's—it's fine." Her smile faltered, and she looked away. "Jasper talked a lot about you since your last visit. A lot for him, I mean. You know how he is. He was angry with me for fighting with you. And he was right. How I feel about the choices you've made doesn't mean I can't be friendly with you. I'm sorry. I'll do better."

Autumn's heart cautiously lifted, then sank back down as she peeled through the words. "But how you feel hasn't changed."

Kelly sank down in her seat, looking desperately like she wanted to be somewhere else.

Her mother sat still a few seconds, looking down at the carpet, before she rose to her paws. "The memorial service is in three days. Jasper and I both want you to be there, and at the wake. Before then, I think you should collect anything you've left in the house of yours that you'd like to keep." She ambled toward the kitchen.

Autumn clenched her fists, taking a deep, ragged breath. "Dammit, Mom!"

She paused, without turning around, puff tail twitching.

"Why the hell can't you be happy for me? Even now? Why can't you be happy that *I'm* happy?"

"That's not—it's—" Evelyn's voice cracked. "How can I do that when you were never happy until you stopped being my son?" She hurried into the kitchen.

Something dark clawed at Autumn's stomach. "Tell Evelyn not to make dinner for me," she said hoarsely. "I'm going to Gimpy's."

"Autumn—" Kelly started.

"Pick me up there on your way home, okay?" She grabbed her jacket and strode out of the house before her sister could respond.

Just outside the driveway, she grew, back to her full size, her right size, heading down the hill. Stick to the open space, follow the creek, just like her dad—her dad had told her—

She stumbled, vision blurring, then dropped to the ground with a tree-rattling thump. When the tears came a moment later, they came in great, wracking sobs, and she wasn't sure they would ever stop.

CHAPTER 23

Steampunk Poet

IT SHOULD HAVE BEEN RAINING THE DAY OF THE FUNERAL.

Autumn had let Kelly buffalo her into being her original size, not even six-foot-nine, for both yesterday's wake and this morning's ceremony. While she'd dressed formally, she did it her own way: a black frock coat with matching leggings and high boots, frilly white blouse, collar traded for a silver choker. And, of course, she kept the black lipstick, nail polish, and heavy eye liner. Her mother hadn't given her the disapproving glance she'd expected so much as a slightly confused one.

But it wasn't raining. It insisted on being aggressively, obstinately beautiful. A cloudless fall sky, cool but not yet cold, leaves just coming into brilliant shades of yellow, gold and orange.

The wake had been...it had been *odd*. They'd held it at the church's social hall. Between the location and the homemade food brought by her parents' friends—with more than a few contributions from Evelyn herself, grief temporarily sublimated into a kitchen frenzy—it felt strangely like church luncheons she dimly remembered being dragged to in her childhood. The hall itself looked, like its parishioners, worse for the wear, but otherwise matched her memories, down to the faint omnipresent scent of the terrible coffee they served here after every service.

While she barely knew anyone at the event, most seemed to know *her.* The vast majority of attendees were there for her parents— retirees they socialized with, mom's knitting or sewing or whatever the hell it was circle, dad's former business partners. She had variants of the same conversation at least a dozen times:

> **Random Old Person:** *So it's…Autumn now, isn't it?*
> **Autumn:** *Yes.*
> **Random Old Person:** *I haven't seen you since you were about [pick a number between seven and sixteen]. You've changed a lot.*
> **Autumn:** *Ha ha.*
> **Random Old Person:** *[shuffles awkwardly] I'm sorry for your loss.*
> **Autumn:** *Thanks.*
> **Random Old Person:** *Jasper was very proud of you, you know, even if he didn't show it.*
> **Autumn:** *[nods mutely]*
> **Random Old Person:** *I know it might be hard, but I hope you can be there for your mother. She'll need support.*
> **Autumn:** *Great catching up.*

The handful of attendees closer to her age were Kelly's friends, not hers; she only remembered one of them from high school. Even so, all of them seemed to take her gender in stride, without the awkward shuffling of the older adults. The one she remembered was a haughty lynx girl she'd hated, but today she was virtually the opposite of Autumn's memory of her, warm and genuinely sympathetic. it wasn't until after Autumn had retreated outside for a breather that she realized the lynx had been wearing a tiny rainbow pride cloisonné pin.

At the funeral now, watching the coffin be lowered into the ground, she finally put her finger on what had made the wake feel so strange to her. It was odd because everyone put so much effort into behaving as if it *wasn't* odd. Most of the conversation she overheard was idle, everyday chatter: acquaintances catching up with one another, discussing plans or making new ones, asking for opinions on trivial topics. Other than the offered condolences, it might have *been* one of those church luncheons.

The service itself had been rote, full of platitudes that described her father in the most banal and generic of terms. What did *living a full life* mean, anyway? He'd had the most pedestrian of lives, moving from blue collar worker to white collar supervisor of blue-collar workers, and even though sixty-seven seemed far away to her, objectively it was an early death. How was that life full?

And had he had a loving family? As the random old people had kept inadvertently pointing out, he hadn't shown love to his family very often or very easily. She'd never been sure if the vague air of disappointment from him was real or a bit of paranoia on her part. At least until her transition. Then it definitely wasn't paranoia.

She flashed back to him calling her "girlie" on two separate occasions in her early teens, the first leaving her crying in her room and the second ending with her screaming "So what?" and stomping off in a confused, angry huff. If he were around right now for her to call him on it, he wouldn't apologize. He'd cock his head and say, "Well, I wasn't wrong, was I?"

Shaking her head at herself, she listened to the priest finish his droning ritual and hand a bowl of flower petals to Evelyn to toss into the open grave. She'd forgotten what religious fable that called back to; something about rebirth, no doubt. It was always rebirth. The priest followed that with his own bowlful of blessed soil, then directed everyone to hold hands while he said a final benediction.

And, all at once, that was that. The small crowd began to drift apart. Cemetery workers began to shovel dirt into the grave in earnest. Autumn remained motionless, watching her father disappear under the earth.

"Kelly tells me you're taking the train back to Mensura this afternoon."

She blinked, turning to look down at her mother. Evelyn had dressed in black, too, as widows traditionally did. It didn't look elegant on her; it made her look small and sad. The older rabbit looked exhausted, but beyond that, Autumn couldn't read her expression. "Yeah," she said softly. "Almost noon on the dot."

"So you have everything from the house you want?"

"There wasn't much left." In truth, everything was left, but it was from a life no longer hers. Clothes, toys (mostly the "manly" ones her mother had started foisting on her in a vain attempt to head off that girlie stuff), flotsam and jetsam from school years. She'd impulsively grabbed a couple books, even stopping to flip back through *Margie*, her favorite book growing up. The story about an adolescent vixen wrestling with faith, puberty, and her divorced mother's interspecies relationships was one of the most celebrated yet most frequently banned YA novels in history; she'd found herself identifying pretty strongly with Margie. This was her second copy of the book. The first one had mysteriously vanished after the Barbie Vixen incident.

Her mother nodded, then looked off into the distance, biting her lip. "I wish things were different between us."

Make it different, then, mom. Tell me I'm your daughter and you love me. Send me a damned birthday card with the right name on it. "I do, too."

After a few more seconds of staring into space, her mother took both her hands, looking up at her face. "Take care."

"You too."

When she walked away, Evelyn didn't look back.

She didn't know how long she kept standing there until Kelly touched her on the arm. "Hey."

"Hey." She took a deep breath. "I guess it's time to get my things, huh?"

"Yeah." Kelly started walking back toward the church's parking lot, Autumn following a pace behind. "You wanna change back to normal clothes before I drop you off at the train station, or you wanna ride back home in that steampunk poet getup?"

"Steampunk poet."

"Figured."

It barely took five minutes to stop back at Kelly's place, get her bag, and be back in the car on the way to the station. They drove in silence for a few minutes, Autumn staring moodily out at the passing scenery. It wasn't especially pretty, but she might not be seeing it again for a long time.

"Thanks for coming out."

She turned to look back at Kelly. "It's not like I had a lot of choice."

"Sure you did." Kelly shrugged. "Even if your last visit eased things a little with dad, things got worse with mom. I wouldn't have blamed you if you'd stayed away."

She smiled a little. "Yeah, you would have."

"No." Her sister looked over at her, serious. "I'd have been upset, because I wanted you to come. But I'd have understood."

"Well, I guess it's some kind of closure." She shrugged. "I feel like...like I'm giving myself permission to shut a door that wasn't healthy for me to keep open."

"Maybe." Kelly sighed, eyes back on the road. "I'll keep talking to her."

"Don't do it on my account."

"It's just..." Kelly trailed off and shook her head, sighing again. "I don't know."

It's just that you want us to be the happy family we never were. Autumn turned back to the window.

The next few minutes fell back to silence, until Kelly pulled into the station's driveway and up to the curb. They both got out of the car.

"Okay." Autumn hesitated. Despite the early hour, she felt like she'd run out of energy for words. "Thanks for the ride. And everything."

"Hey." Kelly gave her a hug. "You'd better keep in touch. Don't make me come up there and box your ears."

She squeezed her sister back. "You know I'll be a hundred feet tall, right?"

"I'll get Saida to lift me up."

"Only if we're still seeing each other."

"If you're not, lift me up to her and I'll box her ears."

"Visit me sometime even if it's not for ear-boxing." Autumn

167

grinned faintly. "And take the train, not the plane. I don't know what you were thinking that first trip."

"I was thinking speed. And I didn't know the train didn't suck."

Autumn watched her sister drive off, then headed into the station to find the departing track.

The train didn't suck, especially compared to the ever-shrinking seats of airplanes, but she found its electric silence a little off-putting today. Fishing around in her bag, she pulled out the copy of *Margie* and began reading.

Her phone buzzed before they'd reached the next station. When she pulled it out, her eyes widened, the miasma lifting a little from her spirit. It was a message from Saida—she'd gotten the gateway working again? And more importantly, wanted to use it?

The note was so short and direct it felt a little inscrutable: *When are you coming back?*

How'd she even know Autumn was gone? Did she know why? So many questions all at once. She typed out, *4 hours. On train back to Mensura now. Where are you?*

It took a few minutes for a non-responsive response: *Talk soon.*

She frowned, running a hand through her hair. Then she shoved the phone back in her pocket and went back to the book.

It was dusk when she got off at the station, hefting her bag up over one shoulder. All right, should she get a taxi, walk back as a little, or size-shift and—

She stopped, staring at the parking lot. Saida sat cross-legged near the back of it, looking intently at the train—although she'd presumably missed Autumn stepping off.

Other passengers glanced in the direction of the giantess, but few showed any reaction beyond that. "First time seeing a giant?" a burly wolf said as he walked past. "You'll get used to 'em."

"No, it's—uh—" She shook her head, shifting her grip on the bag, and hurried out over the asphalt.

Saida saw her approaching long before she got there, of course, the cat's ears perking. She leaned forward, smiling, and Autumn felt her pulse race. This was the first time *she'd* been the small one.

"Hi," the giantess said. "I'm sorry about your father. I know things were strained, but I can only imagine how hard this is."

"Thanks." She approached the cat's closest knee, looking up. "What—I mean—I was hoping I'd hear from you again, but between your troubles at work and the way we left things…"

"We have a lot to talk about." Saida flashed her lopsided smile.

"Okay." She ran a hand through her hair. "I think I'm going to change back to being a giantess and we'll get some drinks. Uh, not that I'm trying to make that a command."

Saida's smile became a full grin. Autumn hadn't fully appreciated how terrifying that set of beautiful teeth could be before now. "We'll talk about that, too."

CHAPTER 24

Severance

"UNDERSTAND IT'S NOT ABOUT YOUR PERFORMANCE." THE company's personnel manager was doing her best to sound sympathetic, but she just sounded sullen. "The board has decided that to take the company to the next level, they—"

Saida kept her tone professionally pleasant. "Need to get rid of any Talirends in Talirend Systems."

Karelle wilted slightly, eyes darting across the table to Raiben.

He kept his own professional veneer of false empathy. "It's never easy, but it's not uncommon for companies to change management as they grow."

"Yes, I'm familiar with CEOs being moved to other C-level suites, or to a chairman of the board position. Is Mradhi keeping his seat on the board?" She knew the answer already, and both of them knew she did. But she wasn't going to let this be too easy.

"We decided that wasn't for the best."

"'We?' Oh, that's right, you took Mradhi's seat on the board." She smiled without a trace of friendliness, sliding the folder of papers in front of Karelle over to her and pulling her own pen out of her suit pocket. "Well, I'm sure 'we' won't have trouble finding the right CEO to take the company to the next level. That's the right phrase, isn't it?"

Raiben's ears skewed, and he didn't reply.

171

"Mmm." She flipped through the papers, beginning to sign document after document. She couldn't say whether these were typical separation agreements or not; it wasn't as if she'd ever been fired from a position like this before. Her jobs before this were secretarial and shitty retail. The non-competition clause was one she expected; the requirement not to "disparage" the company for a similar period seemed fishy, but she'd heard of such things before. And the severance package *was* generous. It might not be the proverbial golden parachute, but Mradhi had been right: it was a full year's worth of salary, and her salary was—had been—pretty damn high.

She frowned, coming across a decidedly less friendly-looking legal document. "The earlier paperwork stipulated I could keep my beacon. Why does this one demand its return?"

"To study its transit logs."

"We've always treated transit logs as private information. It's completely against company policy."

Raiben narrowed his eyes. "Our internal investigation suggests you have *two* beacons, and you've misled us about both its existence and its location. When—not if—we send a security team to retrieve it, we'll make decisions about any further action."

What? They couldn't—but they could, couldn't they? They thought the prototype's secret location must be an illicit vacation home paid with embezzled company funds, or worse, a competitor's office. Unless she erased the logs from the beacon back at her flat, which would get her in goddess knew what trouble, they could use it to just teleport themselves to Mensura. And all hell would break loose.

"We've already cleared the legal issues involved." Karelle looked apologetic but firm.

"And you want my beacon returned to you in..." She looked at the paperwork, and barely managed to keep her voice level. "Fortyeight hours."

Karelle cleared her throat, looking to the side. "Yes, Ms. Talirend. It's a condition of your severance package."

She'd been prepared for them to ask for the impossible. Asking for the possible turned out to be worse. Saida gritted her teeth, signing that form, too, then slid the whole folder back across the table to Karelle.

* * *

The view across the river tonight was beautiful, just enough clouds to bring out all the colors as the sun sank behind the mountains. It was cool on her balcony, but she was on her third *ulvi* and soda and feeling warm enough to mostly ignore the pit in her stomach.

Mostly.

"Saida?"

She squinted, looking around. Was someone in her apartment? Someone calling to her from the street?

"Over here."

It still took her a second to follow the voice—across her balcony to its other side. Tam, the Liliren, perched on the railing in a precarious-looking fashion.

She sat up. "Tam! Get down from there. You know how high up we are?"

He slid down a railing pole to the balcony, looking none the worse for it. "I'm not the one out here sitting on the balcony floor drinking. I'd ask if you were okay, but I'm pretty sure you're not."

She snorted, taking another sip of the drink before setting her glass down. "This isn't doing a good job of convincing me you guys aren't spying on me all the time."

"We're not, I promise. This is just...neighborly concern. I haven't seen you like this before."

"You haven't seen me pushed out of my career with my relationship in shambles and my severance package held hostage by a chauvinist prick before."

"Oh." He rubbed the back of his head. "So is this the kind of thing you should talk about with someone, or the kind of thing you should be left alone for after you promise me you're not taking a dive off your balcony?"

She sighed heavily. "No dives, I promise. I'll go in. Follow if you want." She hauled herself to her paws.

Tam scampered in after her when she took a seat on the sofa, climbing up onto the far armrest. Hard not to notice he always kept well out of arm's reach, but she didn't feel like pressing him on it. "So," he said. "You lost your job and...you've been seeing someone, I guess wherever you go when you use that teleportation gadget, and it's not going well?"

"I lost my job, my brother lost his company. I'm seeing a woman who's probably too young for me and lives in a different world, and she's wonderful but she kinda scares me. And she might think I hate her right now anyway."

"That sounds complicated," Tam said cautiously, taking a seat on the armrest. "And the part about your severance package being held hostage?"

"You know how those teleportation beacons work?"

That made him sound wryly amused. "Sometimes you go over there and press a button and get sent to another teleportation gadget somewhere else."

"That's it. Short form, if I don't return my beacon, I don't get my severance pay and might go to jail. If I do return it, they'll teleport someone to the other side to find out what's there, which would...expose things I need to keep secret."

"That's foreboding." Tam scratched his nose and fell silent a few seconds. "Did you get the beacon put there so you could visit your girl?"

"Huh?"

"I mean, did you already know her and that's why you're going back there, or did you already like the place before you met her?"

Saida sighed, shrugging. "I already loved the place before I met her." She downed the rest of her drink, then got up to pour a fourth one.

"It sounds to me like you should just move there, then. Even if your relationship doesn't work out, you'd be in a place you love."

She stared at him, liquor bottle in hand. "That's not something I can just snap my fingers and do. Especially moving *there*. And it doesn't change anything *here*."

"This is where I guess I prove I'm *not* actually spying on you,

174

because I don't know what you do even when you're here. But it doesn't seem like you have guests over and it doesn't seem like you go out much, except using that teleporter. I can't help but wonder if most of your social life is, well, already over there."

"If I even have a social life at all." She finished pouring and headed back to her seat. "The last few years it's been all work. But I like this place, too. I have a beautiful home."

"It's hard not to notice you said you *like* Stravell, and *love* your girl's land."

She swirled her drink around in her glass and took a sip. Hmm. She'd left out the soda this time, hadn't she? It was still good. Bracing. "Maybe you're reading too much into that."

"But maybe I'm not."

"It's...hard for me to explain just how different it is. Where she lives."

"But you love it. And her."

"I...think so." She shook her head. "But I can't just move there. It'd mean giving up my severance package. It might mean giving up everything."

"I know you Rhas are less nomadic than Liliren, but you still move between cities sometimes."

"Not like this." She looked over at him levelly. "What would you think if I told you that when I said she lives in a different world, I wasn't being metaphorical? That it's a world with different races, different species, and almost everything is on *your* scale, not mine?"

"I'd think I'd need to find some way to cut you off from that *ulvi* despite our size difference." He gave her a curious smile. "You're not telling me that, are you?"

"I'm...not *not* telling you that."

"So you're not not saying you have a secret magical door that only you know about, like from some kind of fantastic children's book. Maybe a Liliren children's book, at that."

"And I'm not not saying we've reached the part of the book where the heroine makes a crucial mistake that lets the devil cross over." She sighed and took a big enough gulp of her drink that she started coughing. "I shouldn't...ugh. Just write this all off as drunken rambling, all right?"

"Mmm." He fell silent a few seconds, then looked up again. "So how does the heroine turn it all around and save the day?"

"I don't know. If it was a Liliren book, how would she do it?"

Tam shrugged. "Probably sacrifice herself nobly."

"Seriously?" Saida sighed. "Your books suck."

"Yeah, a lot of our kids grow up traumatized."

She rolled her eyes, but laughed in spite of herself. "I guess...I don't know. I'd thought they were just going to want the prototype beacon on the other side back. But they want to know where I've been going."

"Do they think you've been engaging in corporate spying, maybe?"

"They might. I also think they want to humiliate me on the way out the door so I know my place."

"That's awful."

"I thought my impossible dilemma was going to be how to get the beacon back from a world it only got to through a one-in-a-million fluke. Instead, it's a choice between protecting myself and protecting that secret magical door."

"Which is more important to you?"

She looked into her glass. "I don't know," she said after a few seconds, very softly.

Tam leaned forward on the armrest. "I bet you do, Saida."

She glanced at him, and fell silent, setting down her glass. It was annoying for someone that small to be that perceptive. Then she gave him a small nod, got up and headed to the kitchen. She started a pot of coffee going, then picked up the phone and dialed Mradhi.

He answered on the fourth ring. "Hello, this is—"

"Hi. It's Saida."

"Oh. How are you holding up?"

"I'm drunk."

"Understandable."

"They want the prototype back, but they want to know where it's been. They want to 'audit' mine. Get records. And Raiben made it clear he'd just send a team through to see where the prototype was if he thought he had to."

"Oh."

"So I think...I think you need to talk me into something, or talk me out of it. I'm not sure which yet."

CHAPTER 25

A Risky Plan

"I KNOW IT'S A RISKY PLAN, BUT—"

"The word I used wasn't 'risky,' it was 'absurd,' and I won't dignify it by calling it a plan." Mradhi lashed his tail. "How much did you say you had to drink?"

Saida sighed, looking up from the couch. He'd been sitting beside her up until a few seconds ago, until he understood exactly what she was proposing. Then, in decidedly un-Mradhi fashion, he'd leapt up for dramatic effect. "What's the non-absurd alternative?"

"Your first, obvious idea. Reset your beacon completely."

"And how do I explain that in a way that doesn't make it look like I have something to hide?"

"I told you, I can have my lawyer do...do something." His tail lashed faster, likely at his inability to be more specific.

"Come on, you know it doesn't matter how good your lawyer is if I do that. Raiben will tie me up until I run out of savings if I make this a legal challenge—and if this gets in front of a judge they're going to set my tail on fire."

"Even in the worst case you're unlikely to serve much time, if any."

"Well, *that's* a relief, isn't it? I'll be unemployed, branded as a possible fraudster, and left bankrupt by legal fees, but at least I won't be in jail long."

"And you won't be a fugitive."

"A fugitive in a place that our world doesn't know exists and that we'd both decided long ago we shouldn't expose. Has any of that changed? If I stay here and play things the 'right' way, what happens? How does Mensura react to an influx of new giants who don't have the best track record with little indigenous people? How does *this* world react to magic and spaceships and the occasional godlike being?"

"For goddess' sake, I said just wipe it all!" He gestured angrily at the beacon. "Nobody's able to send anything back to the prototype. Everything stays safe."

"And I never go back to Mensura."

Mradhi stopped pacing, rubbing his face, then sat down on the couch. "That's not a given. That prototype beacon's still going to be there. I found it once before when I was trying to rescue Arilin. I can find it again."

"You wouldn't have access to the beacon network anymore."

"There *was* no network when I found it the first time. I've been thinking for months about how to create a backward-compatible next generation system. And I know—I think I know—how to engineer it in a way that wouldn't run into any patent violations, since they're mostly my patents."

"How long would that take?"

"A year or two. Maybe three."

"Or more, possibly up to never. And trying just might put *you* in jail."

"No." He shook his head. "It'd survive a court challenge. I might not be able to start work on it for a year, until the non-compete agreements expire."

She got up, refilling her mug. The pot had been on too long and the coffee had started to burn, but it was still drinkable. She missed Higher Grounds, though. "So suppose that's true. It makes my plan reasonable. After I go through, you can reset this beacon. I'll still get the blame for it, and one day you'll be able to get the connection open again."

He tensed, voice rising again. "But we can't—" He abruptly

stopped, looking down, voice dropping. "I can't...if I can't connect to that beacon again..."

She sat down and put her hand on his knee. "I know."

He looked at her pleadingly, then pulled away. "It's insane," he muttered, sipping his own lukewarm coffee.

"What do you think, Tam? I know you're still around."

Mradhi's ears skewed. "Who?"

Saida addressed the open air, ignoring her brother. "I wouldn't have called you out if Mradhi was going to be a problem, I promise."

"You're sure?" a voice came from the far side of the living room. Tam popped up on a bookshelf.

Mradhi stared, setting down his mug. "You've...had a Liliren listening."

"He's my friend. I mean, we don't know each other that well, but we've talked occasionally. We talked a lot today. He kind of, well, helped put the idea in my mind."

Mradhi ran a hand through his hair. "And you're taking life advice from him."

Tam straightened up, looking offended. "Hey, I know what you Rha—well, most of you—think of us, but just because we're tiny compared to you doesn't mean we're stupid."

Mradhi focused a sullen gaze on the little mouse. "I assure you I'm not skeptical of your advice because of either your species or your stature. I'm skeptical because it's insane."

Tam cleared his throat. "With all due respect, the most insane thing I've heard tonight is you two talking about teleporting to a literally different world. And unless both of *you* are insane...it's true, isn't it?"

Mradhi kept his voice perfectly level. "Now that you know, I'm afraid I have to kill you."

Tam squeaked and vanished again.

"Dammit, Mradhi." She cuffed him on the shoulder.

"That's not funny, man." Tam's voice was shaky and even higher-pitched than normal.

Mradhi sighed, folding his arms. "You're safe, as much as I'd rather you help me talk my sister *out* of this idea." He looked to

Saida. "You're talking about moving to a world literally built on a Liliren scale."

"Arilin's lived there for well over a decade."

"Where are you going to stay? You don't know that the school's going to let you live there full-time."

"Why wouldn't they? I'm paying rent for the suite there full-time as it is. If I stop paying for *this* place, it'll cut my housing costs by two-thirds."

"Where are you going to work?"

"If you can get the gateway up and transfer my savings before you reset the beacon, I'll have at least a year of runway to find a job. Hell, maybe two or three."

"Other than the college, who's going to hire a giant?"

"I don't know. Look, I'm not saying this wouldn't be a big risk. But staying is *also* a risk, and not just for me."

Mradhi grunted. "How much of this is about your girlfriend? We both know people who've moved across Stravell to chase lovers they'd only met a few times, and it never worked out well."

"I won't say that's not part of it. But I don't honestly know if she's even going to want to see me again, and I haven't had time to fully work through some...things...between us." She looked up again. "But if I stay, there's no chance to work those things out. The best case is seeing her years in the future, when all my legal issues are behind me and you can work out whatever mad science you need to tap into Talirend's teleportation network. That might be after she's graduated and moved God knows where. And that's assuming you can actually do it at all."

Mradhi twisted his hands in his lap.

"She's making sense," Tam offered, climbing up onto a different furniture piece. "Even though this is a lot to take in. Other worlds, different sizes. Magic."

"It was for me, too. But it's because of that," she pointed at the beacon, "that I truly understand people your size are *people*, not in some kind of nebulous state between Rha and animals. Because of the world over there."

He nodded slowly.

Saida gave the Liliren a small smile, then took her brother's hand. "Mradhi," she said softly.

He turned to look at her, expression halfway between mournful and challenging.

"All of the things you're saying are right. It's a huge risk, with no way back for years, if ever, if it doesn't work out. But you know all the things *I've* been saying are right, too."

His ears slowly lowered, and his expression shifted to just mournful. Finally, he closed his eyes. "What do you need to me to do?"

She squeezed his hand, purring softly. "I want you to get whatever crazy system you set up to transfer money between worlds working one last time. It's not traceable, is it? I mean...back to you."

"It shouldn't be." He swallowed.

"Good. Transfer everything you can, from all the liquid accounts. I've put in orders to liquidate my investment account, too. Keep about ten thousand to cover the rest of this place's lease. You do what you want with whatever I've left here, which I guess is going to be...well, almost everything. There's only so much I can pack into boxes and zap over there. Clothes, sundries, a few personal items. The room there's furnished already, fortunately."

"For Goddess' sake, Saida." He rubbed his face. "Should we go shopping tomorrow?"

She smiled wryly. "They have stores there, you know."

"Not on our scale." His voice remained level, but his eyes glistened. "And you might want to buy anything they don't have there that you're going to miss. You're not going to have a chance to get any more for...for a while."

"Right." She gave a weak laugh. "Maybe that'll give us enough time to come up with something plausible about my disappearance."

He shook his head. "They'll know you've gone to wherever the prototype beacon is. I'll just say I don't know where that might be. What I need to come up with is something plausible about why your beacon here was reset to factory settings." He looked down again, tail flicking.

"An error. Something I programmed in. Who knows. It doesn't matter much. It just matters that they can't go through."

He nodded slightly, still looking down. "That no one can, either way."

She hugged him. "I'll see you again, eventually. You found Arilin with much less to go on. You'll find me."

After a moment, he hugged her back, sniffling. "Let's get some boxes."

"So you're really moving to Fairyland," Tam murmured.

CHAPTER 26

With Fresh Eyes

"WHEW. THAT'S BETTER." AUTUMN BRUSHED OFF, looking down at the train station from the proper vantage point.

"That's an even more amazing outfit at this size." Saida smirked. "And being little around me was that frightening, huh?"

"Kelly called it 'dagger-wielding steampunk poet.' And it wasn't frightening. Exactly." She started walking back toward campus. The roads out here toward the edge of Mensura didn't have signaling for giants—only a few blocks in the city did—but they were multiple lanes with generously wide paved shoulders. Drivers in the outside lanes still tended to swerve unnecessarily wide, but the walks tended to be pretty chill. "It was a hell of a view of you, though. And I have a new appreciation for how big your teeth are. It's just like, that size is claustrophobic now. You don't feel that way?"

Saida followed, walking more carefully, glancing down at every car. "I've rarely been that size. Other than the time you shrank me, it's happened...once with another friend, and once with Kenley." Her ears went flat a moment, until she started speaking again. "And a few times I've been around giants way bigger than even you are, but that's not the same thing." Her ears went flat again as a car passing by honked at her. "What?" she snapped at it.

"They're just making sure you know where they are. Or saying hi. Or saying you have cute toes. Relax. You're one of the most

185

graceful women I've ever met and you're not going to accidentally step on anyone who isn't being an idiot. Also, you didn't actually answer 'yes' or 'no' to my question."

Saida rolled her eyes, starting to walk again. "The answer is that I haven't been that small often enough to have an opinion. Anyway, we have a lot to catch up on."

"My dad died of a surgery complication, I went home for the funeral, and...some of it was harder than I guess I expected, even though I knew the day was coming soon."

She nodded sadly. "And your mom?"

"I think we might have disowned each other."

That earned her a shocked expression. "What?"

"That might be too melodramatic. It's that we both know we'll cause each other less stress if we're not in one another's lives. Anyway, I went to the wake, I went to the funeral, and...I came back here. It feels like so much happened, but I can't think of anything else to say."

Saida stopped at an intersection, looking around, then headed toward the campus gate. She'd started to walk in a faster, more relaxed way, paying attention to the occasional honk but no longer getting visible jitters from it. "What was the service like?"

"Banal. Generic. I don't know if Dad would have liked it much. He was never the religious one." She slowed down, gaze growing distant. "We were never as close as mom and I were, and now I don't know why. Looking back it feels like I had more in common with him than her."

Saida took her hand.

Autumn looked down, smiling a little, and squeezed the cat's velvet paw pad. "Okay, now my turn. All I know is that I stupidly freaked you out so much you had Professor Thorferra come and tell me she'd sent you home, and..." She took a deep breath. "I didn't know if you'd come back at all, or if you'd want to see me again if you *did* come back, or if you wouldn't even be *able* to come back because of whatever shit was going down with your job. What's happening with that? If you're here it's gotten better, right?"

"Goddess." The cat laughed dryly, flicking her tail. "Only in the sense that it's over. Mradhi and I were both fired."

"*What?* Isn't it his damn company?"

"Not anymore." Saida slowed as they walked onto campus proper, looking around with a hard-to-read expression, then picked up speed. "Let's head toward the Beanstalk. I'm going to want a drink or two for all this, and given what *you've* been through, I might not be alone."

"Been there, done that. What do you mean 'not anymore?'"

"Raiben, that exec Mradhi brought in a few months ago, organized a coup, with the help of at least one board member."

"From what you were saying earlier, I thought Mradhi was trying to help Raiben get rid of you!"

"I was worried he might be, even though it didn't seem like him at all. Turns out it wasn't."

"How can they just—just—Lords, I hate capitalism!"

"I know. It's cute."

Autumn shoved Saida lightly in the shoulder. "It's not funny. They screwed you over. And how does this change you being able to get here?"

"That's gotten complicated. Well, I guess you could say it's gotten very simple." They stepped into the Union building. "I could really use that beer."

Autumn frowned. Out of all the things she'd have called Saida, "enigmatic" wouldn't have been one of them, but that was world-class cryptic. She followed the shorter cat into the pub and up toward the counter.

"Do you want to order for both of us, or can I get my own beer?" Saida flashed her a lopsided grin.

Autumn opened her mouth, then closed it, hoping her ears weren't blushing. "Get whatever beer you want," she muttered. "And get me the amber, please. I'll find a seat."

Fortunately, her favorite corner table was free; she headed there before Saida responded. Yes, it had been a joke, but...well, but what? Goddess, she just wasn't ready to deal with anything else heavy. After all the shit that had happened in the past week, the evening she'd had in mind was maybe getting a pizza and beer—by herself—then stumbling back to her dorm room and collapsing. Apparently that wasn't in the playbook just yet, though. Also, where had she picked up "Goddess?" From Saida? She should really ask who the Rha goddess *was* if she was gonna be referring to her in vain.

In another minute or so Saida sat down at the table, setting Autumn's beer in front of her and a lighter beer—it smelled like a pale ale—in front of herself. "I put in a pepperoni and pineapple pizza order, too."

"See, I knew you'd like it. Okay." She clasped her hands in front of her on the table. "So."

"So." Saida took a long sip of her beer. "They—the company— wanted me to turn my teleporter beacon, the one back at my place in Stravell, over to them. Technically I should have been able to keep it as long as I kept paying for it. If I'd taken the severance package, the company would have covered it another year, even. But the whole pretext of getting rid of me and Mradhi was my 'misleading' them about having two beacons instead of one. So they wanted to find out where the other one was by sending a security team over here to get it."

"Holy shit. You're keeping Mensura's existence a little family secret, right?"

She nodded. "Mradhi and I talked a lot about that over the years —I mean, on the one hand it's crazy that we're keeping the existence of other worlds and other races and magic a secret. Maybe it's selfish, too."

"When you get outside of Mensura, people in this world have barely come to grips with giants and magic. And from what everyone who knows tells me, up in the giant lands they've barely come to grips with littles and high technology. So no, it's not selfish. I wouldn't be rushing to set up an inter-dimensional travel agency, either."

"Right. So..." Saida's gaze grew unfocused as she looked off to the side, speaking more slowly. "Just hanging onto my beacon and saying 'no, you can't have it' wouldn't stop them from coming here. Eventually, they'd get a court order. The only answer was wiping my beacon entirely, like a factory reset, so it lost any connection to the one here in Mensura."

"If you did that, you'd never be able to come back here, would you?" She couldn't keep the alarm out of her voice. Saida was back to say goodbye forever, wasn't she? Had she dared one of the Three Lords by thinking *at least my week can't get any worse*?

"No. I wouldn't." The cat looked back at her with a sad smile. "So…I came through first."

Autumn furrowed her brow. First? What did that—

She sat bolt upright, eyes widening, and her breath caught. "You can't go back home anymore?"

Saida took a deep breath, then shook her head. "No. I can't."

"That's—I don't—wow." Autumn ran a hand through her hair. "Saida, no."

The Rha leaned back, looking nonplussed.

"I mean—" Phrasing, rabbit, phrasing. "It's just…right now I feel like I'd be happy if I never saw my hometown again, but I have the option to change my mind. We're suddenly going from 'I need some time apart' to 'I've literally moved to your world and blown up the door behind me.'"

"Autumn." Saida sighed, reaching across the table and touching her hand to the rabbit's. "Like I said at the train station, I want to talk about us soon. But for all the reasons you just went over, I didn't make this move for you. I made it for me."

Well, *that* was hard to read. Or maybe her own feelings were. She'd have felt panicked if Saida had said she *had* moved across the universe for her, but hearing that no, of course she hadn't, was somehow disappointing. She bit her lip. "I don't think I understand."

"Staying in Stravell didn't just mean the possibility of having the gateway between our worlds discovered. It would have meant long legal battles. Possible criminal charges. Maybe even jail. And the best, *best* case would still mean I'd lose my beacon. I wouldn't ever be able to come back here. Even if I got another job that paid well enough for me to rent a new personal one—assuming the company *would* rent me one—I doubt I'd be able to reconnect it to the

Mensura beacon, even if it was still here and working after all that time."

"And coming here is that important to you?"

"I love this place in a way that I haven't loved anywhere else. I know how risky this all is. Mradhi went over virtually ever possible point of failure with me. No job, not even a guarantee of a place to live, literally not fitting into the world."

"So, you're me when I graduate."

Saida laughed, looking more relaxed. "Hopefully you're getting more time to prepare for it."

Autumn grunted, taking a long drink from her beer.

The Rha grinned at that, then took a sip of her own beer, looking thoughtful. "If this had happened a year ago, I don't think I'd have made this same choice. I'd been coming here for years, sure, and I'd already grown to love it, but I'd gotten kind of...disaffected, maybe. The curse had put a big damper on my outlook. Oh, you want me to make a one-way move to a place full of crazy magical beings who might eat me? Thanks, I hate it."

"When you put it that way." She laughed. "What changed?"

"I started looking at Mensura with fresh eyes. Not just at how giants can accommodate littles, but at how littles can accommodate giants. How much I like being in a place where the relationship between the sizes is complicated in a mostly *good* way. And even how the curse might be—at least in part—my attitude." Saida leaned forward, this time clasping the rabbit's hand in hers. "What changed is I met you."

Autumn swallowed, eyes going very wide again.

CHAPTER 27

Big Ideas

"ALL RIGHT, EVERYONE! FIVE MORE MINUTES."

Autumn breathed a sigh of relief as Tom made the announcement. Normally her volunteer shifts at the food bank were a breeze, but during this one, she'd been "less than fully present," as the hyena had put it ten minutes ago. That was right after the second—*second!*—box she'd dropped as she picked it up. The first one she hadn't damaged, but that one had sent tomatoes cascading around the floor —worse, splattering some on impact—and other volunteers ducking and shrieking. The upside of being a giant might be her speed, but the downside was her ability to screw up an awful lot in a single motion. More humiliatingly, she wasn't even having to do that much this time around; they only had maybe half the volunteers they usually did.

Kim had volunteered, though, for the first time. Autumn had texted her earlier this morning asking to talk, and said that she'd drop by Higher Grounds later in the day. Instead of waiting, the goat had decided to meet her here, gamely letting Tom rope her into work.

When the shift ended, Autumn carefully wriggled out through the loading dock, then sat down on the pavement, brushing off.

"You could just shrink yourself to do that, couldn't you?" Kim said, walking out the side door.

"Yeah, I suppose, but I don't want to. It wouldn't feel right."

"And people say us goats are always the stubborn ones."

"Are you sure they're not saying you're stubby?"

"Fuck you."

Usually Tom was out with her can of Diet Dr. Pepper before she got settled, but he hadn't come out yet. A few of the other volunteers had already come out, which meant they'd been dismissed after their final pep talk. A few glanced up at her nervously as they passed by on the way to the parking lot; one, though, the business vixen who volunteered monthly, gave her a cheerful wave as she walked past. She looked down, trying to look as non-threatening as a hundred foot tall rabbit could, and waved back.

The vixen paused, circling back to stop about five yards away from the giantess. "Is everything all right? You seemed..." She swished her tail, clearly thinking. "Distracted."

"That's a gentle way to put it." Autumn flashed a weary smile. "It's been a rough last couple of weeks."

"Oh. Yes." The woman nodded sympathetically. "There's a lot of drama here, but I don't think it affects—although you're an extraordinary volunteer, so it might be different."

Did the vixen somehow know about her personal troubles? She hadn't told Tom. Had Kim? No, the goat looked puzzled, too. Wait. She played the woman's last sentence over in her head. No, she was talking about something else entirely, wasn't she? "Drama here?"

"With the director." She hesitated again, light dawning in her green eyes. "You haven't heard?"

Autumn shook her head. "I've been pretty busy dealing with my own drama. What's been happening?"

"The director was arrested last week. They'd run an overdue audit here, and found they were missing over eight hundred thousand dollars."

"He stole from a *food bank?* What kind of a—Lords, I hate capitalists." Even as she spoke she realized maybe the vixen always dressed in heels and a power suit might be even less receptive than Saida was, but the words came out before she could stop them.

"Sometimes I do, too, and I'm a VP in banking," the vixen said dryly. "But from what this has exposed about the way they've been handling finances here, he got away with this for so long because their controls are virtually non-existent."

The goat snorted. "So you're saying they *need* a capitalist."

The vixen turned to Kim. "They need someone with business sense. Who's also willing to plunge into a giant hornet's nest."

"Now, don't make it sound that bad." Tom had walked out while they were talking. The hyena carried two cans of soda this time, setting the Diet Dr. Pepper down by Autumn and handing the root beer to Kim. "We have auditors cleaning up the mess, the board's already starting an executive search. We should be on even ground in no time."

"That's good to hear." Even from Autumn's altitude, it was impossible to miss the skepticism on the vixen's face as she looked at her phone. "Speaking of board meetings, I have one myself on the other side of town, and I should grab lunch beforehand. I'll see you all in a few weeks."

"Take care, Carolyn." Tom waved cheerfully as the vixen walked toward the parking lot, then looked up at Autumn. "You saw the can, right?" He pointed.

"Yes, I saw the can." She traced the rune in the air quickly, touching the Dr. Pepper to enlarge it to her size.

"So. Your drama."

Autumn paused, realizing both Kim and Tom had spoken at the same time. "Am I being ganged up on?"

"Yeah, watch out, we've got one of your toes partially surrounded." Kim crossed her arms. "No, I was just talking with Tommy after you talked to me this morning—"

"'Tommy,'" Autumn repeated. "You already know each other?"

"I introduced him to his boyfriend." Kim grinned.

The hyena nodded. "So, talk. Relationship issues, not family ones?"

She took a long sip of the soda. "Mmf. All the family issues, but yeah, this is about my long-distance girlfriend. I know I've mentioned her to you, and I've talked about her a lot with Kim."

"Yeah, the cat you want to collar." She grinned lopsidedly. "But from what Judy's said, you and Saida were having some rough patches."

"I shouldn't have let Judy talk me into trying to push that whole collar thing, no. I think we're on more solid ground after last night, although there's a lot still to work out."

"Was last night a deep talk or just great sex?" Tom flashed a particularly hyena grin.

"More cuddling than sex. Well, heavy cuddling. Well—look, the point is that she's not long-distance anymore."

Kim looked like she'd been about to say something else, but lifted her brows. "What?"

"She got pushed out of her company and wasn't going to be able to travel between worlds anymore, so she basically just leapt through for good. No job here, leaving most of her stuff, no promise of—well —anything."

"Wow." Tom's eyes were wide, too. "That's amazing!"

"It's fucking terrifying. She said she didn't do this because of me, but then said that she wouldn't have been willing to do it if her atti-tude toward this place hadn't changed over the last year and it *changed* because of me, and even after all that I still don't know *exactly* where we stand and I'm not sure I know where I *want* us to stand."

"But you *did* have great sex," Tom supplied.

Autumn sighed, giving him a look. He fluttered his eyelashes.

"You wanna keep seeing her?" Kim said.

"Yes."

"Even if she's not, how did Judy put it, kneeling in your hand calling you mistress?"

Tom choked on his soda.

"Even if. You okay there, little hyena?"

He pretended to ignore Autumn's question, looking over at Kim. "When did the rabbits get so scary?"

"It's the black lipstick," the goat said. "So you know what your problem is, Autumn?"

She folded her arms. "The black lipstick?"

"No, the black lipstick is awesome. Your problem is that up until now you couldn't act on any of your fantasies, except maybe for a night or two, and now you can."

"And this is a problem how?"

Tom grinned. "Let me boil down what Kim just said."

Kim swept both arms toward the hyena in a *go on* gesture.

"Shit," Tom pronounced, "just got *real*."

The goat raised her hands over her head. "Ding!"

Oh, come on. That wasn't...um. Autumn ran a hand down the back of one of her ears, then the other. "Look, our problems started when I tried to push her fantasy on her like you and Judy were talking about."

"Whoa." Kim's hands dropped into a time-out gesture. "That is *not* how I remember that conversation. Judy said to let her be the one who decides, not for you to push."

"I didn't mean push that literally." Autumn felt a flush rise to her ears and cheeks, though. Judy had kept using the word *safe*, and while she'd told Professor Thorferra that's what she'd been trying to do with her cousin—make her feel safe—now she couldn't help suspect she'd been focusing more on her own weird fantasies than the cat's. *Then don't try to trick her into going there*, the older Rha had said.

Finally she sighed, looking off to the side. "It's what it looked like Judy was doing with you."

"Holding out her hand and letting me decide whether to climb onto it? That's not pushing. I mean, yeah, by that point it was crystal clear that was an invitation to crazy mad teasing. But it was still an invitation."

Tom put his hands on his hips. "I swear, am I the only one without a giant girlfriend?"

"I thought I was your giant girlfriend, Tom."

"I don't know." He looked up at Autumn in mock skepticism. "You're scarier than I thought."

"I'm trying not to be scary to people I like unless they ask." She twisted a hand in her hair. "What if you're right? What if I'm scared by this *not* being a long-distance relationship anymore?"

"Of course you're scared by it." Kim shrugged. "It's serious. You just have to figure out if you're scared more by breaking it off, or more by making it work."

"'Just,'" Autumn echoed. She took a long sip of the soda and fell silent.

Tom patted her closest paw. "We'll be here for you either way."

"Mmm. Yeah, that reminds me." She waved toward the building. "I have to ask about what Business Fox was talking about, the whole thing with the director and the embezzlement. You say it's being smoothed over?"

"Oh, honey, we are *fucked*." Tom sighed, his ears lowering. "Because it looks like we don't know how to handle our money—and, let's be up front, we don't—donations are falling off the proverbial cliff. Which just makes the stolen money that much more of a problem. We're going to be laying off staff in a month if things don't pick up, and that *might* let us stretch out another two months at best. Or let whoever's left, if I'm one of the layoffs."

"Shit," Kim said. "That's not very smoothed over."

"It is so very bumpy. Carolyn was right about it being hard to find someone to step into the role after this. The board says they're talking to people, but they also say they're 'exploring options,' which is one of those phrases that radiates foreboding."

Autumn grunted, taking another sip of her soda. Would Saida know anything about running a non-profit? She had been in sales or something like that, but hadn't she, like, pretty much started the company with her brother?

"You have a 'sudden idea' kind of look," Kim said.

She shrugged after a moment, taking a big sip of the soda again and looking down. "Well, I already have a lot of other things I need to talk about with Saida, so I can at least ask if she has any advice for the place."

Tom grinned stupidly. "So you're going to ask your giant girlfriend if she has any...big ideas?"

Autumn narrowed her eyes, then lifted up the soda can and started to tip it over him.

"Hey! No!" Tom backed away from the stream of Dr. Pepper,

laughing, then ran to try to get out of her reach as the stream followed. "Stop! I'm sorry!"

CHAPTER 28

Climb On

"WE UNPACKED THEM ALREADY." SAIDA OPENED A CABINET in the kitchen, getting down three wine glasses. "See?"

"Fine, fine." Arilin opened the bottle she'd brought, only fighting a little with Saida's cheap corkscrew. "I hope you brought dishes to replace the ones the college provided, though."

Saida's ears lowered. "Not all of them. Are they going to be taking theirs back?"

"They are. You're going to have to apply for residency status at the college, and assuming they accept the application, they're going to stop treating this as an extended-stay suite and start treating it as an apartment."

Autumn looked over from where she sat on the couch. "It's startling how much you two look alike when you're both in jeans and T-shirts."

Saida frowned. "No, we don't," she protested, virtually at the same time Arilin said the exact same thing. They eyed one another.

"Yeah, that wasn't creepy. So if they're going to treat this as an apartment, are they going to take away the hotel room furniture?"

The older Rha carried the glasses to the living room, setting them down, and sat on the opposite end of the couch from the rabbit, letting Saida take the middle. "Not if she pays to keep renting it. I did that until I could start replacing pieces with my own selections. But the weekly maid service stops."

Saida sighed, picking up the wine-glass. "At least the rent drops."

"To about half what you're paying now."

Autumn had picked up her own glass and was giving the wine a careful sniff. "How much is that?"

"Mine's ten-fifty a month," Arilin replied.

The rabbit's painted eyes widened. "Holy..."

"That's great," Saida protested. "I was paying about two thousand to rent this as a hotel room monthly, and over two thousand a month for my flat back in Stravell."

"I'm pretty sure my parents' mortgage was around eight hundred a month and that was a four-bedroom place."

"Your parents' house almost certainly takes up fewer square feet than Saida's coffee table." Arilin gestured to the table in question. "The college gets away with a tremendous amount of savings by just magically enlarging as much as they can—"

"It's not as easy as saying 'just' makes it sound." Autumn sounded faintly affronted. "And there's a lot of real, physical construction involved either way."

"I helped start the college, so I'm aware. My point is that the one cost magic can't help with is actual land area. Rent for giants is always going to be more expensive, simply because we just take up so much more space. We've been trying to negotiate graduate housing for years, so giants such as yourself—and Saida—have a place to live that *isn't* meant as faculty or student housing."

Saida bit her lip. Once she'd gotten over the shock of her cousin's surprise move to Mensura, Arilin had gone into planning overdrive mode, almost instantly pulling together the paperwork the younger Rha would need to stay here, none of which she'd understood. There weren't any giants living on campus who weren't either students or college employees—Saida had blithely assumed they'd keep making an exception for her. What was the real difference between renting the place as a hotel room for literally years and shifting to renting it as an apartment?

But there was a host of differences, legally speaking. Leases.

Liability clauses. Personal property insurance. Goddess Arvya, proof of income. How could she manage that when she didn't have any? Show her bank statement and prove she could pay the rent for a couple years even with no job? That, only assuming Mradhi could finish all the transfers before shutting down the beacon. She'd checked her account earlier today, and her liquid accounts from back home—the checking and the savings—had come through, but the investment funds hadn't. When she'd been Autumn's age, what she had in her checking account now would have sounded like a fortune, but it wasn't; it was maybe four months of runway, and she had no idea how long finding a job would take. Or what kind of job she could find. She might end up working at the Beanstalk, not just eating there.

Back home. Her vision threatened to blur momentarily. Not home anymore.

She stole a glance at the beacon. Its connection status lights were still on.

"—pay that much," Autumn was saying. Saida blinked, focusing on the conversation.

"If you check rental prices of little-sized apartments throughout the city, you'll find the prices Saida and I are paying aren't out of line. But for now, it's rather a moot point. This is the only housing our size. There are some entrepreneurs looking to establish a mixed use development off-campus, closer to the mountains, but it's challenging. Honestly, we hadn't realized how much of an economy we'd have to try and create along with the college."

"I don't remember orientation going over the part about not being able to find a place to live or work after graduation." Autumn half-smiled, but Saida could see the underlying dismay in her eyes. She put her free hand on the rabbit's knee.

Arilin looked surprised. "It does." She paused, then tilted her head, sighing. "With students who've entered as giants. I suppose you'll get the after-graduation advice in your senior year that our giant students do, but you got the orientation for littles, didn't you."

"I know I'm not the first size-shifting student the school's had."

"No." Arilin shook her head. "But you may be the first who used size magic with the intent of a permanent change. I know you're the first who used transformation magic for a gender transition."

"Magic history books are full of trans people! There's evidence that trans people are more likely to have magical talent, or at least be drawn to magical studies."

"I didn't say you're the first in your world's history, Autumn, but you are the first *here*. As an institution we're less than a decade old, and there's still a lot we're learning ourselves."

Autumn frowned thoughtfully and nodded.

"It's interesting, though." Arilin swirled the wine in her glass. "Giants and magic are past history, or just folk legend, to much of the world, so we've tried to be...as low profile as a place like this possible can be, so littles can take years to get comfortable with the notion. And giants can get comfortable with littles, for that matter. But a side effect of that seems to be that most of our students aren't here for the academics, or even the novelty. They're here because something in them tells them they have to be."

Saida took another sip, too, and then set the glass down, looking around the apartment. Her apartment, assuming her life got back on the rails. The evening of unpacking had emptied the boxes faster than she'd imagined, but she'd brought less on this move than her last one. "I wonder if that's what happened to me."

"I don't wonder that at all." Arilin finished her wine, then stood up and took her glass to the sink. "I have papers to grade, so I'll take my leave. I suspect you two have a great deal to talk about."

Autumn nodded, expression shifting to thinly veiled nervousness. "Yeah."

Arilin crossed over and gave Saida a light, quick hug. "Get that residency application going, and get it to me along with what you can about your finances. I'll talk with the facilities director and see if I still have a few strings to pull."

"I didn't think this would be so much trouble." She hugged back, tail flicking.

Arilin chuckled. "Our family seems prone to leap into uncharted territory. Or occasionally get pushed. But it usually works out."

After her cousin had left, Saida headed back to the couch to sit down by the rabbit. "So." She folded her hands in her lap. "We talked about a lot yesterday, but we still need to talk about us."

Autumn nodded mutely, looking down at the coffee table rather than down at the cat.

Saida put her hand on the rabbit's knee again. "Don't be so tense. You know this isn't going to be the start of a 'it's not you, it's me' talk, right?"

She shifted her gaze to Saida and smiled crookedly. "I guess it still feels like there's a good chance of an 'actually, it really *is* you' talk coming."

"Even after last night?"

"Great sex doesn't mean a 'maybe we should just be friends with benefits' speech isn't coming. I'm glad I made you love Mensura again, and maybe even look at your curse a different way, but that's not *our* relationship. So." She took a deep breath. "What *is* our relationship?"

"Do you want to just be friends with benefits?"

"I don't know. I mean, I'd take it. But...if I could, I'd take more."

"Yeah." Saida bit her lip. This morning, before Autumn had arrived, things seemed clear, but now it seemed like all her words had vanished, crushed to dust. "My curse feels like it shouldn't have anything to do with our relationship, but it's what we keep dancing around. Or running aground on."

"No." Autumn sighed, sinking back in the couch and folding her arms around herself. "It's what led me to shoving you into weird fantasies I didn't even know I had before meeting you, and I let those nearly break us up almost as soon as it started to feel like there was an 'us' to break."

"You definitely threw me off by pushing like that. But a lot of what scared me about that was that it worked."

"Did it? You were just going along with the pushy rabbit girl until she pushed too far and you were like, 'look, I'm supposed to be your girlfriend, not your fucking pet.'" Autumn's voice shook.

"That's what I've been trying to answer for myself for weeks. I'd think—well, pretty much what you just said, in pretty much those words." She tilted her head. "But then I'd flash back to sitting at your paws. Or being in your hand. And..." She felt the heat rise in her ears, but didn't try to fight the blush. "I caught myself wondering whether those had to be mutually exclusive."

Autumn stiffened, eyes widening again. She didn't meet Saida's gaze. "You're going to have to be clearer or this is really going to screw with me."

"I mean..." Saida closed her eyes. What *did* she mean? Not that she wanted to be Autumn's pet. Exactly. Well, maybe kind of. "I mean I do want to be your girlfriend, Autumn, not just your friend. I want to try to make this work long-term. And I mean that I kind of...kind of liked..." She found her own voice shaking, but took a deep breath and pressed ahead. "You...taking control that way."

The rabbit swallowed, but otherwise went very still, eyes fully on Saida now.

"I was scared about...Goddess, it's tough to figure out the words. I didn't—I thought—"

"You didn't know if it was you going along with me, even subconsciously, or if it was Kenley." Autumn took Saida's hand, sighing, and looked at the ceiling. "I thought I was, I don't know, going to help you with that, too. Somehow. I thought I didn't need to ask for permission." She looked back down. "I'm so sorry."

Saida slid over on the couch until she pressed against Autumn's side, her hand still entwined with the rabbit's. "You're forgiven. I know you're not him. You're nothing like him. It's just...hard to act like I know that."

"Instead of picking you up, I should hold out my hand and let you decide whether to climb on."

"If I did, what would you do?"

Autumn looked down at her, breathing faster, and took long seconds to answer. "Whatever my little cat gave me permission to," she said softly.

Saida couldn't stop a little squirm and purr at *my little cat*, and the grin that blossomed over the rabbit's face just made her squirm more. "She might give you permission to do nearly anything."

Autumn's voice had dropped to a near whisper. "Would she want me to take control, the way only a giantess can?"

"I think she would," she breathed.

The rabbit licked her lips slowly, tongue extended enough to show its silver stud. "May I make my cat...my *little* cat?"

Saida felt herself blush again, purr breaking up as her breath became even faster. "Oh, yes."

Autumn traced a rune in the air, and left it hanging there, glittering in rainbow iridescence. Then, instead of touching the Rha with a finger, she gave her a light, lingering kiss.

The world blurred.

When her vision cleared, Saida was just where she expected—in her now giant-seeming (it *was* giant, and now she was this world's normal, wasn't she?) room, lost on a sofa cushion, colossal girlfriend towering over her. A huge hand came down right next to her, bone-white furred palm up, painted black claws glittering.

Taking a deep breath, she climbed on.

CHAPTER 29

Expectations

As she woke up, Autumn blinked blearily at the sheets, then the nightstand. Something felt off. She'd woken up in Saida's bed before, but never alone. Where—

Oh. She lifted her head off the pillow to see Saida's little form lying to one side, still asleep, barely making an indent in the blue pillowcase. She'd wanted to sleep on the rabbit's body somewhere, but Autumn had heard from other giants that it could be too dangerous for the littles, and so hadn't given Saida permission to do that. She might ask Judy for advice, though; somehow she had a feeling the raccoon would have practical experience.

After a moment's consideration, she gave the Rha a very light kiss. "Good morning, little cat."

Saida's eyelids fluttered, then went very wide for a moment. Then she gave Autumn's nose a kiss. "Good morning, giantess."

Both of them sat up, the rabbit on the bed and the cat on the pillow. "This is such a strange view." Saida ran a hand through her hair. "I've been giant relative to the world, and I've been the same size as it, but this might be the longest I've spent *tiny* relative to it."

Autumn grinned, looking down. "I'd probably be a wreck over it."

"You don't like being this size even when it's what matches your surroundings."

She shook her head. "Cars should be smaller than my paws." Stretching—more showily than she usually would, in the hopes that it would earn her another appreciative stare—she got up. "I remember you had a coffeemaker?"

"Uh." Saida looked gratifyingly wide-eyed. "Yes, on the counter near the microwave."

"Okay." She padded into the kitchen, then stopped. Oh, wait. Saida had that weird beaker-like thing she made coffee in, didn't she? She remembered watching the cat heat water separately and pour it in, with some kind of paper filter that started out square but unfolded into a cone. She ran a hand through her hair, then walked back to the bed, holding out her hand by the cat. "Hop on. You're giving me directions on how to use your mad science coffee thing."

The cat laughed, climbing onto her hand. "It's easy to use, really."

"Mmm." She walked back to the kitchen more slowly, doing her best to keep her hand level. She'd watched Professor Thorferra and other staff members hold little students like this on occasion seemingly without any care in the world, but she found it surprisingly nerve-wracking. Twisting your wrist enough to keep your palm parallel to the floor wasn't that comfortable, and not only could a misstep or stumble send her passenger flying, letting her hand bounce with her movement might, too. Or relaxing too much and letting her palm tilt. Or maybe just letting the ride become too jarring.

The coffee was by the brewer, too, a brand she'd never heard of in slightly strange pouch packaging. Saida had said she'd brought coffee from Stravell before, or whatever their version of coffee was. She carefully set the Rha down on the counter by the bag. "So I should measure some of this into the grinder, which is...right there. How much?"

"Four level scoops. And start the kettle going. You want three-quarters of a liter. Well, according to the measuring cup."

She laughed. "Having everything scaled up and just rolling with it threw me for a while when I was first giant." She got the kettle going, then found the scoop in question and emptied the beans into the grinder. Once she had the coffee ground, she looked down at the cat, who was staring around her own kitchen like it was an alien landscape. "And?"

Saida looked back up. "Okay, get a filter," she pointed, "and don't unfold it, just pull one of the corners out. It makes a cone with one layer on one side and three on the other."

"Got it." She followed the instructions, and shortly started pouring the water in. "This seems very old school. They don't have electric coffee brewers in Stravell?"

"They do, but they're not as good."

"You're channeling the goat."

Saida laughed. "The last step is making me big again, so I can actually enjoy the cup of coffee with you instead of swimming in it."

"I was thinking about dipping you in my mug and sucking the coffee out of your fur."

The cat's green eyes grew gratifyingly big again. "You can't... um...I mean..."

She grinned as predatorily as she could manage. "Choose your next words *very* carefully."

Saida whimpered audibly, although Autumn knew her noises well enough now to be able to tell it wasn't truly fear. "It'd be nice to have coffee with you on the couch side by side."

"I suppose it would." She finished pouring the water and set the kettle aside; it'd take another minute for it to finish draining through the grounds. "All right, hop on." She held out her hand.

Saida let out a shaky breath and climbed onto her palm. She curled her fingers around the cat this time so she could crouch without worrying, set her tiny girlfriend down, then cast the size-shifting spell, touching Saida's head with a claw tip.

The cat sparkled a moment, then abruptly took up her normal amount of space, the displaced air a brief gust of wind that blew a few papers off the counter.

Saida took a couple seconds to get her balance, then gave Autumn a hug. "Thanks."

She returned the hug and nipped Saida's ear. "Anytime, except maybe when I want to keep you pocket-sized."

"Ha ha." The Rha got down two mugs.

"That's just asking me to follow through, you know."

Saida's ears blushed, but she grinned. "I know." She took a sip of the coffee, then headed over to the bedroom closet to put on clothes.

Autumn paused a moment, unable to shake the image of putting a hand on her hip and saying, *did I give you permission to dress?* But —as much as it felt more like a joke than a real demand to her—she'd better not push her luck.

"What's so funny?" Saida gave her a suspicious look, her T-shirt half on.

"Nothing, except for you half-dressed." She set down the mug and went to get her own clothes. "But I remembered I have some business stuff to talk to you about."

Saida finished dressing and got her mug, then headed to the couch. "Wait, what? Little Miss Down With the System wants some business advice?" She fluttered her eyelashes.

Autumn sat down next to her and pointed at her paw with her free hand. "Do *not* think I won't shrink you and put you in my sandal."

The Rha made a *hmf* noise, although her ears colored slightly.

"Oh ho." She brushed her lips against a fuzzy cat ear. "Does that secretly make you squirm?"

Saida poked her leg with four claw tips, just hard enough to be a little painful. "Business advice."

"Ow. Okay, you know I volunteer at a food bank."

She nodded, sipping her coffee and leaning back. "You've mentioned it."

"Well, they're having big problems."

"What kind?"

"The kind where the executive director steals nearly a million dollars from an organization that's already running on a shoestring."

The cat lifted her brows. "Okay, that's big."

"So they need lots of money in a hurry *and* to find a new executive director. But it sounds like they're in trouble for not having caught their old director in time, which makes it hard for them to raise money or hire someone."

"Why would...hmm. I guess they didn't have proper auditing controls?"

"I guess." Tom had said it looked like they couldn't handle their money, which sounded like the same thing. Right?

"That's pretty terrible."

She nodded. "So what can they do?"

Saida blinked, setting down her mug. "You want me to give *them* business advice?"

"Yeah."

The cat sighed, shaking her head. "I don't know the first thing about non-profits."

"I guess it's just like any other business, except that they don't have be profitable."

"That's like saying 'it's just like any other lake, except that it doesn't have to have water.'"

Autumn tossed a throw pillow at her. "Come on."

"Seriously, I don't know." She spread her hands. "I'd need to learn all the basics about them. How much they bring in, how much they spend, what their typical revenue centers are."

"Donations."

"Sure, but what's the breakdown between individual donors and corporate donors?" The cat started ticking things off on her fingers. "Cash versus goods? One-time versus recurring? How much food is purchased versus donated? How much waste is there? How many people do they serve? Do they offer rewards for donations, or is the good feeling enough? What promises of transparency can they offer? I'm running out of fingers."

Autumn ran a hand through her hair. "I thought you didn't know the first thing about non-profits."

"I don't." Saida shrugged. "Not at the business level. This is just basic groundwork stuff. I'd need answers to those questions to even sound like I know what I'm talking about."

How many answer did she have to those questions? The orientation covered some of that, she was sure, but she didn't remember much of it now. "I think they get most of the food from wholesalers, or maybe some government program. I'm sure they have, like, thousands of families depending on them."

Saida nodded, picking up her mug again. "I hope they come through it."

"If you had answers..."

"I'd share them." The cat lifted her brows, taking another sip of coffee.

"No, I mean answers to your questions. Can you go talk to Tom? He's some kind of manager there. He'd be able to tell you all you needed to know."

Saida shifted more uncomfortably, tail flicking. "I don't think I'd be able to tell him anything he needed to know."

She grinned impishly. "Can I make it a command?"

"If you're trying to go down that path, I don't think you're supposed to ask me for permission to give me an order."

"I know, but 'I order you to go help the food bank' sounds *really* silly."

The cat chuckled. "Yes." She sipped more of her coffee, relaxing again.

"So will you?"

That got Saida to pause and look uncomfortable again. No, maybe more irritated than uncomfortable. "Look, there's nothing—"

"I'm just asking you to talk. That's all." It shouldn't be that big of a deal, should it?

Saida sighed melodramatically. "If I have time and you can schedule things with him, you can walk me over there, sure."

"Don't sound so enthusiastic."

The cat tilted her head. "I just don't want you to have unrealistic expectations about what I can do."

No, you clearly just don't want to do it. Autumn kept the acerbic retort to herself, though. To be fair, Saida had a hell of a lot on her mind right now. "It's fine."

Saida pursed her lips, clearly picking up from the rabbit's tone that it wasn't completely fine. Then she frowned, looking past Autumn.

"What?" Autumn looked in the same direction. The beacon?

"The light's off." Saida got up and crossed over to it. "It's lost the link. Mradhi must have cut it off."

Autumn crossed over to her, putting a hand on her shoulder. "You knew that was coming, though."

"I know. It's just...let me check." Saida hurried over to her tablet computer, letting the rabbit's hand fall off her. "No email," she muttered to herself, swiping and tapping furiously. "Oh, come on."

"What's happening?"

"I don't think it's here. It's not here." She tapped some more, then leaned heavily against the desk, nearly dropping the tablet. "It's not here."

"What isn't?"

"My money. Nearly all my money." She closed her eyes. "Mradhi must have had to break the link before my investment transfers could go through."

"How much do you have without that?"

She shook her head. "Fifteen thousand. Maybe."

"Oh." She'd been expecting a much lower number. "That's a lot. You should be fine."

Saida gave her a baleful look. "It's *not* a lot."

"Maybe not compared to what you're used to, but—" She cut herself off again. Between the crazy notion that fifteen thousand was a small amount of money and Saida's attitude toward the food bank, this was heading toward an argument about capitalism more real than their usual jests, and she didn't want to leave on that note. So instead she just gave the cat a hug. "We'll work it out. I have to get to class." Not entirely true, but she did have a class later.

Saida hugged back, tail lashing, and gave her a kiss—then started poking at the tablet again furiously. As Autumn headed out, she didn't look up.

CHAPTER 30
Compatible

"What if we're just not that compatible?"

Judy rolled her eyes, setting her paper coffee cup down on the table in front of the sofa she and Autumn sat on, and sighed. "She moved here from another *world* to be with you, sugar."

"She went out of her way to make it clear it wasn't just about me." Autumn shook her head, looking around the Union's common area rather than directly at the raccoon.

"That's good."

"How is that good?"

"It means she's not an idiot." Judy picked up her coffee again. "How many stories have you heard about people moving halfway across the country to chase after someone that end in 'and they lived happily ever after' versus 'and they ended up alone, broke, and in a city they didn't know?' She's here to be with someone she loves, but also to be in a city she loves."

"So she can end up alone and broke in a city she *does* know." Autumn picked up her own coffee.

"She's not alone, unless you're planning to break up with her over one...honestly, the way you described it, that was barely even a disagreement."

"She just looks at the world like a capitalist. That's so not me."

Judy sighed. "Sugar, I don't like to get into politics, but even if you don't like 'big corporations,'" she made air quotes with her fingers, "that doesn't mean you have to be against the concept of money."

"She was a vice-president of sales or something!"

"At a family-owned boutique business her brother started. How many employees did the company even have?"

"I don't know. She said she had three salespeople working under her."

The raccoon spread her hands. "That sounds like the whole thing was barely bigger than the coffee shop Kim works at."

"They weren't selling coffee, they were selling teleporter gadgets for big businesses and the ultra-rich."

"All right. And?" Judy sighed, picking up her coffee again. "Look, I may just be a naive raccoon girl from lands whose corporations aren't much like the crazy multinationals you have in these parts, and maybe back in Saida's place, too. But it's hard for me to see much difference between a business like Higher Grounds, or a street vendor, or someone selling art online—or alien cats selling teleporters." She tapped Autumn lightly on the shoulder. "But the important part is that we're not talking about some kind of abstract evil rich person here. We're talking about your girlfriend who's lost her job, her home, and her savings."

"I know." She sighed, slumping forward. "I guess I'm really overthinking this. This isn't like me."

Judy laughed. "Sweetie, it's so like you it's painful. You get yourself all hung up on the small things to keep your mind off the big ones."

She looked askance at the raccoon. "What big ones?"

"The worry that Saida's the one, and you're going to blow it by letting her go. Couple that with the worry that she *isn't* the one and you're going to blow it by hanging on."

Autumn slumped down more, staring dolefully-on at the raccoon, who looked back with a serene smile. "That is way more insightful than I wish it was." She groaned. "Three Lords, am I just looking for an excuse to break up before things get any more serious?"

"You'd hardly be the first."

She fell silent, sipping her coffee and staring into space. They were supposed to be meeting Saida here...well, any minute now, to head to an early dinner at the Beanstalk. She hadn't even *thought* the phrase "break up" since that period right after their first impromptu date, when it had looked like the Rha was blowing her off, and here she was just blurting it out.

At length, she drained the rest of the cup and set it down on the table again. "Have you felt this way?"

"Wondering if someone I'd been dating was the one for me? The capital-O One?"

"Yeah."

"I did. When I was younger, dating in secondary school. What you'd call high school here. I wasn't a popular girl. When someone paid attention to me I fell hard, and when they stopped I fell apart."

"You—you!—weren't popular." Autumn lifted a brow, half-grinning.

"I was fat, I was short, I'd gotten cripplingly shy because of all the teasing. And I didn't have a lick of fashion sense back then. I dressed like a tent. So all attention felt special, even if there was always a little voice in the back of mind saying 'he's just taking pity on you' or 'she can't find anyone else.'" She smiled, but it looked uncharacteristically melancholy. "It didn't help that sometimes the voice was right."

Autumn folded her hands in her lap, nodding a little. She'd been neither short nor fat, but she'd been teased for her appearance enough. And as her dad had said, she'd been a wallflower.

"So." Judy slapped her own knee. "I could give you the talk about how I had to start seeing myself as beautiful, and about how I don't think a capital-O One is what I want. I don't think it's what I need, either. But that's me. The question is whether it's what *you* want, and only you know the answer to that. But it's okay to be happy with someone for a time and move on. Most of us want companionship, most of us want sex. But not everyone wants both or even either, and maybe when we do, it's not from the same people. I wouldn't be surprised if I settle down in a decade or two with someone I *love,* but not someone who's one of my *lovers.* As romantic as the idea of destined true love can be, it can also be poisonous."

"That's profound, but I'm not sure it's comforting." She stroked along one of her ears. "Or very helpful. I think you just found a fancy way to say you don't want to be tied down."

The raccoon grinned more slyly. "Depends on who's got the ropes, sugar."

"Ha ha." She looked down at her coffee cup, wishing she could zap it into a very high-ABV beer. That was a class of spell that turned out to be way harder and fiddlier than you'd guess before you started studying magic, though.

Judy's smile grew softer. "I could say 'just follow your heart,' because as sappy as it sounds, I mean it. But hearts get us lost. If you let yourself get serious with someone, you're still going to have fights. And you're going to be hurt."

"I'm not expecting a storybook romance. Even though I guess a wizard in training falling in love with a cursed woman from another world is pretty fantastic." Autumn sighed. "I just feel like I've been at the lowest low back home and right up to the highest high when she was waiting for me when I came back, then all—all upside-down since then."

"So are you going to feel more right-side up if you break it off?"

"No." She hesitated, then shook her head. "No."

"Then that's what matters."

She smiled wanly. "First you talk me into seeing that Saida's problems are bigger than I wanted to admit, and now you're telling me how I feel is more important than anything else?"

"No. I'm telling you that if a relationship makes you feel bad, you're not doing your partner a favor by staying in it."

That made sense. She might still be feeling out just what it was she had with Saida. She didn't know if *she* believed in, as Judy put it, "the capital-O One." But maybe Judy was right that at the end of the day, that didn't matter so much. Whatever she had with the Rha, it *definitely* didn't make her feel bad.

"Speaking of partners." Judy nodded in the direction of the hallway that lead toward the Beanstalk.

"Huh?" She turned around to see Saida walking out, waving. Autumn stood up, too, spreading her hands. "We were supposed to meet out here, not in there! How long have you been waiting?"

"I wasn't." The Rha hugged Autumn lightly, tail swishing. "Not exactly. I've been scoping out places on campus that might have open jobs. Hopefully something in an office, but..." She shrugged.

Judy gave her a reproachful look. "You can't be thinking about being a waitress at the Beanstalk, sugar."

Autumn bristled at the implied condescension. Before she could say anything, Judy poked her in the side. "I mean she's overqualified."

"That's not a real thing!"

"No, it is." Saida sighed, leading them back slowly toward the pub. "It's not a real barrier to getting a job that's mostly staffed by student help, because they don't expect most employees to stick around. But anyone offering me a salary position will look at my résumé and think 'We're offering her a fraction of what she was making. She's heading out the door the moment anything else opens.'"

That was completely logical, and completely insane. "But you're a giant!" Autumn said incredulously. "What the hell is going to open for you that *isn't* on campus?"

"I don't know. I'm trying not to dwell on it. Oh. I spoke with your friend Tom. We didn't do much more than set up a meeting tomorrow, though."

Judy flashed Autumn a smug glance behind the Rha's back, as if to say, *see? She cares more than you think.* Autumn couldn't figure out how to communicate *this just means she wants me to stop sulking* silently, so settled for an exasperated glare.

CHAPTER 31

Measure of Efficiency

SAIDA WAITED OUTSIDE AUTUMN'S DORM ROOM AS THE rabbit locked the door, then led her back out down the hall.

"I've never seen you in a business suit before. You really pull it off."

"Thanks. Although it just makes me look even more like my cousin."

"Maybe." Autumn shrugged, looking down at the cat as they stepped outside. "You move differently than she does, though. And the clothes fall differently. Three Lords, that makes me sound like Judy."

"Kind of." Saida laughed. "But you have a strong fashion sense yourself."

Autumn hadn't planned to join her at this meeting with her friend at the food bank, but Saida had insisted. It felt wise to bring along a known friendly giant. As nonchalant as the littles in the city seemed to be, she knew the relationship with the college had some very jagged edges to it, and just because Tom liked Autumn didn't mean he'd automatically warm to someone else he was ankle-height to.

"Mmm." Autumn shrugged self-consciously.

By now, walking down little city streets with traffic around her paws—well, no, it didn't feel normal, but it didn't feel crazy. It did make her unexpectedly maudlin, though: when was the next time she'd ever ride in, let alone drive, a car?

They didn't stay in the section with the clever signaling for giants for very long. The rabbit led them out toward an older, more run-down area. It wasn't like the strange no-man's land directly adjoining the college, but it had a sense of exhaustion to it. She suspected if she were walking here as a little, with her eyes at street level, the houses would remind her of places she'd grown up, when her mother lived paycheck to paycheck.

"It's up there." Autumn pointed toward where the houses merged into a light industrial area, not far from one of the city's few elevated highways.

"So we don't have to step over that. Good."

"No, we don't, and we're not allowed to step over raised roads and tracks in the city. I mean, nobody's going to run after us and stick a ticket to our heels, but they'll raise shit with the college."

"Huh." She stopped herself from asking why—a moment's thought made it clear. A four-lane road like the one ahead would force her to take a long, heavy stride over it, without being able to clearly see what her leading sandal was coming down on. Even if the step didn't wreck anything, if she got surprised or just stepped on something sharp—or wheeled—and lost her balance, it'd be a catastrophe.

"Head down the street behind the food bank. It's wide and opens up into a big concrete lot that's giant-friendly."

She nodded. "Got it." The road was just about traffic free, but parked cars lined both sides of the street, making walking difficult. Most of the cars looked old; some of them looked like they might not be able to move unless she gave them a good kick. And in the swath of green space under that overpass, were those *tents?* She pointed. "There's...camping?"

"A homeless encampment." Autumn looked back at her with a raised brow.

"Oh." Her ears lowered.

The lot was easy enough to find, a wide concrete plain behind the well-kept warehouse building. Brushing off a space, she sat down,

Autumn next to her. A couple staff members, including a forklift driver, had paused to gawk at the cat. She waved, setting her tablet in her lap and folding her hands on top of it.

"Hi!" A hyena was jogging out of the building, waving up. "Saida? Thanks for coming by. I'm Tom." He came to a stop a few yards away, waving to Autumn, too. She'd been somehow expecting someone, well, frumpy. With form-hugging jeans and a teal T-shirt one size too small, Tom would be better described as "fashionably ripped."

"You're welcome. Nice to meet you." She drummed her fingers on the tablet's cover. "I don't know a lot—well, anything—about non-profits specifically, other than what I looked up about the food bank, so I apologize in advance if I talk about things that don't apply."

"It's okay." He shrugged, grinning. "This is pretty informal. So, Marc and I are kind of the acting directors." He gestured at a wolf closer to the warehouse, who waved back. "You have more business experience than I do, and probably more than he does. And even though this is a non-profit, it's still a business."

She nodded, flipping the tablet open and tapping over to her notes. "One that's been operating for just over twelve years."

Tom studied the tablet with slightly wide eyes. "Yeah. Well, I've been working here five years. Sorry I'm staring, but somehow I didn't think, uh, giants had computers."

Autumn snorted. "Our keyboards only have four keys: fee, fi, fo, and fum."

Saida elbowed the rabbit. "So Autumn explained the crisis you're in, with a former CEO stealing a lot of money. I have a few naïve questions that'll help me understand the business, I hope. You don't give food directly to people who need it, you give it to other organizations that do. A lot of church groups, food pantries, and other aid organizations. Some school programs."

"Yes." A few other people had stopped to stand nearby the three —Marc, a second wolf, and a vixen dressed in a smart business suit. "Um. This other wolf is Jan, our warehouse supervisor, and the vixen here is Carolyn, a long-time volunteer who just joined our board to try and help dig us out. Carolyn, this is Saida, um, Autumn's giant business woman friend."

She nodded. "I've seen her around town."

Saida smiled, then turned back to her own screen. "You get most of the food as," she flipped through the annual report on her screen, "in-kind donations from...grocery stores?"

"Some grocers, some of the wholesalers who sell to the grocery stores. But we buy about two-thirds of the food we distribute."

"So cash funding's the big thing you need."

"Right."

She rotated the tablet, splitting the screen so she could keep the report up on side and open a notes app on the other, then scribbled with the stylus. "It looked like you had one point two million dollars in reserve at the end of this auditing period, but this report is from two years ago. Is this the most recent audited statement you have?"

"Um, probably." Tom ran a hand through his hair. "We knew we'd been having problems with the most recent audit that should have been done last year, but we didn't know until last week why."

"Your former CEO didn't want an independent audit. How much do you have left in reserve now?"

"About two hundred thousand."

"And donations are dropping."

"Yes. Also, some big corporate restricted matches that usually unlock by now haven't because of the whole auditing mess. A restricted donation is one with some kind of performance measure attached to it, and since we don't have a verified audit from last year..." He spread his hands.

"Right." She tapped the stylus against the tablet. "Well, job one has to be getting that audit out, even if it's a provisional one."

"The board's supervising that now, and the unfinished audit from last year is being expedited," Carolyn said, tail swishing. She tilted her head, studying Saida more keenly. "Pardon my boldness, but what's your background?"

"I'm—uh, I was a VP of sales. Autumn thought I might have some advice for Tom." The vixen might have been a fifteenth Saida's height, but she had the presence—well, the presence the Rha had tried for in client meetings. She'd probably be formidable to meet across a negotiating table.

Carolyn glanced up at the rabbit giantess. "Really. Interesting." She smiled slightly, tail giving another swish, then looked back to Saida. "So do you have some?"

"Well." She turned back to the hyena, who was looking back and forth between short business vixen and giant business cat with a mildly wary expression. "It sounds like your first job is rebuilding trust with your biggest donors. The audit's important because you need to be absolutely transparent about the size of the hole the food bank is in. And you need to identify two or three operational areas you can immediately improve from where the last CEO left you."

"Like what?" Marc said.

She tapped the stylus again. "What's a measure of efficiency you use in your business?"

Autumn shifted, frowning. "It's not a business like your old one was," she murmured. "Helping people doesn't have to be efficient."

She looked up at the rabbit. "No, but efficiency doesn't have to be corporate speak for being cold and ruthless, either. If you and I both did the same service for people, but I could do it for half the cost you could without cutting corners, I'd be able to help twice as many people for the same amount of donations."

"We measure cost per meal," Tom offered. "We can get a food pantry a healthy meal for about fifty cents."

"Is that good? What's the industry average?"

Autumn flinched visibly at the corporate speak. Saida patted her knee. The vixen watched them, looking distinctly amused.

"It's...actually a little on the high side."

"That could be one of your goals. Say you wanted to get it down to, I don't know, forty cents a meal. Is the cost a blocker for food pantries and other agencies using you? If it is, lowering it gives you another target: expand your reach by, say, twenty-five percent. And lastly, do you do...oh, what are they called? Food drives."

"Yes. But I think you'd tell us they're not very efficient." Tom grinned up weakly. "They're probably part of why our per-meal cost is too high."

"I can see that, but they raise visibility. Maybe you could couple it with a marketing campaign to raise awareness about how you're becoming a new kind of food bank."

His ears skewed. "We're becoming a new kind of food bank?"

"Well—" she waved a hand. "We'd have to work on that. I mean, *you* would have to work on it. You don't want to spout an empty buzz phrase. But you need to make the point that you're not the food bank that's in the news now. You're restructured, you're taking steps to stay transparent, you're serving more people, you're stretching donor money farther."

"Huh. Okay." He and Marc glanced at one another, then both nodded.

"I don't know if any of this is helpful."

"No, it is. I think. I don't know what we can do until we have a new CEO, and they're going to have their own ideas, but maybe this'll guide us in searching."

She doubted it; she felt like she'd been rambling stream-of-consciousness, despite her notes. "Okay. Well, I should—"

"Can you shrink?"

"What?" She looked down at Carolyn, who was furiously typing on her phone.

"Can you shrink?" the vixen repeated, without looking up. "I'd love it if you could run through this as a presentation to the rest of the board in a couple days."

"I...well, I can be shrunk. I can do it over the phone, though, if you can set up a conference call."

She put her phone away, looking up now. "It'd be better if you could do it in person, but the next meeting's in a conference room at my bank, and while it may be a big ask—no pun intended—it'd be *much* easier if you could adopt to our scale."

She nodded slowly. "Okay."

"Thank you so much, Saida." Carolyn beamed, then looked at her watch. "I need to be on my way. I'll be in touch. Bring a C.V., if you have one."

Saida blinked, and ran a hand through her hair as the vixen strode away.

CHAPTER 32

Worth the Risk

"BEING LATE WITH A MAJOR COMPONENT OF YOUR coursework is...unlike you, Miss Caligo." Professor Snep laced his fingers together, looking across his desk at her with an expression that managed to be simultaneously stone-faced and disapproving.

"I know. It's..." No, don't tell him you forgot, even though it's technically true. Tell him *why* you forgot. "I've had some pretty unusual stresses this last quarter."

"Such as." His tone remained too flat to make it sound like a question.

"My father dying, my mother all but disowning me, my girl-friend moving here from another world."

He pursed his lips, leaning back. "You do have my sympathies for the first two. My concern with your work, however, still stands."

She rubbed her forehead. "I'm almost done with the research. I might have been finished already if I hadn't gone down a dead end studying Brinsan."

"What, pray tell, does Brinsan have to do with transmutation of state?"

"Uh." She cleared her throat. "He was interested in conversion of matter to energy and vice-versa, and that usually requires trans-mutation—"

"As a side effect."

"But, uh, that's a matter of perspective. I mean, you convert water to ice and it gives off energy in the process, and whether the ice or the energy is the side effect depends on which one you're trying to capture, right? Most of his spells are actually really *fast* at transmutation of state, but they give off a lot of energy as a byproduct. I mean, energy is what he was going for, but if there's a way to adapt that to be more efficient, it might be faster than the standard transmutation spells."

"Or the tradeoff inherent in transmutation is efficiency versus speed."

"Maybe."

"Given that you described this line of research as a 'dead end,' Miss Caligo, that would suggest a more definitive no."

"Or that I just haven't cracked it yet. But I didn't want to delay the project. Uh, any more." She cleared her throat, wishing Snep would just goddamn *blink* more often instead of staring at her so intently like this.

"Wise." He leaned back, folding his arms across his ruffled shirt, and sighed. "While I wanted to express my...concern, I didn't ask you to meet to chastise you for your work ethic, which is on balance excellent."

She nodded. "Thank you, sir."

"Shortly after you started studying with me, I asked you where you see yourself after graduation, and you had no real answer. Do you have one now?"

"Not, uh, not really."

"Your graduation may be as little as a year away, depending on the path you choose to take. It's time for you to consider that path more seriously."

"I don't know anything more about giant lands than what I've learned in classes here. I was hoping to arrange a visit across the Chasm later this year."

"So you feel your future most likely lies there."

She cleared her throat. "It's literally the only place I fit other than campus, so it seems like it's worth investigating options."

"I suspect it would be a difficult road. As much as one may

wish to avoid sweeping generalizations about other cultures, the idea of a giant who grew up as a little might be met with...hostility."

"I know I'm not the only one, historically speaking."

"And I know you've read those histories."

She sighed, looking away. "Yeah." They were centuries old and all had the feeling of being apocryphal, but the half-dozen she'd read were all positioned as stories about littles masquerading as giants until their deception was unmasked and they were driven out. (Or in two tellings, eaten. That progression had been something all students, particularly littles, had to come to grips with: first learning that what they "knew" about giants was wrong, then learning there was *some* truth to the stories about giants being horrible to those ankle-high to them after all.)

"Miss Heath is doing well with her combinatory alchemy."

Autumn furrowed her brow. What? Jen, her little lab partner? "Uh, yeah. She's really smart about that sort of magic, once you get her to slow down."

"Something you've been more successful at than I have been." He leaned forward. "I'd like you to consider being my teaching assistant next semester."

She'd never heard of Snep having a TA before. In fact, she'd heard that he used to disparage the idea of having one, on the grounds that he'd spend more time instructing any assistant than he would just instructing the class. "Why?" she blurted.

Both his brows lifted and he remained silent for several seconds. "I would like you to consider continuing your magical education after graduation, with an eye toward becoming an instructor at the college."

She blinked, stifling a laugh she knew would come out as slightly crazed. He wanted her to consider *what*? "You—uh—I'm flattered, sir, really. But I don't know how to teach magic!"

"You *have* been teaching magic. You're knowledgeable, inquisitive, and patient."

"Half the students think I look intimidating as hell."

He remained expressionless. "Another point in your favor."

"There isn't any post-degree program for magic. Or anything else. Is there?"

"That program would be becoming my apprentice, Miss Caligo."

* * *

"Do you think I would make a good teacher?"

Saida looked up from her papers distractedly. "What?"

They'd had dinner together over here at Saida's place, both of them working in the kitchen. Despite the Rha's insistence that she knew almost nothing about cooking, she'd definitely been the lead, giving Autumn quick tips on both pan sizes and knife skills as she'd whirled around the countertop. It wasn't until they were sitting down to eat that she'd realized she couldn't remember either of them asking the other one if they were free. Either they'd made plans she'd forgotten about, or she'd made an assumption Saida hadn't challenged her on. Or both. Saida's meeting with the food bank's board was tomorrow, and she'd need Autumn around to make her the right size. So it felt natural.

After dinner, she'd settled in on the couch to do some homework, while Saida had sat down at her desk to—well, also do homework, effectively, for the meeting. But she couldn't shake the conversation she'd had earlier in the day with Snep. "It's, um. Professor Snep wants me to be his teaching assistant next semester."

"That sounds good."

"I don't think he's ever had a TA before. And I think he wants me to study to be a professor here."

That got Saida to set down her papers, looking across at the rabbit with a more engaged expression. "Did he say that?"

"Not in so many words. But he wants me to stay on after graduation as his apprentice."

Saida rubbed the back of her ear. "If this wasn't a magic college, I'd say that sounded creepy, but I guess it isn't in this context. Has he taken on other apprentices?"

She shook her head. "Not as far as I know, and nobody else I've talked to has ever heard of it, either."

"Oh." Saida flicked her tail. She didn't say *that's back to being a little creepy*, but it was clearly in her tone.

"I don't think he's attracted to me, if that's what you're thinking. I think he just..." Just what? She couldn't think of any way to finish the sentence that didn't sound awkward.

"Sees something special in you."

She smiled faintly. "You're making it sound a little creepy again."

"No, I really mean it. It sounds like he thinks you're going to be a...I don't know what the proper terminology is, so I'm going with 'badass supreme sorceress.'"

Autumn felt her ears color. "I think..." She twisted a hand in her hair. "I guess he thinks I have—uh—some potential."

Saida grinned. "I've talked to a couple other Magic Arts Program students who struggle with pretty basic stuff, at least compared to what you do when you literally snap your fingers."

She shrugged. "I'm good at a couple of things that I came here specifically to learn, and I like the research. That makes me an obsessive, not the kind of generalist the school's going to need for MAP faculty."

Saida shook her head. "You're too tall to sell yourself short."

She rolled her eyes.

The cat grinned again, then tilted her head. "Seriously, this sounds like a great opportunity. I know you're not sure what you could do after college, and I'm not sure if I could get a job anywhere but Mensura as a giantess, so if we stay together, it's either going to mean living here or striking out to giant lands. And from what I've heard, those might not be that welcoming to giants who didn't grow up there."

"Yeah. No, they apparently aren't." She sighed.

"So why not give it a shot? What are you afraid of?"

"Abject horrible failure," she said promptly. "That's not a deep one."

Saida got up and walked over to sit by her. "Take the TA position and see how it goes." She smiled up. "Don't look at it as a life commitment, look at it as testing the waters."

"I guess you're right. It's just—I never had an idea of what I wanted to be when I grew up, beyond this." She waved a hand at herself. "And I know 'giantess' isn't a career choice. But even if I'm studying to be a magician, I never once thought of myself as professor material."

"I didn't grow up thinking 'one day, I want to be leading the sales team at a company commercializing mad science.' Most people don't figure out what they're really going to be until they're an adult. Sometimes—maybe more often than not—it feels like we fall into it more than choose it. This is an opportunity to choose. Even if it doesn't end up working out, it's worth the risk."

Compared to the risks Saida had been taking lately, it barely qualified as a risk at all, did it? The worst outcome if she became a TA would be a bad semester followed by just being back to where she was now. Was she really worried the worst outcome was following in Professor Snep's footsteps?

Her own words to Judy echoed in her head. *Am I just looking for an excuse to break up before things get any more serious?*

No. She wasn't, dammit. "Yes," she agreed. "You're right. It is."

Saida tilted her head, smiling up at her curiously. "That's more steel than you usually have in your tone. I think I like it."

She traced a rune in the air, and touched her finger to Saida's nose. The rune dissolved into sparkling red flowers floating down around the cat's head and shoulders. "I want to be a badass supreme sorceress. With my little cat by my side." She pulled Saida firmly against her.

The Rha purred, her ears coloring. "Or in your hand?"

She leaned down to touch her lips to the cat's ears. "Or my pocket," she murmured. "Or my bra. Or my sandal."

Saida squirmed, poking her in the side. "Do not step on your girlfriend."

"I'd just be trapping her under my toes. And only if she was naughty."

That earned her another poke. "What does 'naughty' mean?"

Autumn twisted around to face Saida and leaned forward, using her larger size to force the cat to lean back. "Let's find out."

"I don't want to be under your paws!" Saida pushed back with a laugh.

"Are you sure? I've seen you give them *really* interesting glances when you're little."

"That's because they're huge! And maybe kind of—oof." Saida fell back on her back on the couch.

Autumn stretched out over her, elbows to either side of the cat's head. "Kind of oof?"

"Cute! Bunny paws are cute."

She grinned victoriously. "I do hope you remember our safe word from the other night, because I'm going to shrink you now."

"Don't you dare!" Saida's convincingly cross look was undercut by the purr. And the lack of safe word.

Autumn leaned down and gave her ear a slow, wet lick, and the cat shuddered. Perhaps that effect wasn't part of the curse after all, but it was still glorious to take advantage of. "Don't you—rrr—"

Surreptitiously tracing another rune in the air, Autumn opened her mouth wide, then closed it around Saida's other ear. The cat shrank instantly, her head in the rabbit's mouth now, not just her ear. She squealed.

Autumn drew her girlfriend completely into her muzzle, feeling the cat squirming almost violently as the lick became full-body. For a brief moment she had the temptation—just like she had the one other time she'd held the cat fully in her mouth like this—to tilt her head back and swallow, but she couldn't *quite* work up the nerve. But the little Rha's combination of frantic protests and increasingly aroused moaning set her own body tingling with almost embarrassing speed. Rolling onto her back, she quickly shrugged out of her jeans.

CHAPTER 33

Options to Consider

As Saida walked down the street, high-heeled sandals clacking on the sidewalk, she found herself doing something she hadn't done in the month since she'd left Stravell: constantly looking up.

This was a view of Mensura she'd never had before. She'd be towering over other pedestrians, even most buildings. And while she'd been "little" on campus, it was always with Autumn, in spaces scaled to Autumn's size. Now, she was neither giant nor little, neither macro nor micro. The campus frowned on the word *normal* due to the connotations of bias—shouldn't all sizes be seen as normal?—but she found herself unexpectedly buoyant at just matching everything again.

Even as a giantess she wouldn't have loomed over most of these buildings, though. Regulations kept Mensura's downtown core off-limits to giants due to the high potential for accidental damage. While it didn't have any true skyscrapers by the standards she'd grown up with, the office buildings around her regularly rose a dozen stories, and a handful more than doubled that. On the street level, she passed by the kinds of shops she'd expect to find serving weekday workers: coffee shops, office supplies, all manner of little delis and cafés with food that ranged from what she'd seen on campus—and not too far from what she'd seen in Stravell—to highly exotic. She'd had a bagel before, but what was a "matar paneer?" Or a "pupusa?" She'd have to investigate.

From down here, the whole city had that mix of familiar and exotic, though. And she'd never in her life been surrounded by thousands of non-Rha. As a giantess in Mensura, even a "crowd" of other giants never meant more than a few dozen other people. And here she was now in a city as densely packed as any she'd ever seen, but full of cats and rats and wolves and foxes and raccoons and bears and Goddess knew what else. It was a strange thrill she doubted she could explain to anyone, other than maybe Arilin.

She checked her phone. The bank should be one more block in this direction, right? Ah, there it was, across the street, eighteen or nineteen stories of austere concrete and glass. Clean lines, if too industrial for her tastes. Even so, it was amusing how much it looked like the kind of buildings financial firms in Stravell favored, too. As many small differences as there were, there were far more similarities.

When she reached the building, she'd half-expected to find an actual bank branch on the street level. But she found only a marble-floored lobby, a bored-looking wolf in a security uniform sitting behind an information desk. Carolyn said she'd meet her "downstairs," but she was a few minutes early. She headed over to a settee against one wall, taking a seat to one side and taking out her tablet. Arilin had loaned her the cables she'd need to connect it to a projector; she'd spent last night making slightly better charts, although it still wasn't a full-blown slide show.

Was she nervous? Maybe *anxious* was a better word. It wasn't like her career depended on the impression she made, but on the flip side, she didn't exactly have a career currently—so she might at least be making valuable connections. The career she'd had until recently was all about networking, and she'd been good at it.

Putting the tablet back in its case, she paused, seeing her C.V. in the document pocket. She pulled it out, scanning it, and sighed. There was only so much she could do to downplay the Cat From Another World vibe; anyone trying to check her references would be shit out of luck. They could talk with Arilin, and she had a letter of reference she'd gotten from Mradhi before she'd made the leap, and…

that was it. Two people, both related to her, only one of whom had actually worked with her—and they couldn't verify he or his company even existed.

She closed the leather portfolio case and drummed her fingers against it. Why *had* Carolyn asked for her C.V., anyway? Maybe some of the other board members were more skeptical than the vixen, and would demand documentation to show Saida knew what she was talking about. But—

"Saida!"

She looked up to see Carolyn approaching from the elevator bank, waving, dressed just as power-professionally as the first time they'd met. "You didn't have any trouble finding the place, did you? This must be a very different view for you." She grinned.

"No, it was easy to find, Ms. Thompson." Saida rose to her feet, chuckling. "And where I used to live, I'm at this scale relative to everything else. So this feels surprisingly natural."

"Excellent. It's nice to be able to see all of you at once. The meeting room is on the sixteenth floor." She motioned the cat to follow.

Saida did, stepping into the elevator with Carolyn. "You know, I didn't get a chance to ask why you wanted me to bring along my C.V."

"Questions might come up." She swished her tail, grinning a little. "It's good to be prepared, don't you think?"

"Of course. It's just rare to have anyone ask for that outside of the context of a job application."

"Mmm-hmm." The elevator door opened on the sixteenth floor.

"This isn't secretly an interview, is it?" She half-smiled.

Carolyn put her hand on Saida's arm, steering her down the hall. "After the presentation, we might have some options for you to consider."

Saida's ears splayed.

* * *

Saida hadn't been back in the Beanstalk as a little since that first meeting with Autumn's sister Kelly, and she'd forgotten how disorienting it could be. When she caught sight of her girlfriend—easier said than done, given not only how many other giants there were but how the room's design partially hid tables and booths—she took a moment to find the correct pathway arcing toward the table, then hurried over.

The rabbit saw her before she waved, smiling as the cat walked down the final few steps onto a wide leaf over Autumn's table, holding its own appropriately sized tabletop. "You know, I don't think I've set up a date here with a little before."

"Well, I've never been on a date with a giant as a little here before, so we're even." She waved back at the path she'd taken. "I'd forgotten that at this size, this place is as much of a theme park as a restaurant."

"I remember, sort of. I still prefer being up here." She picked up her beer—from here, it looked like a slightly sudsy water tower—and took a sip. "So, how did it go?"

"It went...well. It wasn't what I expected."

Before she could figure out how to explain that, a waitress appeared—a squirrel on Autumn's scale, one who'd probably be taller than Saida even at her original size. "What can I get you, sweetie?"

"Two slices of pepperoni and pineapple, and a glass of the stout, please."

She nodded, turning away and almost bouncing off. Saida couldn't help but stare at the cloud of tail.

"Hey." Autumn snapped her black-tipped claws over Saida's head. "Don't stare at her tail when mine's right here. Also, that was a really cryptic answer to my question."

"Yeah. I'm still trying to figure things out myself." She ran a hand through her hair, then leaned back, looking up. "I think they want to offer me a job. There's nothing formal on the table yet, but the implication...I mean, it was more text than subtext."

"Really? That's great!" Autumn smiled, leaning in closer. "What kind of job..." Her eyes widened. "Holy shit, they want you to be the new CEO."

Saida cleared her throat. "Ms. Thompson—Carolyn, the vixen— does. I'm not sure how enthusiastic the rest of the board is about the idea, but they were impressed by my presentation."

"That's amazing!"

A raccoon on Saida's scale walked up behind her with her beer. Goddess, did he teleport? Were there hidden staff-only access points...somewhere? "Uh, thanks."

"No prob. Your pizza'll be up soon."

She nodded, and looked back up to Autumn. "It's...yeah, it is."

"You don't sound like you've convinced yourself of that."

Saida took a sip of the beer, and looked off into the distance across the pub. She was used to thinking of the Beanstalk as relatively cozy, not objectively huge. "I've never run a non-profit. Hell, I've never run a for-profit, either. I just—I don't know this space at all. I'd be managing more people than ever before, too." She sighed, looking back up. "There's a big difference between selling teleporters to companies and gazillionaires and getting food to homeless shelters and soup kitchens. If you don't sell somebody a teleporter, it just means they have to travel like normal people. If a food bank screws up, people go hungry. They could even starve."

Autumn took another sip of her beer, then drummed her fingers on the table, under the leaf Saida's table sat on. "Do you want it?"

She shrugged. "You know what they say. Count your catmint sprouts, not your seeds."

The rabbit squinted down at her. "No, I don't know that saying at all, and it's pretty weird. And you're ducking my question again."

"I think...I think I do. It'd just be such a big change."

"Says the woman who recently moved between worlds."

"Ha ha."

The giant squirrel waitress appeared, carrying a tray with Autumn's pizza slices on it—and the raccoon waiter, who carried a tray with Saida's. "Clever," Autumn said.

"Thanks, sweetie," the squirrel said with a wink.

"It's efficient," the raccoon said with a grin.

"What is that?" Saida squinted skeptically at Autumn's pizza after the waitstaff headed off. "It isn't even red."

"No sauce. Almonds, grapes, and gorgonzola."

"That is really fancy for a college pizza joint and also sounds disgusting."

Autumn snorted. "It's the weekly special, and it's great. Look, what are you worried about? If they don't make an offer, you're just where you are now anyway. If they do, it means they *really* want you. They'd have to make a lot of accommodations for a giantess."

Saida found herself watching Autumn's throat as she swallowed, and she sat on her tail to keep it from twitching. She took a big bite of her own pizza, then took a deep breath. "That's maybe part of what I'm worried about."

"What do you mean?"

"If they actually made me an offer—" She waved her free hand at herself. "They'd expect me to stay this size, not be yours."

Autumn choked on her pizza.

CHAPTER 34

A Crazy Thought

SAIDA TILTED HER HEAD UP TO LOOK AT AUTUMN, staying nestled against her side on the couch. "What's on your mind? It's clearly not the movie."

"Mmm." She pursed her lips at the romantic comedy playing on the TV. "I don't think I've seen this one, but I feel like I could almost quote the dialogue word for word anyway. So I guess my mind's drifting."

"To what?"

"You spending most of your time small." She grinned. "Well, smaller."

Saida snorted. "Don't count your shrunken girlfriends before they get the job offer."

"Is that another bizarre Rha aphorism?"

Saida poked her in the side. "I mean it. It's silly of me to be making plans without even a signal an offer is coming, so it's even sillier of you to fantasize about that."

"I didn't say I was fantasizing about it. I *am*, but I didn't say it." Autumn grinned. "Seriously, though, this is something we have to think about. I'd have to be available to shrink you in the mornings and grow you in the evenings."

"It'd be more practical if I just stayed small the whole week, I think."

"How could you—you wouldn't fit!" She gestured around the apartment. "You couldn't live here!"

Saida shrugged. "I'd have to get a place that's little-sized for the week. Ideally, I could afford to keep both this place and a studio closer to downtown, although that'd depend on the salary I could get wherever I ended up. But that might be something I'd need to do even if I don't get an offer from the food bank."

"Why?" She furrowed her brow.

"Going downtown, seeing all the businesses there, the offices, the people..." Saida leaned back against the couch, looking up at Autumn again. "It made realize that I might be thinking too small by staying big. As a giant, my work options are limited to campus. As a little, a lot of positions I have relevant experience for open up."

"Yeah, but that's just so..." She trailed off. She couldn't imagine being trapped as a little day and night for an office job, returning to her correct size only on weekends. How could Saida, who grew up giant, even think about it? But back in Stravell she hadn't been a giant, not in a relative sense. And she certainly hadn't grown up knowing she was the wrong size. "I guess it's not something I'd considered."

"It's not something I'd considered, either." Saida smiled more, tilting her head. "But it's something you *wouldn't* consider. For you, towering over the world has to be the rule, not the exception. For me, though—as much as I hate to say 'it's all relative,' it really is. I love towering over the world, too, but I'm remembering how much I also love fitting perfectly in it." She grinned more impishly. "And thanks to a certain rabbit, I've started seeing more appeal in being doll-sized."

Autumn smiled sheepishly. But Saida's words still made her head spin. "So you're really thinking of living as a little most of the time."

Saida sat up, leaning forward to pick up her drink. "It's not something I'm committed to. But it's an option I should keep open."

"Wow. Everything you're saying makes sense, but—wow." She frowned. "Although I'm not sure the part about keeping two places makes sense. I know you used to do that, but you literally lived in two worlds, and you were making a big VP kind of salary."

Saida smiled. "This wouldn't be living in two worlds as literally, no, but in a way it still would be. Shrinking in the morning, commuting off campus, commuting back in the evening and shifting back up to full size—that's complicated. What if I stay late at work, or have an evening meeting? And if I stayed small during the week, well, like you said, I couldn't keep living here."

Autumn leaned back, crossing her arms. She didn't want to go around in circles on this; maybe Saida was right. It just seemed so... not just expensive, but wasteful to have two places to live, no matter how convenient. "Would they pay you enough to keep two places in the same city like this?"

"I think so. Mensura's rents don't look like they're far off from where I lived in Stravell, and I'd only be looking for a studio. So even though there's be a premium for living downtown, it'd be less than half of what I was paying for my old place."

"But you'd still be paying for *this* place. How much would your total rent go up?"

"About double."

"Three Lords." She shifted position on the couch, scowling to herself. There had to be some way...

Autumn looked back down at Saida, biting her lip. "I kind of have a crazy thought."

"Like?"

"What if I moved in with you?"

Saida's eyes widened slightly.

"The scholarship I'm on has a housing allowance which just goes straight to the school now, but it could go to your rent. And if I'm here, that solves the problems with you needing me to shift your size."

Saida smiled, but furrowed her brows, clearly working through this. After a moment, though, she shook her head. "It doesn't make your schedule line up with mine. Or solve the problems of not being able to do *anything* in this place when I'm the wrong size. I don't know if the school even runs the little-sized buses out here, since it's a giant-only section of campus."

"They do. And it'd help with the schedule, even if it wouldn't solve it. Maybe you'd still need the place in the city, but your total rent would only be fifty percent higher."

Saida pursed her lips, tail flicking, and drummed her fingers on the armrest. At length, she looked up at the rabbit with a searching expression. "Forget all the finances and the mechanics for a moment. If they didn't matter at all, would you *want* to move in with me?"

Autumn swallowed. That was the real question, wasn't it? She'd had a roommate her first year here, a requirement for all freshmen staying on campus. Honestly, it hadn't been as bad as she liked to remember it as being. But it hadn't been good, either. Her only other experience living with people was back home, and she'd had her own room then. This would be sharing a single bedroom—barely more than a studio—with someone else, someone who had a very different outlook on the world than anyone else she'd known.

And someone she was in love with. Her girlfriend. Her little cat.

She nodded slowly, looking back into Saida's eyes. "I'm willing to try. Would you want me to?"

Saida let out a long, slow breath, then took another one, running a hand through her hair. Then she smiled up. "I'm willing to try."

Autumn pulled the cat close again, gently, and kissed her.

* * *

"This is a damn quick change from 'I'm just not sure we're compatible,' sugar." The raccoon hefted a box of books, grunting softly.

Autumn snorted at Judy, picking up a box of her own. "That was a while ago."

"A month. It was barely a month ago." They headed out of the dorm, adding the boxes to a slightly haphazard stack on a low—for giants—push truck.

"Are you telling me I'm rushing into this?" Autumn crossed her arms. If Judy was going to get into that conversation with her, it might have been better to do it before she was almost all packed.

"What's important is, what do *you* tell you?" Judy leaned against the cart, breathing hard.

"Well, remembering that conversation we had from not quite a month ago, what I'm telling me is that this is a relationship that doesn't make me feel bad. It makes me feel really good so far."

"And you're not still worried she's just too capitalist?" Judy's grin edged into a smirk.

"I'm grudgingly admitting that her business background might be just what the food bank needs after all. Even if it doesn't pan out, it'd be selfish of me to hold her back from doing what she's good at because it doesn't mesh with my anarchist streak."

Judy started trudging back toward the dorm. "Wasn't she supposed to have been here helping you move by now?"

"After her lunch with Professor Thorferra."

Judy looked at her watch. "I suppose it's still lunchtime. We could have just waited. Or waited to move until tomorrow."

"I guess." She sighed. "It just feels like I should move as fast as I can. I don't know." All the big stuff from the room was already on the truck, not that there'd been a whole lot; she just had some clothes left now, which Judy had already frowned at and repacked.

"It keeps you from overthinking it until you get cold paws."

"Stop psychoanalyzing me."

"Stop psychoanalyzing you correctly, you mean." Judy picked up the box of clothes.

"Yes. That." She picked up another box—the last box—and they both headed back outside.

Judy laughed, then hummed as she set the box down on the cart. "Saida's not going to—" She looked off to the side. "Right on cue."

Autumn looked, too, as Saida hurried over, waving. "Not going to what?"

"Not going to have anything to do, since we just finished loading up the truck." She grinned. "How was your lunch with your cousin?"

The Rha's ears folded down. "Running long, evidently."

"No, we're just that fast, sugar," Judy said, waving a hand dismissively. "Did the professor have any advice for you?"

"No, just an attentive ear. She's impressed that I'm 'finding solid ground so quickly.' Which is funny, because I feel like I'm skydiving, waiting for the parachute to open."

Judy tilted her head, looking blank.

"When littles—and Rha, I guess—jump out of airplanes, parachutes are kind of like sails that open to catch the wind and slow them down."

"I don't know why a little would want to go *up* in an aeroplane. Why in the heavens would they want to jump *out* of one?"

Autumn and Saida looked at each other. "You know, objectively, that's a great question," Autumn said. Both of them laughed; Judy looked puzzled, and just shook her head.

"You've got all the boxes down?" Saida put her hands on her hips. "There's nothing left for me to do?"

"You can push the truck along. It's magically assisted, so it should be pretty easy."

"Um, sure." Saida started pushing. After an initial grunt, the cart started rolling almost of its own accord, keeping pace ahead of the Rha. Autumn and Judy walked to either side of her.

"Arilin did mention a complication. There's safety rules about littles and giants living together on campus. Even though we're both giants, since I might be spending a lot of time little, we might run into problems."

"Oh." Autumn furrowed her brow. "I thought that rule only applied to students."

"No, and besides, you're a student. Arilin wasn't sure what we needed to do to be in compliance."

Judy grinned. "You'll need somewhere in your shared living space that's set up for your size. I mean, your little size."

"Like what?" Saida snorted. "A dollhouse?"

"The official term is 'nested living space.' But you could sure call it that if you want." Judy's grin grew wickedly wide.

Saida's ears flattened.

"Can I keep it on the nightstand?" Autumn tried to sound joking, but couldn't keep actual eagerness out of her tone.

"I am *not*—" Saida started to say.

"If the nightstand's big enough, of course!" Judy cut in.

The Rha narrowed her eyes at the raccoon. "You're enjoying this way too much for a bystander."

"Don't worry, sugar." Judy squeezed Saida's shoulder. "I won't play with Autumn's doll unless she gives me permission."

Saida spluttered. Autumn tried, unsuccessfully, not to giggle.

CHAPTER 35

Before She Finally...

"BAD NEWS?"

Saida blinked over at Autumn as the Rha stepped back in from the patio. "What?" She put away her phone.

The rabbit tilted her head. "Your expression is hard to read, but it's not happy."

She shook her head, sitting down on the couch. "No, not bad news at all." Usually the rabbit was the more teasingly cryptic one; maybe she could play this for a minute or two. "I'm just a little shell-shocked. Things are suddenly moving...fast."

Autumn sat down next to her. "I know. They are for me, too. But don't keep me in suspense. Did they give you an answer?"

"They gave me an answer." Saida managed to keep her face and tone completely blank.

That earned her a gratifyingly exasperated glare from the rabbit. "For fuck's sake, what was it?" Autumn snapped.

"They offered me the job."

It took Autumn a full second to process Saida's studied bland-ness. Then she yelped, bouncing in place. "You got the job? You jerk!" She pulled the cat into a tight hug. "You got the job!"

Saida hugged back, purring. "I haven't accepted the offer yet, but I will. It's higher than I was expecting. By a lot. More than I'd been making."

Autumn pulled back, eyes widening. "Holy shit, from a *food bank*?"

"It's a non-profit, but I guess it's still a CEO position. This is a drop from the previous executive's salary."

"Really? Why? It's not because you're a woman, is it?"

"I think it's because the last guy was a crook and it's an important symbolic gesture. If things work out, I could push to go up in a year or two, but I don't know if I'd want to. I'd rather more money go to the actual mission."

"I swear you're just trying to confound my stereotypes."

"Maybe." Saida laughed. "I wasn't focused on making money claw over paw back in Stravell; it felt like it all just *happened*. Having a brother starting the business in the first place, being the first person he turned to, just kind of...having the company grow out from us. I didn't think about charity work, what non-profits do, much back then. And a food bank isn't as glamorous, as whiz-bang science fiction-ish. But to the people it's important to, it's..." She shrugged. "It's everything."

Autumn smiled at that, giving the cat a nuzzle on the cheek.

Saida purred, leaning against her. "So, we need to talk about getting that nested living thing. Apparently we'll need it set up within sixty days to stay compliant with the lease."

"Yep." The rabbit grinned a little. "I won't force you to use it."

Saida poked Autumn in the side. "You think you can just make me?"

"We both *know* I can just make you." Autumn licked the edge of her ear, slowly and just wetly enough to make her squirm. "But it's not hot if you don't want it."

After all these months, she still wasn't sure she liked Snep's not-so-tacit implication that her reaction to licks—and tongues and teeth —stemmed from her own suppressed desires rather than Kenley's machinations. She cleared her throat, feeling her ears burn. "We'll talk about it once we see what it actually is."

"Oh, will we." Autumn licked her lips slowly, tongue extending just far enough to show the stud.

"Behave, you. We need to have this conversation." She poked Autumn in the nose with a claw.

"We do. But we also need to celebrate." The rabbit caught her hand with her own larger one, then traced a rune in the air with her other hand.

"Don't you dare!" Her tail lashed more. Should she break out the safe word? She hadn't used it yet, and—well, it seemed silly to do that in the middle of a serious conversation. And it wasn't as if being shrunk by Autumn's touch was all that bad.

Autumn finished the rune, still holding Saida's hand, then caught one of the cat's fingers between her lips.

All at once Saida found herself dangling from the rabbit's giant mouth, her hand starting to slip along the glossy black lip. She yelped, trying to get her other hand up on—oh, that didn't help at all. "Autumn!" She scrabbled to pull herself up. *"Autumn!"*

The rabbit opened her jaws. With a startled shriek, Saida fell— about five feet, onto Autumn's furry palm. "Yes, little cat?" She fluttered her eyelashes.

Saida just stared up, breathing hard. "When I get big again—" she started to mutter.

"When I *make* you big again, you mean." Autumn couldn't keep a grin off her face. "So. You were saying we need to talk about living arrangements when you're little like this."

"This isn't the easiest condition to have a serious conversation in."

"Look, if you're thinking about spending the bulk of your time little, you'll have to get used to having serious conversations with me like this. But maybe this will be easier." Autumn lowered her hand, setting her down on the couch close to one of the armrests. Then the rabbit stretched out on her stomach, paws in the air nearly a hundred feet away. Autumn's lovely muzzle hovered close overhead, and her hands, with their surprisingly intimidating glossy black claws, came to rest on either side of the Rha.

"Yeah." She swallowed. "Um. Easier." Her tail lashed, slapping the cushioned armrest. "So I guess I can...talk to the leasing office about the...nested...thing..."

"Nested living space. I looked it up. It's kind of cool. It has its own kitchenette and bathroom, privacy curtains, sometimes even an elevator. You have to pick where you want it ahead of time, though, because it's installed, not just set down. And they need to install an entrance for you into the place at that size, a little door in the big door."

Saida nodded, listening, then pursed her lips. "That makes it sound like a pet door."

"Mmm-hmm. I swear I wasn't thinking about getting you a leash and collar."

She narrowed her eyes up at the rabbit. "You couldn't even find them in this size."

Autumn poked her lightly with one of those fearsome claws. "You may *feel* like you're a few inches high, but you're five foot seven, remember? Finding them in that size is easy. I'd get you a green one, so it matched your eyes."

"For someone who's not thinking about collaring me, that's awfully specific."

"It's just that when I'm not thinking about it, I'm specifically not thinking about you wearing a green one." She grinned.

Saida could tell her ears were flushed again. She tried to counterbalance that with a scowl. "You're terrible."

"I am, but that's because it turns you on so much. So what else do we need to talk about before I finally swallow you whole?"

"You're just saying that to get me flustered."

"You're already flustered." She lowered her muzzle down toward the little Rha. "I'm saying it to get you frightened and aroused all at once."

Saida swallowed, watching those black lips descend, the fine chains on Autumn's choker jangling softly. "It's working. I, well, my weekday home in the city, although you don't need to worry too much about that. You're—"

Autumn touched her nose to Saida's chest. She scooted back, only to find herself pressing into one of the rabbit's furred hands. She cleared her throat and finished, "You're, uh, not likely to be visiting me there."

"Probably not." Autumn's breath ruffled the cat's fur as she spoke softly. "Maybe you can get a studio with a balcony, though, so I can grab you off it like a proper monster."

She squirmed as the rabbit's lips touched her. "I don't think there are any high-rises in the parts of town giants are welcome."

Autumn blew over her. "I'll crouch."

Saida found herself squirming again just from the breathing. Moisture in the breath? The glimpse of the tongue? Remembering Autumn, that very first night they'd met, talking about how she'd try swallowing someone if she knew they could come back? The way when her thoughts drifted to being trapped *right there* with Autumn tilting her head back, it became less nightmare than erotic dream? Her breath was—sweet—but more—

"Did you take a breath freshener...?"

"I wouldn't want to have bad breath with my little cat in my hand, let alone my mouth, would I? So I chewed on some mint." She blew over the Rha again. "Catmint."

Saida whimpered. "I mentioned you were terrible, right?"

She laughed. "I think we're going to have a lot of fun living together, little cat."

Saida didn't try to fight the blush this time. "There's still the question of where to put this 'nested living space.' It sounds like you know more about the requirements than I do."

"It needs a wall with a power outlet and a way to make a water connection. It needs to be on a raised platform, high enough that a giant can't accidentally step on it. And it needs around three hundred square feet of surface area, plus whatever they need for an elevator or staircase."

"Three hundred square feet? That's more than half the apartment—oh, right."

"Oh, right." Autumn grinned. "To me, and to you when you're bigger, that's more like twelve inches by sixteen inches. I think the total living space is closer to thirteen feet by eighteen feet. Anyway, it'd fit on the nightstand. Not that we have to put it there, but I think it would be...I think it'd be nice."

"When you're not sleeping by your girlfriend's side, you'd like her by your side in a dollhouse." It was Saida's turn to grin impishly.

"It sounds sweet and weirdly romantic and somehow very, very hot." Autumn sounded sheepish. "But if you think somewhere else would be better, that's absolutely—"

"I'd love to be your doll." It came out before she'd given herself time to consider it, but: it was true.

Autumn blushed, and pressed her nose to Saida's chest.

"Rrf." She squirmed, hands on the rabbit's nose, feeling herself get more tingly-prickly. "Uh. There's—um. Can they make a water connection there? It's not a shared wall with a bathroom or a kitchen."

Autumn kept her muzzle right in front the little cat as she answered, making her look at her teeth, tongue and throat again— and making that sweet, slightly intoxicating breath blow around her inescapably. "They said there are water pipes there, because this is a multi-unit connection. So it's mostly paying for installation costs plus a deposit."

"Oh. Good."

Autumn drew back and bit her lip. "I'm going to give you a command or two now, I think."

"All right."

"And you remember the safe word? Because you just might need to scream it." She tilted her chin up, exposing her long throat, and swallowed audibly, making her throat ruff ripple.

"Yes. I do." Saida's voice wavered as her heart raced.

"Strip."

She did so, setting her clothes off to the side, past one of the rabbit's giant hands.

Autumn pulled back enough to watch, then slowly drew her tongue up the Rha's nude body, knees to face. Saida closed her eyes, leaning in, whimper edging over into a moan.

When she opened her eyes, Autumn simply opened her mouth, lower jaw touching the couch, upper jaw high enough that the square front teeth loomed over Saida's head. The next command was unspoken, but crystal clear.

Taking a deep breath of catmint, she crawled into the rabbit's mouth.

The jaws closed, teeth just behind her paws. Autumn lifted her tongue, pinning her against the ribbed palate, heat and moisture building rapidly in near-total darkness, leaving just touch and scent and sound as overwhelming sensations. The "floor" of tongue shifted, rubbing, until the stud pressed up hard between her legs. She gasped, bucking reflexively, finding herself held in place. Goddess, her fur was already soaked, and—mff—

Everything shifted as the rabbit tilted her head back and sucked her forward. She slid helplessly, yelping and spluttering. The sounds became not just fluid wetness but a short, breathy moan vibrating her whole body. She knew that sound, knew what it meant Autumn felt now, too. It scared her and elated her in equal measure.

The giantess shifted the pressure, making her slide forward in a slick rush of saliva, paws bumping the back of those huge front teeth once more. Then a disorienting whirl, a shift in gravity, ending with sliding back down again. Was she upside down? Autumn had rolled onto her back, hadn't she? Another faster, breathier bone-rattling moan filled her mind with images of just what her giant girlfriend was doing out there, just what she thought of having *her* in *here*.

Even without another press, another tease, Saida found herself shuddering, and the shuddering wouldn't stop. Another moan, more urgent—two moans, both hers and Autumn's. "Yes," she gasped, jamming herself against the tongue, against the stud. Oh, goddess, did she mean she wanted the climax, or to be swallowed? It could be taken either way.

And—it didn't matter.

The shudder became a spasm, her back arching, body twisting. She felt her lover shudder, too, all around her. "Yes! Y—"

Her scream compressed into a tight, hot blur as she slid down Autumn's throat, ears ringing with both the rabbit's squeal and her own.

CHAPTER 36
Live it Up

AUTUMN TURNED FROM LISTLESSLY STARING AT THE ceiling to squint at the bedside clock.

2:46.

She looked back at the ceiling, putting a hand on her stomach. Anything she could have felt—or imagined feeling—was long gone.

Three Lords, how could she have *done* that?

(Very easily.)

Why had she—

(Because she wanted to, and because Saida—she hoped—wanted her to. Because it was somehow incredibly sexy. Because every minute of it had been so intense, she got aroused just remembering she'd done it.)

But when would Saida come back?

(Not yet.)

She closed her eyes, rubbing over them.

(*Would* Saida come back? Nobody *else* did. Maybe the whole "curse" was a delusion. Maybe Saida hadn't had the nerve to tell her she'd been lying. Maybe she'd missed the safe word. Maybe —maybe—)

She covered her face with the bed's other pillow, groaning, and lay in the near-darkness. Alone. As exhausted as she felt, sleep had to come sometime, whether or not she wanted it to.

When her eyes snapped open again, the pillow was off her face, and the sheets were twisted around her. She'd slept for a moment, barely, only to be snared by an already-fading nightmare of the previous evening, stripped of all its romance and fetish-fuel sexiness. Now what she felt in her stomach was unsettled, knotty nausea.

Whining, she rolled over to look at the clock again. 3:02. Oh, Three Lords. She rolled onto her back again and collided with another body.

She sat up abruptly, screaming.

Saida blinked drowsily. "Mmm?" The Rha had just a moment to look surprised before she started to bubble, dissolve and melt.

Autumn's scream rose in pitch, even as she felt someone hug her. That made her scream even louder.

"Shh. Shh. Stop." Saida nuzzled her neck, holding her tightly. "It's okay. Stop."

Was she really awake now? Saida was really—

She frantically fumbled for the bedside light, snapping the switch on. It temporarily blinded her. Saida made a *mewp!* noise.

But she was really there. Back to her normal, giant size, in bed, sitting next to her.

"You—you're—"

"I'm okay." Saida kissed her nose. "Oh, sweetie, I'm fine. I'm fine."

"I didn't—didn't..." Autumn sniffed, rubbing at her eyes, and took a deep breath. "How did you—you weren't here, you were gone, and suddenly you're back?"

"That's the way it happens." The Rha sighed, smiling, rubbing the rabbit's shoulders. "I've never had anyone here before, though. I just wake up in bed, and what happened feels like a very real dream. Did I just...teleport in, or what?"

"I don't know. I guess I finally fell asleep and when I woke up from a *really* fucked-up nightmare you were hugging me." She sniffed again. "I didn't know what to expect. I should have asked. I didn't know when you'd come back, how you'd come back. I started wondering *if* you'd come back. I didn't even ask if—if this what you wanted."

"Yes, you did." Saida gave her a kiss on the cheek. "I mean, you made it very clear what might be coming, asked about the safe word, and..." She cleared her throat, purring unevenly. "I'm pretty sure you could tell what my reaction was."

"Yeah." She smiled weakly. "It's just the, uh, part afterward I started to get real worried about." She patted her stomach.

The Rha gave her a lopsided smile in return. "Just say that's the least romantic part, but I've figured out how to make things quick and leave it at that."

Autumn shook her head, and ran her hand through her hair. Then she fell back on the bed, staring at the ceiling again. "At least now I might have a chance to get back to sleep."

"That'd be good." Saida smiled down, then snuggled up next to the larger rabbit.

"Yeah." Autumn kissed the cat, smiling back, and sighed deeply.

They lay in silence a minute or two, until Saida spoke in a hesitant whisper. "Did you...I mean, um. Did you like..."

"Swallowing you whole?"

"At the time it seemed like you did, but you seemed so broken up a few minutes ago, I'm second-guessing myself now."

"It was so hot it kind of scares me. On the one hand, I don't know if I could bring myself to do it again for a while, and on the other, I want to do it again so bad it almost hurts."

"Wow." Saida laughed softly, giving her throat a kiss. "Now I have a new mixed emotion of shock-gratification to go along with fright-arousal."

* * *

"Do they even *do* a Sunday dinner this early?" Autumn glanced between Saida and the closed door to Chimayo. When she'd suggested going out for lunch a few hours ago, the Rha had said they should eat light because she'd made early dinner reservations. She hadn't mentioned where she'd made them, although as far as Autumn knew, unless they both shrank down—an option her girlfriend wasn't likely to spring on her without warning—it was either here or the Union Cafe. Saida had said it was fine if they went "casual, but dressy casual," which made her long for Judy's advice. When she'd made that joke on the way over, Saida told her she looked lovely, then added that Judy was on the way to meet them—it'd be a double-date with Kim.

"Yes, they do. We're just here a little early. There's some folks waiting outside the street-level door, too." She waved a hand at a handful of littles visible past the railing overlooking the campus.

"Mmm."

Judy arrived a few minutes later, Kim on her shoulder. The raccoon looked positively thrilled—and naturally, her idea of "dressy casual" made Autumn feel like she might as well be wearing a burlap sack. As for the goat, her jeans were unripped, her T-shirt was a solid, logo-free color, and she wore a simple gold chain necklace. It—well, it manage to make her look a lot dressier than normal. Judy probably had something to do with that.

"Oh, this is so lovely." Judy clasped her hands together, studying the restaurant.

Kim studied it, too, expression more dismayed than pleased. "I'm not going to be able to afford the appetizers here. Are they going to charge me for going in? I think I feel money being tugged out of my wallet just for getting this close." She slapped a hand over her pocket.

"Hush." Judy patted her with a finger. "We'll manage."

"It's covered," Saida said.

Judy shook her head. "Sugar, you may be getting an income soon, but you don't have one now. And you don't need to—"

"Really." Saida held up both her hands. "It's fine. Trust me. I've worked something out."

"You staying to wash the dishes?" Kim snorted.

Autumn poked the cat in the side. "She knows the owner, and she means she's name-dropping to get a discount."

Saida batted her hand away. "I know this isn't our 'first date' restaurant, but it's still special to me because of you."

Judy furrowed her brows. "Isn't the owner some kind of celebrity? Or do you mean the owner of this location?"

Autumn started, "She means—"

The door opened, first a crack, then all the way, as the tigress she recognized from their first visit held it open. "Hello. Talirend party?"

"Yes." Saida waved, motioning the rest forward.

"Three giants, one little." She checked her tablet and nodded, smiling. "Right this way."

They followed her in. The giant side of the restaurant was empty; two or three parties were being led into the little dining room visible as a balcony to them.

The tigress didn't stop there, though; she walked through the entrance to the kitchen. Judy stopped in confusion; Autumn slowed, glancing at Saida, who spread her hands in a "no clue" motion.

"Right this way," the tigress repeated, motioning.

Proportionally, the giant side of the kitchen was surprisingly small. Maybe they just did the final prep and plating here. They could look directly into the main kitchen on the little side, though— the floor on that side became a counter on the giant side. Two cooks on their scale, a wolf and a squirrel, stood nearby. The wolf nodded solemnly to them as they entered; the squirrel smiled briefly, although she kept glancing into the little kitchen. Autumn guessed she was some kind of coordinator between the two sides.

The tigress led them to a table at the side of the kitchen, just slightly set into a carpeted alcove. The silent wolf followed, and both of them pulled out the chairs.

"You booked us at the chef's table?" Kim stared at Saida. "I didn't know they even *had* a chef's table for giants."

The tigress smiled. "It's only by special request."

Judy gave Saida a raised-brow look as she sat down. "Now I *am* starting to think you're showing off, sugar."

"I didn't request it," Saida protested, still standing. She looked to the tigress. "Are you sure—"

"No, you didn't. I did."

Autumn looked over at the new, distinctly amused voice. A coyote woman, a few feet shorter than Saida, walked over from around the kitchen corner. Brilliant red hair was tied back in a ponytail; the rest of her fur, at least what wasn't covered by her chef's whites, seemed just as vibrantly colored. And she looked awfully familiar. Cooking shows her mom had watched occasionally?

"Chipotle! I didn't know you were in town!" Saida and the coyote hugged. "And my size on top of it."

The chef laughed. "I try to get to each restaurant for a week at least three times a year. Your timing was just good luck. And I'm giant tonight because how else would I help serve you? Sit. Introduce me to your friends."

Saida sat down. "This is Autumn, my girlfriend."

"Nice to meet you, Autumn."

The rabbit took Chipotle's offered hand. "I'm pretty sure I've seen you on television."

"You might have." The coyote grinned, turning to the raccoon.

"And this is Judy, and the goat on her shoulder is Kim." Saida indicated each one.

"It's a pleasure to meet you," Judy said, shaking Chipotle's hand.

"Likewise, Judy." The coyote smiled, then leaned toward Kim slightly, holding out a finger.

Kim touched the coyote's claw and bleated. "Oh my god I have like three of your cookbooks and I can't figure out how to cook anything in them but they're all so amazing and I was saving up to get dinner here sometime and now I'm at the chef's table and—"

"It's nice to meet you, too, Kim. Take a breath and relax. You're all guests of the house tonight." Chipotle smiled, without showing much tooth, and straightened up, clasping her hands in front of her. "So, welcome to Chimayo. We're going to do tonight's tasting menu, with a bit of adjustment for each of you based on your species like we always do. There'll be nine courses—"

Kim bleated again, sinking back against Judy's neck fur.

"—and there's a wine pairing with each course. Hanson and I will be taking care of you tonight." She indicated the wolf, who nodded once more.

"Chipotle, that's...more than I was expecting." Saida smiled nervously.

"I said you're my *guests*. Live it up, fluffy." Chipotle slapped the Rha's back, and headed away.

As soon as she left the table, Autumn, Saida, and Judy all stared at Kim.

"Shut up I'm a big fan okay," the goat muttered, ears and cheeks bright red. "I didn't know you *knew* her, Saida!"

"I didn't know she was such a big deal." The Rha grinned faintly.

"She won *Iron Chef*, twice!"

"I don't know what that means, but I guess it's impressive. I mostly just know her as Arilin's friend and business partner."

Judy blinked. "Arilin, as in Professor Thorferra?"

Saida nodded.

"Wow."

Hanson set down wine glasses, along with small plates that each bore a single small cookie. Three of the cookies were giant-sized; the fourth cookie was sized for Kim, but came not only on its own plate but on its own table and chair, which Chipotle herself carefully set down on the middle of the big table. Judy gently set the starstruck goat down by it.

"An amuse-bouche of smoked chile shortbread," Hanson noted. He poured three glasses of white wine; Kim's was already poured, sized for her.

"It's not chocolate?" Autumn blinked, picking up her cookie and taking a nibble. Her ears stood up. "Oh." It definitely wasn't: it had a hint of chocolate, but had just as much smoke and pepper to it. A hidden jelly center packed a more distinct punch.

"Oh, wow," Kim mumbled, sinking down in her chair as she ate the not-quite-a-cookie. "But...how did Chef Layotl get to be giant? Her own magic rabbit?"

Autumn snorted.

"Sarah, I'd bet." Saida nibbled her own cookie. "A red wolf singer friend of ours who's got a lot of magic of her own."

Red wolf singer, named... Autumn narrowed her eyes. "You don't mean Sarah Wylde of Obsidian Rose, do you?"

Saida finished her cookie, nodding. "Chipotle's half-sister is in the band."

"Three Lords." She'd loved that group a few years ago, although they'd gotten too pop-rock for her tastes lately.

Saida blinked. "Um...?"

Hanson deftly removed their plates, as silently as ever, replacing them with bowls, each containing a tiny "flower" made of blue corn tortillas. A little assistant hopped off the wolf's tray to do the same for Kim as Chipotle approached with a pitcher of soup.

"Never mind." Autumn picked up her glass. "Toast me before I kill you."

The Rha laughed, picking up her glass and tapping it to Autumn's. Judy clinked hers, too.

Epilogue

"SUCH A PSYCHEDELIC CAMPUS."

Saida looked up from her phone at her ride share driver, a greying lynx with one hand on the wheel and his eyes on the side of the road. "Hmm?"

"Like a drug trip, ma'am." He swerved to pass a minivan merely doing the speed limit, then waved at the buildings in the distance. "Half for guys our size, half for ones with paws bigger than this car."

"I know what 'psychedelic' means, but I'd never thought of the college that way. Normal is relative, I suppose. Is this your first ride out here?" Half the time she got the same driver, a chatty young fennec who seemed almost too enthusiastic about the campus. She suspected a lot of drivers just wouldn't pick up rides going any farther than the main gate.

"Nah, I've dropped off a couple of parents, a kid or two. Never somebody who looks like an executive going home on a Friday evening."

"Ah."

She'd never appreciated just how many miles of roads the campus had for littles until she'd started doing this commute. The first couple of weeks on the job she'd taken buses, but it required two transfers and a lot of walking, making a twenty minute commute into a seventy-minute one. It exhausted her enough that she'd considered just buying a car, no matter how ludicrous it was to have one she could only drive when she was this size. But Kim had talked her into trying ride sharing, and it was mostly working out. Even so, she missed the sports coupe she'd had back in Stravell. One day.

"So," the driver prompted. "What brings you out here, ma'am?"

"Oh, just like you said. I'm going home."

He furrowed his brow, grunting, and fell silent.

The road took a circuitous loop from the college's southern gate, around part of the Union building, then back down toward the southeast corner. The "depot" they were en route to was little more than a bus stop; littles rarely came here unless they were trekking on to dare the Giants' Club or visiting the giant staff housing looming a quarter-mile away.

"So right here?" he said as they pulled up toward the shelter. She could see his eyes on the gargantuan buildings in the distance—the row of motel-like suites for giants she'd be heading toward.

"Yes, this is fine. Thank you." She smiled briefly as she got out of the car, then pulled out her phone again to give him a tip and a quick rating. Five stars, which she wasn't sure he deserved, but if he ever got her again he might be less nonplussed about it all.

The walk toward her apartment—hers and Autumn's—took her along one of the few areas on the campus with no subtle architectural separation between giant and little space. The sidewalk was sized only for giants, with yellow diamond warning signs on her scale showing the silhouette of a giant paw coming down on a hapless stick figure and the warnings STAY TO WALKWAY EDGE and STAY ALERT. The roofline of those suites started nearly twelve stories up. Even the trees—evergreens imported from giant lands that reached six hundred feet high when full-grown—had seemed *small* before this became her normal size. Now they seemed impossibly huge.

At least, they did when she thought about them. She was coming up on her first anniversary with Autumn, and this had long since become her normal view of the campus, the buildings, the trees, her home. Not that Saida didn't still spend a lot of time as a giantess, but every workday, at the least, she was like this, and at home she was... usually, whatever size Autumn wanted.

The suite's original giant-sized door had been joined by a little-sized one to the side, similar to the setup her cousin's office had. As she'd expected, Autumn wasn't home yet; she knew the rabbit's class schedule, but Thursdays were usually a study session. Even so, she'd be by later to pick Saida up—literally—for a date at the Beanstalk.

She made her way across the floor, letting herself take in the scale of the furniture more than she usually did, until she reached the bedroom and walked the spiral stairs along the nightstand's leg up to her "nested living space." Inside, it was about as nice as the room outside; that had surprised her at first, but Judy had pointed out that it shouldn't—despite jokes about it being a dollhouse, it was just like any other manufactured home. Just one that happened to have a panoramic view of a bed bigger than a tennis court.

She'd gotten a coffee and sat down to listen to a podcast when she heard Autumn come in. Saida tensed, but grinned in spite of herself. There was one definite way it *was* more dollhouse than manufactured home. The house shook faintly with the rabbit's approaching footsteps—then a few sharp thumps vibrated through the walls as the giantess unlatched the roof and lifted it off. Autumn had teased her about being able to do that before they'd had the living space installed, but when they discovered that was actually an available option, she'd left the choice up to Saida.

The giant rabbit leaned over, hovering her hand near her pet girl-friend. "How was your day?"

"Fine." She blew a kiss up. "When do we need to be there?"

"Now. They're already there waiting."

"They? You didn't say we were meeting anyone."

Autumn just grinned. "Ready?"

She set down her coffee mug. "Yes, I just need to—"

Before she finished Autumn closed her fingers around her, enveloping her in white fur and setting her down on her shoulder. Saida huffed, but took her seat. A leash at her scale hooked onto one of the rings on Autumn's choker; Saida wrapped her arm around it for safety as the giantess started walking.

When they reached the Beanstalk, Autumn beelined toward their table. Two littles already sat at the table on the "leaf" talking with one another, although they stopped and stared as Autumn approached, Saida now in hand. The rabbit let Saida hop off with some measure of dignity.

Who—well, she recognized one of the littles. Kelly, Autumn's sister, who greeted her by raising up her beer. "Hey." She grinned. "Don't worry, I'm not here because of a family disaster this time. I'm in town on business."

She'd forgotten how strong Kelly looked. Since they'd last met, the rabbit had trimmed her head-fur to a near buzz cut, which somehow just amplified that look. "I wasn't *too* worried. But a little." She grinned lopsidedly. "I haven't seen you in nearly a year. How've you been?"

The fourth person was a thin vixen in tight jeans and a pink blouse. Her hair was nearly waist-length, tied back in a ponytail. She smiled at Saida timidly, but didn't say anything. Mostly she was staring at Autumn. Saida recognized the overwhelmed expression.

"Yeah, about that long. Shit. I'm, uh, I've been good." Kelly waved at the vixen. "This is Kate." A self-conscious note crept into her voice, as if she were finishing the introduction in an unfamiliar way. "My girlfriend. Uh, Kate, this is Autumn," she waved up, "my sister."

"N-nice to meet you." Kate waved nervously.

"Nice to meet you, too, Kate." Autumn slid into her seat.

"Oh." Saida blinked. "Oh!"

Kelly cleared her throat, looking flustered. "Yeah. Oh."

Saida smiled, offering a hand to Kate. "I'm Saida."

Kate took her hand, smiling stiffly. It was still a pretty smile. "Nice to meet you, too. I, um, wasn't sure whether to expect one or two giantesses, from what Kelly was saying." She swallowed.

"That's, well, complicated."

"It...sounds like it."

"Kate came with me on the trip because she's never seen a giant and she wanted to meet the family member I could introduce her to." Kelly smiled wryly.

"And because it's our first trip together anywhere." Kate smiled, too, then looked up at Autumn and around the rest of the room. "It must sound awfully silly to say that I didn't expect everything to be... so big. But it's true."

"No, I understand." Saida took a seat, realizing there was a third beer waiting on the little table for her, and a giant beer waiting for Autumn. "What, did you order for me?"

"I called ahead," Autumn said. "Put in the pizza order, too."

"How do you know I wasn't going to order something different?"

"How do you know I didn't order you something different?"

Saida sighed, rolling her eyes, and picked up the beer. "So how long have you two been dating?"

"About six months," Kate said.

"Although we've known each other over a year." Kelly rubbed the back of her head. "It took me that long to...I mean, Kate's pretty...open, and I guess I've been...figuring a lot out. I still am."

"Without asking me." Autumn took a big sip of her beer. "Because surely I wouldn't have had anything to say about figuring yourself out."

"You're kinda my role model for this, you big idiot." Kelly snorted. "Besides, I remember telling you I thought I might like girls back at Gimpy's."

"You did?"

"Yeah, I did. We were both on our fourth daiquiri, but I did. You said it was cute and I punched you."

Autumn grunted. "C'mon, you made it sound abstract, not that you liked a *specific* girl." She held out a finger right by Kelly. "Also, it *is* cute. Go on, punch me again."

"Asshole."

Kate leaned toward Saida. "Are they always like this?" she murmured.

"Pretty much."

The vixen smiled again, straightening up, although her eyes lingered on Saida's neck. "That's a pretty collar. It matches your eyes."

"Thanks." It had taken Saida much less time than she'd imagined it would to stop feeling self-conscious about wearing it. It *was* a pretty collar, a polished, high-gloss green, as fashionable as any choker necklace.

"So...what's it like to switch back and forth between being a giant and normal-size? I guess I should say 'little,' right?"

"Right. Well, giant is how I grew up, but I was in a place where everything was on my scale, so I didn't *feel* giant. Coming here was kind of a thrill because everything's ankle-high to me. Everything off-campus, at least. But..." She tilted her head, considering, then took a sip of the beer and shrugged. "I like being a weekend giant."

"With Autumn's magic." Kate glanced up at the towering rabbit, then back to the Rha. Autumn and Kelly seemed to be verbally sparring with one another, not paying attention as Kate continued in a lower voice. "Doesn't that...um. I'm trying to think on how to phrase this. It kind of makes you very dependent." Her gaze flicked down to the collar for a split-second again.

"There's a lot of trust involved. But there always is, if you're a little around giants."

"Yeah, I guess so." Kate leaned back, tail swishing, and sipped her own beer as she glanced around. "I've heard about giants, seen pictures, but...wow."

Saida grinned. "So do you like being a little around giants, or would you be just as happy to not visit again?"

"Oh, it's, well, it's intimidating. But I'm glad I came." She took another long sip, looking reflective. "I think if I really had a choice," she continued slowly, "I'd rather be a giant around littles, though."

Kelly stopped mid-sentence and narrowed her eyes at her girlfriend. "What, just being a half a foot taller than I am isn't enough?"

Kate's ears folded back, although she grinned. "I'm just—"

"Being a lot taller could be arranged," Autumn cut in.

"Don't even start!" Kelly looked at Kate. "You're kidding, right?"

The vixen chewed on her claw tip and giggled. "Well..."

"This is your fault." Kelly pointed at both the Rha and the rabbit.

Saida gave her best innocent-cat smile. "It's not our fault we're a cute couple."

Kate giggled again. "You are."

Saida smiled more. "So are you."

Kelly took the vixen's hand with an uncharacteristically shy smile.

Autumn leaned over the table. "Do you think we should give them ideas, little cat?"

"Absolutely not," Kelly barked, simultaneously with Kate murmuring, "Maybe."

The pizza arrived then, distracting everyone but Autumn from the Rha's blush.

Acknowledgments

Saida & Autumn wouldn't have been possible without the support of my Patrons. The following folks supported me for at least three months during the time I was writing (and posting) the first draft:

applestooranges, Ashlandic, Balina, Becky Cascane, c, Cebula-san, Chaos Potato, David Chappell, David Green, Dissident Love, Dracur, DragonessSapphire, Eric S, hippiewerewolf, Jakebe, Jayne Folest, Jspeed, Jvore1, K Boudjan, Kagur, Kalessan, KenCougr, Kitana, Krell, Kryp7ic, Kyrugii, Leishmania, Lukas Schmidt, Macciavelo, Meow Wei, Monki Lufi, MoonlightUmbry, MrPerson, Narzain, Ndoto, Nines Kitsune, Ninesyllables, NotNotton, Odddice, Raventail, Redstiza, Rob, Rooth, Saga, Sean Grave, Silas Mousehold, Silberlynx, sp, StarryAqua, Tommi Cat, Ulfra Wolfe, Valeska Voss, WoofWoof, Xipher

About the Author

In universe, Arilin Thorferra is Saida Talirend's cousin and a professor at Mensura College. In the real world, she's an award-winning author and a long-time member of the furry and macrophile community. She is the author of the short novel *Goddess* (available in print and ebook from FurPlanet), the screenplay *Red Savina,* and many short stories about furry giants.

Find her work at https://giants-club.net/
and https://www.furaffinity.net/user/arilin/

www.ingramcontent.com/pod-product-compliance
Lightning Source LLC
Chambersburg PA
CBHW070844250626
47159CB00003B/925